A HIDD

Thana stepped back and admired the old piece of furniture. She lay down and, sure enough, there was the secret drawer.

What she found was a notebook with a name written on the inside cover. A name that made her look at her hands in horror as if expecting to see them covered in blood. A name that recalled the night two innocent people had been cut to ribbons in their beds in the great Tinley murder case.

She gasped with excitement. For here in the Blue Bazaar she had found a document that had lain hidden for seventeen years. A document that gave her the answer to a mystery that had never been solved; now she knew the astonishing identity of the person who had murdered Patrick Meadows and his ten-year-old son!

...A DANGEROUS SECRET

Murder Ink.® Mysteries

Scene Of The Crime™ Mysteries

A Scene Of The Crime™ Mystery

Spence
at the
Blue Bazaar

Michael Allen

A DELL BOOK

Published by
Dell Publishing Co., Inc.
1 Dag Hammarskjold Plaza
New York, New York 10017

All the characters and events
portrayed in this story are fictitious.

Dell ® TM 681510, Dell Publishing Co., Inc.

ISBN: 0-440-18308-1

Reprinted by arrangement with Walker and Company
Printed in the United States of America
First Dell printing—August 1981

Spence
at the
Blue Bazaar

1

The sleepy English village of Tinley, on the northern edge of Southshire, was about to be treated to its first see-through blouse—but unfortunately the only man around at the time was seventy-two years old and totally blind.

It was 3 o'clock in the afternoon on a Monday in late April; the village green in Tinley was deserted except for one old-age pensioner (male) sitting on a bench. The see-through blouse was worn by a gorgeous creature who called herself Thana; she also called herself Melody McFee, and from time to time she had lived and worked under at least three other names in addition to her real one.

Thana was tall for a girl, with long flashing legs on high heels; she had blonde shoulder-length hair, blue eyes, and the best complexion that Estée Lauder could concoct. She looked to be in her early twenties, but in fact she had been born in Tinley thirty years previously. Her bust was particularly spectacular, which was only right considering the small fortune which had been spent on it, and she had dark, prominent nipples, which showed up clearly under the delicately patterned material of her blouse.

In addition to the white see-through top, Thana was wearing a dark-blue cardigan slung carelessly around her shoulders. Below the waist she had on a black pencil skirt with a twelve-inch slash in each side, black stockings of the old-fashioned thigh-length variety, and a garter belt. No knickers. Strong men sitting opposite her on the Underground, when she was wearing this outfit, had been known to start biting their knuckles and mumbling incoherently.

Thana had walked half a mile from the Blue Bazaar nightclub on the London Road, where she was staying, and now stood facing the village green. To reach this point she had had to walk past 200 houses on a new estate, none of which had been there when she had last seen the village; now, however, she was back in territory which she recognized. To her right were the post office, the pub, and the garage; in the distance was the vicarage, and beyond that the church. Nothing seemed to have changed much here, anyway.

She noticed the blind man sitting on the bench facing the village green, his white stick held between his knees, and she decided to go and speak to him; it was time she found someone who could bring her up to date on the latest gossip. She realized as she approached the old man that he was not an inhabitant she had known in her youth, but perhaps, she decided, that was just as well. And even a relative newcomer might still be a useful source of information.

'Good afternoon,' she began, as she sat down.

The blind man had sensed her approach, of course, and now he turned his pale face towards her. Thana could see herself dazzlingly reflected in his dark glasses: it was almost a shock to her to see how incredibly beautiful she looked.

'Good afternoon,' said the blind man in return.

Thana looked at him carefully and decided he was a retired minor civil servant. She knew the type well: dirty old lechers to a man, in her view. This particular specimen was wearing a sports jacket and flannels, and a grey panama hat, which he now lifted politely. His hair was a whiter shade of grey than the hat.

'Lovely day,' he continued.

'Very nice,' said Thana. 'Very nice . . . Roll on summer.'

'And so say all of us.' The blind man chuckled, but a little uneasily. Thana's perfume was coming strongly downwind at him and he wondered what sort of a woman he was dealing with. The clip-clop of the high heels on the road had led him to expect a woman, and the deep, throaty, sophisticated voice had told him that she was probably a woman of class; he had begun to wonder whether she might be staying with the Colonel. But now this powerful, almost overwhelmingly erotic scent came rolling over him, and the phrase 'whore's parlour' floated into his mind. He hoped desperately that Mrs Amble in the post office was not observing the scene, but he was very much afraid that she would be—and she was. Word would get back to his wife within the hour.

'Well,' said Thana, 'it's very quiet here, isn't it? This is the first time I've been back here for some years, and I'd forgotten how peaceful it is.'

'Oh, it's peaceful enough now,' said the blind man. 'But wait till the kids get out of school—then it'll change.'

Thana leaned back on the bench and contemplated the village green. Judging by the ropes round a square in the middle it was still used for cricket in the summer. 'It's a beautiful old village, isn't it?' she said.

'Ah. Used to be.'

'You mean it's changed?'

'Oh, yes. Oh, yes . . . A lot. Even in the time I've here. The wife and I retired here seven years ago, looking for a bit of peace and quiet. And what happened? After two years they built a damn great housing estate. Just over there.' He pointed.

'Oh, yes,' said Thana. 'Yes, I walked through that way just now. I expect that's changed the whole tone of the place.'

'My word, you can say that again,' said the blind man. 'Altered the whole character of the village completely. Place is full of strangers . . . Not,' he added hastily, 'that there's anything wrong in that. I'm a stranger here myself, in a manner of speaking . . . But the new people don't work here, you see. Just use the place as a dormitory.'

'Ah, yes,' said Thana. 'Yes. Commute to London, I suppose?'

'That's right . . . It's only an hour by train, and they seem to think that's nothing nowadays. And they work in Tallmead too, some of them. But they're never here, you see, that's the point. Off early in the morning, back last thing at night. Their kids run wild in the meantime and what their wives get up to is nobody's business.'

On reflection the blind man rather regretted that last remark. After all, this glamour-puss, whoever she was, might well be a wife on the loose herself.

'What about you?' he continued cautiously. 'Staying with friends or just here for the day?'

'Neither,' said Thana. She let him dangle for a few seconds and then added: 'My work brings me here.'

The blind man waggled his stick in the dust while he tried to pluck up the courage to probe further. Thana let him off lightly.

'I'm working at the Blue Bazaar,' she told him.

'Oh,' said the blind man knowingly, as if all had been revealed at last. 'Yes, at the Blue Bazaar. I see. You'll be in the cabaret, I expect.'

'Yes, that's right. For a week, starting tonight.'

'Ah, yes, I see.' And in his mind's eye the blind man could see. After all, it was only last week that Rupert Fuller—a dirty old bugger if ever there was one—had given him a graphic description at the over-60's club of the stripper they'd had at the Blue Bazaar in Christmas week. A coloured girl by all accounts, with a bum like a horse and shameless with it. In the darkened cinema of his mind the blind man had had many an action replay from that one already. And he no longer had any doubt about what the girl sitting beside him was—a stripper if ever he smelt one. 'Ah, yes, I see now,' he repeated.

Thana was quite amused. She had never been leered at by a blind man before, but there was, she reflected, a first time for everything.

'I knew that house when old Mrs Prentice lived there,' said the blind man thoughtfully. 'The Blue Bazaar I mean. Used to be a private house, you know, before they converted it. It was ten times too big for Mrs Prentice, of course, but she wouldn't move. Stayed to the bitter end. My wife used to play bridge with her . . . The house has been built on to now, I gather.'

'Oh, yes,' Thana agreed, 'It's been quite extensively altered. The upstairs is much the same, but they've built on a large cabaret room at the back. It's really quite impressive. For a provincial place, at any rate.'

'Get some big stars there, now, so they say.'

'Yes, indeed,' Thana agreed. Such as me, you ignorant, black-eyed moron, she felt like saying. Goddamn Liza Minelli and Marilyn Monroe and Elizabeth Taylor herself, all rolled into one, that's me, and don't you ever forget it. But she held her tongue. There was no future in preaching that particular gospel to a burnt-out, broken-down pensioner. She felt restless again and began to look around.

'After she died,' the blind man continued, 'it was empty for quite a while. Mrs Prentice, I mean. After she died the house stood empty for nearly a year. No one wanted it. But then Mrs Cordwright got interested. Came into a lot of money, so they say, so she bought it for that son of hers. And now him and his friend, Mr Read, and Mrs Cordwright, they all three run it together. But I expect you've come across them already.'

'Some of them,' said Thana absently.

'And of course Lester Read, he never was short of money anyway, or so I hear. He gave up teaching at Tallmead to do some writing, years ago, but I've never met anyone that heard of him publishing anything. So he can't have been short of a few bob to support himself.'

'Yes,' said Thana. 'I think he's pretty well placed.'

She shifted her position on the bench as if to move on, but the blind man's voice became urgent. He found that perfume of hers rather pleasing, after all.

'Of course, the Colonel tried to block it, you know,' he told her.

That stopped Thana in her tracks all right. She was interested in the Colonel. Tell me more, she thought.

'Tried to block what?'

'The Blue Bazaar.'

'Oh, he did, did he?' She settled back on the bench again.

'Oh, yes. Yes. Tried everything he knew. Said it would lower the tone, you know. Having a nightclub in the village. Well, on the outskirts of it, anyway. Yes, he was very much against it. . . . Not that he had a leg to stand on, mind you, because he was the one that sold off a perfectly good farm so they could build the new housing estate. And that lowered the tone if anything did.'

'I see . . .' said Thana. More interesting by the minute.

'Oh, yes. Yes, made a small fortune out of that, did the Colonel.'

The words 'small fortune' rang up pound signs in the back of Thana's brain. Sneaky bastard, that Colonel, she thought, pleading dire poverty when all the time he was rolling in it from a land deal. Oh, yes, no doubt about it, it was worth coming back to the old village, just to poke around; the visit was paying dividends already.

'He didn't win, though, did he?' said Thana.

'Who, the Colonel?'

'Yes.'

'No, no, he didn't win. The nightclub was opened in a very short time. But him and the Vicar, they put up a good fight, I'll say that for them. Tried all they could to block it. But times are changing, you see. Who would have thought a few years ago that today Tinley would have its own nightclub?'

'Who indeed?' said Thana. And who would have thought, she asked herself, who would have thought, say fifteen years ago, that I would be back here today like this—the new me, stopping the traffic and killing them all stone dead with desire and envy and lust. Dropping their jaws with astonishment, setting the wives against the husbands and generally showing them who's boss.

Without a word of good-bye she stood up and walked briskly away, the breeze pressing the see-through blouse tight against her breasts, thighs flashing and hips swinging and her blonde hair glistening in the sun.

Mrs Amble in the post office watched her go. She tried hard to remember where she had seen that face before.

2

Thana headed towards the church tower on the other side of the village green. It wasn't that she was particularly attracted to churches—far from it—but something the blind man had said had resolved a doubt in her mind.

She reached the far side of the green and began to walk down the lane which led to the fourteenth-century church. The vicarage appeared on her left: it was a mid-nineteenth-century building, a relic of an age when the Vicar could still find and afford servants to cater for his numerous dependents; it was large, rambling, and covered with ivy; when the present Vicar died, the Church would probably sell it, together with the land it stood on, and a local builder would step in and put up five other houses, if not ten, in its place.

Thana examined the vicarage carefully, looking for signs of life. But none were to be seen. Nor did the house seem to have changed much in the twelve years since she had last set eyes on it: the paint was still green, and still peeling off the window-frames; the roof lacked a few tiles. With a sigh she moved on into the churchyard.

A mound of freshly-turned earth denoted that Tinley churchyard was still used for its original purpose: burying people. Other recent graves were indicated by clean white marble and affectionately-laid flowers, some of them plastic.

Thana wandered amongst the gravestones, the names on them bringing to mind many faces from the distant past. But one face stayed in the background; for in a far corner, on the other side of the church, was the grave of her mother. Thana did not even allow herself to think about that: the memory of her mother's death was altogether too painful even to be allowed on to the fringes of her consciousness.

Suddenly Thana became aware that she was being watched. She turned, the breeze blowing her cardigan out behind her. In the shadow of the church door she saw an elderly man in a dark suit; he was short, and rather stout, and wore glasses. He took a hesitant step forward and peered at her sharply, his mouth slightly open as if not believing what he saw. As he moved and lifted his head Thana saw the white dog-collar around his neck, and she realized who it was: it was the Vicar, Albert Barndean. It was the glasses which had thrown her for a moment, for twelve years ago he had not worn them.

For some time, neither of them was able to decide afterwards for how long, the Vicar and Thana stared at each other. The Vicar had never, in all his sixty-four years, seen anyone quite like the person who now stood beneath the trees on the perimeter of his churchyard. She was tall, dressed strikingly and brazenly in black and white, and there was something horribly disturbing about her. Out of long years of habit Thana stood with her body held in a defiantly provocative posture, one leg bent slightly at the knee, the breasts thrust forward. There was a sense of gloating evil about her which would have been highly unsettling in itself. But that wasn't all.

As Albert Barndean came out of his dark church into the April sunlight, and as the woman turned towards him, he had thought for one appalling, hideous moment that his mind had given way and he was seeing a projection of what he feared most. But almost instantly he had had to reject that idea, and settle for the truth. For this wasn't an illusion—this was a real, live person, which was even worse. A person who looked so incredibly like—

But no. No. It wasn't after all. It couldn't possibly be.

The Vicar shook his head and blinked rapidly to clear his vision. And as he did so he broke the spell. Thana began to move. She walked down the gravel path towards him, her arms swinging free and relaxed, a half-smile on her face.

Silly old bugger, she thought, taking it so badly.

She walked past him, out through the churchyard gate, and back towards the village green.

Albert Barndean stood by the church door for a long time. His heart pounded in anguish, as it did with increasing frequency these days. No doubt he ought to see a doctor, but he couldn't bring himself to do so. He just leaned against the comforting cool stone of the church and waited for the pain to pass, or for death to come. He didn't mind which. And after a while he felt better.

Then he went back into the church to pray.

Thana retraced her route over the village green and headed towards the post office. She was quite unruffled by the traumatic disturbance she had left behind her: conscience, concern for others, and a sense of moderation in flaunting her sex appeal, none of these were her strong points.

She entered the post office, making the bell clang loudly above her head. Mrs Amble, the post-mistress, moved away from the window where she had been watching Thana's approach, and returned to the counter to serve her. Disapproval was stamped in every line of her face, but she was outwardly polite.

'Yes, my dear? And what can I do for you?'

'A packet of Embassy Number One, please,' said Thana, who didn't smoke but had to buy something.

Mrs Amble turned awkwardly to the shelf behind her. She was well into her fifties, heavily corseted, with badly swollen ankles. Standing around in the shop all day didn't help, but she had kept the village post office for thirty-four years now and she was determined to keep it for a good few years yet. She would rather drop dead from exhaustion than miss anything that happened in Tinley.

Thana wrinkled her nose in disgust as she looked around her. There was a different layout to the shop now but it still smelt the same.

'There you are,' said Mrs Amble, sliding the cigarettes across the counter. 'Lovely day, isn't it?'

'Very nice,' agreed Thana, and extracted a pound note from her cardigan pocket. She decided to do a little stirring. 'Tell me,' she continued, 'does Colonel Host-Wall still live in the village?'

Mrs Amble's eyes narrowed into suspicious slits as she counted out Thana's change; she was not a good dissembler and if there was one thing that got her back up, as she had frequently remarked to anyone willing to listen, it was shameless hussies flaunting themselves. Why, as recently as six years ago her husband Will had made a fool of himself over—but never mind about that. Back to Colonel Host-Wall, who was old enough to know better than to get himself mixed up with *this*.

'Why yes,' said Mrs Amble politely. 'Colonel Host-Wall, he still lives in the village, yes.' And why would you be wanting to know about him? she felt like adding.

'Still in that big house?' asked Thana. 'Up at the end of the long drive there?'

'Yes, that's right . . . Been there before, have you?'

'Not for a long time,' breathed Thana happily. 'But I have been there before, yes.'

'Oh,' said Mrs Amble thoughtfully. She filed this information away in her data-bank, letting it rattle around against other known facts about Colonel Host-Wall, who many years earlier might have been known as the Squire.

'A lovely man, the Colonel,' said Thana gleefully, thinking to herself that it really didn't do for a man to tell lies to old Thana Melody McFee, by God. No sir, it didn't pay at all. Pleading poverty and near-bankruptcy when all the time you were sitting on a small fortune raised from the sale of land to some greasy little speculative builder, that didn't win you any favours at all.

'Yes, you could say he was lovely,' said Mrs Amble, thinking that that was not quite the description she would have applied to a skinny-looking sixty-year-old snob who was too damn proud to come into the village shop but whose shirts were fraying at the collars. 'Yes, you could say that,' she repeated. 'Did you want to have a word with him, then?'

'Oh, I think I'll look him up some time this week,' said Thana gaily. 'I'm here until Saturday, you know. At the Blue Bazaar.'

'Oh, really?' Mrs Amble's eyes opened wide, but she found herself in a bit of a quandary. Blue Bazaar equalled sexual and alcoholic temptation, and hence trouble with husband Will, who she was damn sure had been known to sneak off there with his mates from time to time. But on the other hand, a slice of the Blue Bazaar's takings did end up in Mrs Amble's till from time to time, because Mrs Cordwright and her son, whatever else might be said about them—and a lot of hard things were said, let's face it—Mrs Cordwright and her son were not snobs. And even when they came into money and were able to start up that nightclub of theirs, and make even more money by all accounts, even then they still kept on coming to the village shop. And stopping for a nice long gossip too, with lots of interesting bits of news about all those people you see on the telly. So it didn't do to criticize the Blue Bazaar out loud. You had to hedge your bets.

'Oh,' said Mrs Amble again, at her thirty-words-to-the-minute Southshire pace. 'Because I was just thinking, you see. If you was wanting to have a word with the Colonel, you could do it now. Because he's just driven past my door and stopped at the garage.'

Thana left the village shop rather faster than she had gone in, and Mrs Amble took down a packet of Persil Automatic from the window in order to get a better view of what was going to happen next.

Sure enough, there was a rather elderly Bentley drawn up in front of the petrol pumps, and there standing beside it was Colonel Brian Host-Wall himself.

Thana took one look and decided that the Colonel was frailer and shabbier than when she had last seen him. All that inbreeding was catching up with him at last, apparently. And what on earth had he done to his hair, for Christ's sake? Dyed it brown by the look of it, and left his grey moustache untouched! Well, really. And that sports jacket and those cavalry-twill trousers—which jumble sale had he bought those at? Ah well, she thought, now to teach the old bastard a lesson.

The Colonel was standing beside the petrol pump, watching the numbers go round, blissfully unaware of Thana approaching on his left flank. He didn't know it yet but old age was bringing tunnel vision as one of its many undesirable side-effects.

Amazing how little petrol you got for a pound nowadays, he thought. It was no good, the Bentley would have to go.

'Well hello, Colonel!' said Thana heartily, and slapped him hard on the back.

The Colonel took some moments to realize who it was that had accosted him, and when the dreadful truth did become clear, and quite inescapable, he understood for the very first time what it was to wish that the ground would open up and swallow you. He looked around, desperately hoping that no one was watching, and all he saw was the garage-hand at the petrol pump grinning fit to split his face in half, Mrs Amble staring through the post office window, and even the blind man sitting on the bench had his head turned this way.

'Hello, Colonel!' Thana repeated joyfully. 'How lovely to see you again after all this time.'

'Oh—um—er—don't believe we've . . . Can't quite recall?' muttered the Colonel, wondering frantically how to disentangle himself from this one. The sun was no help, shining through Thana's blouse to light up everything she'd got.

'Surely you haven't forgotten me?' asked Thana, as if horrified by the very possibility.

The Colonel's mouth seemed to have dried up on him and his face turned as grey as his moustache. 'Why, um, no,' he said at last. 'Miss—um—McFee, isn't it?'

'That's right,' said Thana, flashing a big smile at the garage-hand. 'I knew you'd remember if you put your mind to it.'

'The golf club, wasn't it?' said the Colonel. 'Can't just remember who introduced us . . .'

'Not the golf club, darling,' said Thana. 'The Whiplash Club, actually, off Dean Street.'

'Ha, ha, ha,' said the Colonel, anxious to prove what a good sport he was, able to spot a joke when he saw one. 'Ha, ha, ha. Well, lovely to see you again, but must pay for the petrol, you know. Ask you to excuse me and all that.' He pulled out his wallet and crammed panic-stricken pound notes into the attendant's hand.

'I think you ought to get in touch with me before long, Colonel,' said Thana pointedly. Her smile had gone now. 'The stock market is going up and I want to take advantage of it. Know what I mean?' She placed her hand on the Colonel's arm and squeezed it hard. He jerked away in revulsion. 'Know what I mean?' Thana repeated, as the Colonel climbed into his ancient Bentley. 'I think we could double our money. In fact we *must* double our money.'

The Colonel didn't answer. He started the car and accelerated hard away from the garage. Thana watched him go with a frown on her face. The garage attendant stood and stared at her tits.

Stupid bastard, thought Thana. Stupid, frightened bastard. Well, he would pay for it, that much was certain. Pay for his arrogance, his rudeness and the preservation of his smutty little secret. Pay and pay and pay.

3

Thana went back to her room at the Blue Bazaar and rested on her bed for an hour. She started to read *Death in Venice* by Thomas Mann, which a very good friend of hers had recommended, but really she found it awfully boring and tedious—it made her rather glad she hadn't bothered to see the film.

Towards 7 o'clock that evening Thana persuaded the chef at the Blue Bazaar, who had a room just along the corridor, to make her a meal. After that she faithfully took her daily dose of tablets: three red ones and a torpedo-shaped green one for luck. Following the meal and the tablets Thana felt a *lot* better, so doubt about it, so she took her tape-recorder down to the cabaret room and persuaded one of the musicians to help her set it up. Thana always stripped to a tape—she felt it was so much more reliable than a different group of musicians each week, some of whom couldn't read dots anyway. Her favourite recording was Jimmy Smith's 'Walk on the Wild Side', which, let's face it darling, was a *very* appropriate title.

While the musician was adjusting the balance of Thana's stereo-speakers she was approached by David Cordwright, one of the joint owners of the Blue Bazaar. He left his mother's side and came over to ask Thana if all was well.

'Fine, thank you, darling,' said Thana, giving him

a big toothy grin for old times' sake. Twelve years
ago she and David Cordwright had known each other
quite well, by sight at any rate, but neither yesterday
nor today had David given any indication that he recognized her, and Thana didn't prompt him. Twelve
years was quite a long time, she reflected, and she
had changed quite a bit, after all. Yes, quite a bit,
one way and another. David, she decided, hadn't
changed as much—particularly in his relationship with
his mother.

David Cordwright was thirty-three, tall and slim,
with brown, straight hair which was neatly parted on
the left and brushed down flat. He was almost ex-
cessively handsome and beautifully dressed in a con-
servatively-tailored dark-grey suit. He had been trained
in the hotel and catering industry, and he looked the
part: discreet, capable, never raising his voice. His
mother always spoke of him as a sensitive boy, but only
his fingernails, bitten back deep into the quick, be-
trayed any lack of confidence or the existence of any
tension.

'Right, then, Thana,' said Cordwright with a pleasant smile, 'let me tell you the drill. We always have the
stripper on first here. The audience have got used
to it over the years. No offence.'

'None taken,' said Thana.

'Of course strip is the big attraction,' Cordwright
continued. 'We all know that—'

'Of course.'

'But we find it better from the point of view of local
politics to pretend that it's really only a minor
part of the show, and that what everyone's really
come to see is the singer or the magician or whatever.
Know what I mean?'

'Absolutely,' said Thana. Very smooth, she thought. Very smooth, David, but still a little bit dependent on Mummy, I see.

David's mother, Mrs Jennifer Cordwright, hovered in the background, briefing a new member of the bar staff on the use of the cash register. Mrs Cordwright was in her mid-fifties; her hair was grey but it did not age her unduly, which was the only reason she hadn't dyed it. She was of average height and weight and gave the impression of being a wiry and vigorous person perhaps five years younger than she was. She was very elegantly dressed in a navy-blue costume and a blouse of a lighter blue which matched her eyes.

After a few moments Mrs Cordwright saw Thana looking at her and came over and introduced herself. They had not met before—not for twelve years, anyway, and Mrs Cordwright certainly didn't remember that. She stood with her hands neatly folded in front of her, just as she had been taught to do in finishing-school thirty-seven years earlier.

'Well, my dear,' said Mrs Cordwright—the accent was South Kensington rather than Southshire—'I hear you've been causing a few ripples down in the village.'

Thana put her head back and laughed. 'The word soon gets around,' she said. Just like the old days, she nearly added, but caught herself just in time.

'It does indeed,' said Mrs Cordwright sternly. She contrived to look pleased and yet slightly displeased at one and the same time. 'One has to be a little bit careful, you know . . .'

Oh, does one, thought Thana.

'Contact with the public is all to the good. We like our artistes to mix with the customers, both inside and outside the club. But one has to be careful not to become, shall we say, over-familiar. Particularly with the older generation of residents. Know what I mean?'

'I think so,' said Thana. 'Yes, I think so. You're talking about the Colonel.'

'Yes . . . You see, the village divides into two, Thana. There's a very small group, shrinking with every passing year, who are the long-term residents. We all know each other very well, perhaps too well, and the grapevine operates amongst us with no trouble at all. And then there's a much larger group of new-comers. They all live on the new estate, between here and the village proper, and they often go for years before they so much as know the next-door neighbour's name. Now the newcomers you can frater-nize with as much as you like—flirt with them out-rageously if you wish. They're a permissive, sophis-ticated breed, by and large. But the old guard—well, I'd be grateful if you'd tread rather carefully.'

Thana nodded. 'I'll bear it in mind,' she said.

'Now—how's everything? Got your equipment ready?'

'No problems,' said Thana.

Mrs Cordwright seemed pleased. 'Good. Well, if you want me I'll be on reception tonight. I don't work every night but I normally come in on Mondays to see that everything's fixed for the week. I'm also in the office for at least part of each day, keeping an eye on things, so if there's anything worrying you at all don't hesitate to come and see me.'

Thana promised faithfully that she wouldn't hesi-tate.

'Good, that's splendid. Now let's see . . . You've met my son David, of course. And the other person you

ought to know here is Mr Read.' She indicated a
chubby middle-aged man with black hair, dark eyes
and the ruddy complexion of a solid drinker. 'The
three of us are the joint owners of the Blue Bazaar,
you know, so we're all equally qualified to deal with
any problems. You only have to ask.'

After a few more minutes of casual conversation
Mrs Cordwright moved off to reception, and Thana
took the trouble to introduce herself to the third
partner in the club, Lester Read. Lester was another
person Thana had known before she left the village,
but the memory of Thana's previous existence was
even less well fixed in Lester's mind than it was in
the others'. He was polite, but distant. Not very interested in this week's stripper, which was hardly surprising, Thana decided, considering that he was as
queer as a summer snowstorm.

Time passed. The club filled up—quite a good crowd
for a Monday—and Thana prepared for the 10 o'clock
cabaret. She performed with pleasure, as usual, and
then returned to her room. She sat on the bed with
her back against the headboard, selected a new paperback from the stock she always carried, and began to
read.

But before long she found her mind drifting away
from the book in her hand. Images of the past began
to float above the printed page: memories of her childhood, of her mother and father, of the joys and dis-
asters of the past. She set the book down in her lap.

Perhaps in some ways it had been a mistake to
come back to Tinley. Perhaps the past was better left
alone, particularly when some of it was so painful
and hard to contemplate. But if one must think of

the past, then why not concentrate on the happy days?
On the days, for instance, spent in her grandmother's
house.

Despite herself, tears came to Thana's eyes as she
thought of her grandmother, now long since dead.
That had been the beginning of the end, when her
grandmother had died. And that had been where the
love of show-business had all begun. It was dressing
up in Grandma's bedroom that had started it all,
taking the clothes out of the dressing-table drawers
and holding them up against the tall mirror on the
wardrobe.

Taking the clothes out of the dressing-table drawers, the silk and satin underwear so shining and soft
and thrilling . . .

Taking the clothes out of the dressing-table, just
like the one here, and putting them on and enjoying
the feel of them and wanting to wear them always
and be admired.

Taking the clothes out of the dressing-table just
like the one here.

Taking the clothes . . .

Just like the one here!

The thought hit Thana with an almost physical
force, making her gasp. She leapt off the bed and
crossed the room, staring hard at the dressing-table to
the right of the window.

Something made her pause and draw the curtains
shut, so that no one outside could possibly share her
discovery, and then she approached the dressing-table
again and examined it carefully.

She ran her fingers over the dark oak. It was Victorian, she thought, monstrously ugly, of course, the
kind of thing you wouldn't get five pounds for if you

sent it to an auction sale today. There was one long drawer running the full width of the piece, two smaller drawers above that, and two tiny drawers on the flat surface below the mirrors; there were three mirrors in all, adjustable so that milady could see her face from all angles.

Yes, there was no doubt about it. Thana ran her hand over the pattern cut into the wood. Yes, it was the very same dressing-table, the same piece of furniture Grandma had once owned, all those years ago.

And why not? What was so extraordinary about that, after all? Grandma had lived in the village, and when she died Thana's mother and father had not wanted the old lady's furniture. And so naturally it had all been sold. And then one day whoever had bought it had died, equally naturally. And along had come Mrs Cordwright and her son David, and his long-time lover Lester Read, all wanting to start up a nightclub in old Mrs Prentice's house. And so they had bought a load of old furniture cheap, just to fill up the bedrooms for the staff and the cabaret people.

Yes, it was all quite understandable, once you started to think about it. But what a surprise, nonetheless.

Thana stepped back and admired the old piece of furniture. It really was rather revolting in many ways, but she had great affection for it. She wondered vaguely if Mrs Cordwright and company would sell it to her, just for old times' sake. But no. Perhaps not. Best not to even hint at any connection with the past. However, it *was* nice to see the old thing again, to think about all the happy times in those satin knickers and petticoats, and playing games with the

secret drawer underneath, and reading the old news-
papers in the bottom of the other drawers, and—

Just a minute.

Thana clutched her temples as she remembered.
Now there was a thought. The secret drawer underneath.

Thana could remember the first time Grandma
had shown her that secret drawer. It wasn't so very
secret really—anybody who could reach underneath
could open it if they knew what to do, and you could
even see it if you crawled on the floor. But on the
whole most people didn't go crawling around on bedroom floors. Well, Thana could think of a few who
had, but they hadn't been looking for concealed drawers at the time. No—it was just that the two upper
drawers in the main body of the dressing-table were
slightly shorter than the lower drawer, and behind
one of them, accessible only from underneath, was a
small drawer in which valuables could be kept, some
six inches by four inches in size. Grandma had always
said that Grandpa had kept something very precious
indeed in there, but she would never say what it was,
despite lots and lots of teasing and pleas and tears.
Whatever it was, Grandma had thought it quite a
joke.

Thana lay down on her back on the carpet. She
could smell dust and floorboards, just as she had
done all those years before. And sure enough, there
was the secret drawer. She reached up and released
the catch; it was stiff, and she had to pull hard, and
when the drawer did come open the weight of something in it almost caused her to drop it.

She wriggled out from under the dressing-table and
took her find over to the light.

What she had found was a notebook, almost exactly the same size as the drawer itself. Thana opened it. There was a name on the inside of the cover: Patrick Meadows.

Patrick Meadows.

Now then. Thana sat down on the bed and tried to think of the owner of that name.

Patrick Meadows.

Ah, yes. The teacher.

Dear God, Patrick Meadows had been dead for years and years and years. What was his notebook doing in Grandma's dressing-table? Could he have bought it when Grandma died? Well, yes, he could. Why not? He was living in the village when Grandma died, he and his young son. He could have bought the dressing-table and found the drawer and kept something in it, just like Grandpa. Kept it hidden from his son. Until one night they were both cut to ribbons in their beds of course. In the great Tinley murder case.

Thana looked down at her hands in horror, as if expecting to see them covered in blood. But there was no blood. Only a blue-covered notebook containing—well, containing what?

Thana opened the notebook again and skimmed through it. It was clearly a diary or a journal of some kind, and words began to spring out of the page at her. Short words, rude words, crude words. No wonder Patrick Meadows had kept this hidden.

Thana resumed her previous position on the bed, back against the headboard, feet up, and began to read. And as the minutes ticked by and page followed page Thana became more and more engrossed. And when she had read the final entry, for a Sunday in

August, seventeen years earlier, Thana was so euphoric that she could hardly contain herself.

She climbed off the bed and paced ecstatically around the room, clasping her hands together, biting her lower lip, and giving thanks to the God she didn't believe in for presenting her with such a gift.

For here in the Blue Bazaar she had found a document which had lain hidden for nearly seventeen years. A document which gave her the answer to a mystery which had never previously been solved: namely, who had murdered Patrick Meadows and his ten-year-old son.

Meadows had had no inkling that he was going to be killed, and the journal therefore contained no direct accusation of anyone. But the entry for that Sunday in August, so long ago, had given Thana, with her local knowledge, an insight into the *motive* for the murder. And a glimpse of the truth like that was of inestimable value to someone with Thana's talents— someone who was well practised in the arts of blackmail, someone who would never hesitate to apply the stimulus of guilty knowledge, to apply pressure to a victim's throat, time and time and time again.

For nearly an hour Thana was almost beside herself with joy, delirious with a sense of power and new-found wealth. She thought lovingly of the furs and jewels and expensive perfumes that would be hers, of the prospect of unlimited quantities of top-quality marijuana and cocaine, of the beautiful furnishings and elegant dresses that she would buy . . . And for a while it was all just so exciting that she could hardly bear it.

In the end, of course, it was all to prove far too

much for Thana to bear. For within a very short time, the discovery which Thana had expected would bring her a steady supply of everything that she held dear in life, in fact brought her nothing but pain and fear.

And, rapidly following on from that, an appalling, hideous death.

4

It was half-past midnight now, and Charlie Booth—formerly Detective Chief Superintendent Charles Booth, head of the Southshire CID, had only just drifted off to sleep.

Then the phone at his bedside started to ring. And wouldn't stop ringing. Just like the old days.

Booth reached out and picked the phone off the hook, one eye glancing at the luminous dial of the bedside clock out of sheer habit. Was there never to be any peace, not even in retirement? His wife slept on, also like the old days.

' 'Lo?' grunted Booth.

The pay-phone pips sounded at the other end and Booth waited patiently until the money went in and the line became clear.

'Hello?' he said again.

'Hello!' The voice at the other end of the line was bright, light and cheerful. And something about it, some overtone coming through the static and the fuzziness on the line, something about the voice prompted Booth to wake up fast and take notice.

'Is that Detective Chief Superintendent Charles Booth of the Southshire CID?' the voice continued. It was a slightly singsong voice, almost pedantic in its enunciation of the words. The voice of a woman, was Booth's immediate conclusion—but a decidedly unusual type of woman. He was fully awake now; he pulled himself upright in the bed.

'Charles Booth, that's me,' he said. This was no time to start explaining about coronaries and retirement on doctor's orders. He had only retired a month ago, anyway.

'Oh, good,' said the voice. 'Splendid, splendid. Absolutely super in fact.'

'And who am I talking to?' asked Booth.

There was a happy chuckle at the other end of the line—a curiously throaty chuckle. 'Oh, let's just say that I'm a friend . . . Yes, that will do. A lady friend, of course. A lady friend from way back.'

That noise wasn't static on the line after all, Booth decided. It was something else, something regular, vibrating or thumping in the background. A generator perhaps? Or a pump?

'Right then, milady,' said Booth. 'What can I do for you?'

'Well now, Superintendent, it's like this. Seventeen years ago there was a murder committed in a boring little village called Tinley.'

'A double murder to be precise,' Booth corrected her.

'Why yes, that's right, I was forgetting. A schoolteacher called Patrick Meadows and his young son— they both had their throats cut.'

'Yes,' said Booth cautiously. 'I remember.'

'You were in charge of that investigation, Superintendent.'

'I was for twenty-four hours. Till the Yard was called in.'

'Ah, yes. But you were the *local* man.'

Still that rhythmical booming, faint but persistent in the background.

'Well, what about it?'

'Well, Superintendent, to the best of my knowledge and belief the person who committed that double murder was never caught.'

'Quite right,' said Booth, trying hard not to sound as bitter as he felt. Someone within the tiny community of Tinley had been a killer, he had been quite convinced of that at the time and nothing had happened since to change his mind. But neither Booth nor Scotland Yard had ever been able to pin it down, never been able to make even an educated guess at who had done it, much less bring anyone to court. 'Yes, you're quite right,' Booth continued. 'The murder was never solved.'

'Ah, good. Well now, Superintendent, can I take it, then, that you'd still be interested in finding out who killed Patrick Meadows and his son?'

Booth's heart gave an unhealthy lurch at the very thought. 'You certainly can,' he said fiercely. 'Have you got some new evidence?'

The caller laughed softly. 'No, not really. Old evidence is what I'd call it.' Another laugh. 'Yes, very old evidence indeed. But can I take it that a person could still be tried and convicted for that crime?'

'Yes,' said Booth. 'Of course.'

'There's no statute of limitations on murder, then?'

Been watching too many films, thought Booth. 'No, no statute of limitations . . . Look I'd be very happy to meet you to talk over what you've found. What about—'

'No, no, no, no, no. No meetings, Superintendent.'

'Oh. All right then. If you prefer, we can do it on

the phone. Perhaps that's better really. More anony-mous. You can talk more freely.'

'Precisely.'

Booth gathered his thoughts together. He had to concentrate hard or his chance would slip away. 'I take it from what you've said that the murderer is still alive?'

'Oh, yes. Very much so.'

Booth was very careful about what he said next. 'It's a funny thing about Tinley,' he continued thoughtfully. 'You wouldn't expect a murder to hap-pen in a quiet place like that. Nice little village.'

'Well, it used to be, Superintendent. Used to be. It's changed a lot.'

'But there's still a few people around, though—peo-ple who were there seventeen years ago.'

'Oh, yes, half a dozen maybe. . . . But you're being a little bit naughty, Superintendent.'

'Am I?'

'Oh, yes, definitely a little bit naughty. You nearly got me going there, 'cos I'm a terrible gossip and I love a little chat. But you're trying to pump me, aren't you? Trying to draw me out. But you've told me all I want to know so you mustn't try to keep me hang-ing on.'

'Now just a minute,' said Booth firmly.

'Yes?'

The booming on the line became louder for a moment and then ceased.

'I take it you know who committed that murder?'

'Oh, yes.'

'You've got proof?'

'Yes.'

'Certain proof?'

'Well, let's put it this way, Superintendent—I think the person who did the deed will think so.'

Did the deed, thought Booth. What a peculiar thing to say about a crime like that. He was finding it hard to believe that his caller was 100 per cent sane. And yet he believed her all right. No two ways about that.

'I see.' said Booth slowly. 'So you're going to put the squeeze on, are you?'

Another throaty chuckle was part of his answer. 'The thought had crossed my mind,' the caller continued. 'I think it would be worth my while. But don't feel bad about it, Mr. Booth, it wasn't your fault that the investigation dragged on for so long. It was a very clever crime—very clever indeed.'

'That's just the point,' said Booth. 'You've got a murderer there who was clever and cool, and totally ruthless. Take a tip from an old copper, my dear. Pass the evidence on to me and leave well alone.'

'Don't worry, darling,' said the voice on the other end with an unexpectedly hard edge. 'I know even more about blackmail than you do.'

And then the line went dead.

Booth remained sitting upright in his bed for a long time, staring into the darkness, listening to the tick of the clock and his wife's steady breathing. He felt all of his fifty-five years old, and then some.

In his own eyes that first and only defeat on a murder case had scarred his whole career as head of the Southshire CID. And yet no one else had held it against him. The Yard had been called in almost immediately and not even the Yard had been able to crack it. So no one had blamed Booth. Only Booth had blamed himself. Because in his heart of hearts he had known that it was a local crime, and the local man ought to have solved it. And now, seventeen years later, here was a phone-call in the middle of the night to tell him that he had been right all along. There was evidence about and he ought to have found it.

Booth asked himself what he would give to find the solution to that double murder after all this time—and he realized that he would give everything he had that he could part with without grieving his wife.

He went downstairs and wrote out the telephone conversation in longhand, word for word; the heart attack had done nothing to impair his memory. Then he had a large whisky and soda and returned to bed.

But he slept fitfully, his dreams troubled by the gaping wounds in the throats of the schoolteacher and his young son, wounds he had not seen for seventeen years. He could still see the blood, though, all over the sheets. And in his dream it was still warm.

5

The following morning ex-Detective Chief Superintendent Booth had an early breakfast and then drove into Wellbridge, the county town. He parked his car in a new multi-storey car park and walked the last fifty yards to the county police headquarters.

Booth was a big man, six feet tall and fourteen stone. He was still carrying too much weight, so his doctor said, though it was coming down steadily; his suits were beginning to hang loose on him. His face was thinner now than before his heart attack, his complexion still healthy enough and his black hair only just beginning to turn grey; but those who knew him well could see clearly what the last year had taken out of him and were glad to see him retired, with the pressure removed.

With a cheery wave to one or two men he knew, Booth went up the stairs to his old office, now occupied by his successor as head of the Southshire CID, Detective Chief Superintendent Ben Spence. It was only twenty-past 8 even now, but Booth had every confidence that Spence would be sitting at his desk, and he was.

They greeted each other warmly, using each other's first names with relief after all those years of the formality which was best preserved in a disciplined force.

'Well, Charlie,' said Spence after a few moments'

preliminary chat, 'at this time of the morning it must be business. What have you got for me?'

Booth's big hand groped in the inside pocket of his double-breasted jacket and emerged with the hand-written transcript of his telephone conversation of the early hours. He passed it over without comment and stood gazing out of the window while Spence digested it.

'Well,' said Spence eventually. 'It *reads* convincing-ly . . . Did it sound convincing?'

Booth turned away from the window and sat down again. 'Oh, yes. I think the woman was telling the truth, more or less. Do you remember the case?'

'Barely,' said Spence. 'I'd only been in the force a year or two—signed up on my twentieth birthday. So perhaps you'd better tell me about it.'

Booth took out a pipe and began to fill it. 'Well—it was seventeen years ago. I was in much the same position then as you are now, and much the same age. Just been made head of the CID, at an earlier age than most people thought decent, and a lot of passed-over mediocrities would have been very happy to see me fall flat on my face. Anyway, it all started one Monday afternoon in summer—eighth of August it was. The postman in Tinley was doing his second delivery, about 2 o'clock, and he noticed that the paper and the milk hadn't been taken in at one of the houses.'

'Fairly isolated house, wasn't it,' asked Spence.

'Yes, that's right. It had been a tied cottage at one time, and it wasn't in the main part of the village at all, it was about three-quarters of a mile to the north. It was down a little lane off the road which led to the manor house. And in those days Colonel Host-

Wall really was the lord of the manor. The house belonged to him as a matter of fact, this teacher feller rented it from him.'

'And the teacher was a widower, I believe.'

'Yes, that's right. Patrick Meadows, his name was. His wife had been killed in a road accident five years earlier. He had a son, though, ten years old . . . Anyway, the postman decided that something was wrong. It was the summer holidays you see, and he expected to see the teacher and his son out in the garden. And what with the papers and the milk not being taken in he thought perhaps they were ill, so he went upstairs. What he saw there made him sick all over the floor, and then he called us. . . . It was a very hot day I remember, the flies as thick as you like, even then. So you can imagine how much I enjoyed that part of the proceedings.'

Spence grinned. Booth's squeamishness and dislike of blood had been the subject of much amusement in the force—and occasionally a matter for bitter comment when it was felt that he had failed to pay sufficient attention to a particularly gory case.

'Well,' Booth continued, 'we went in there, Alf Simmonds and me, and on the ground floor everything looked reasonably OK. No disturbance at all. But in the main bedroom we found Patrick Meadows, the father, with his throat savagely cut, Almost severed with one stroke, delivered with enormous power. And in the other bedroom, the boy, same thing. But for that nosy postman they might have been there for days before anyone missed them.'

'What was the weapon?'

'Their own carving knife, left in the boy's bedroom. No prints on it.'

'Killed during the night were they?'

'Oh, yes, on the Sunday night, or rather Monday morning, about 2 or 3 a.m.'

'Any disturbance upstairs?'

'No, not to speak of. We did wonder if someone had gone through the papers on Meadows's desk, but we couldn't be sure . . . Well, we did all the usual things—set up the investigation, talked to people, but after twenty-four hours the old man called in the Yard. Fair enough, I suppose—it was obvious by then that it wasn't going to be a simple case. Not by a long shot.'

'Who did the Yard send?'

'Oh, a bloke called Renton. Him and his sergeant. Couple of gentlemen they were, out of the old school. Hard as nails, of course, but they had some respect for our feelings, mine in particular, and I wouldn't hear a word said against them. Not now, anyway, looking back with a bit more experience. I don't think they had more than two hours' sleep a night, either of them, for the first month.'

'Didn't get anywhere, though, did they?'

'No. Never learnt a damn thing. The only thing which even approached a clue was something we kept pretty quiet about at the time. One man came forward and said that at 2 o'clock on the Monday morning he'd seen a man smoking a pipe and wearing a trilby hat, walking through the village. We kept that piece of information to ourselves at the time.'

'How old was this man?'

'Which one?'

'The one that was seen.'

'Oh, middle-aged.'

'Your informant couldn't identify him, I suppose?'

'No, no.'

'Did he talk to him or challenge him?'

'No. And the man with the pipe didn't see our informant, either.'

'I see. And what was your informant doing out at that time?'

'Well, he said he couldn't sleep, but we didn't believe that, of course. He was none too bright, but that was his story and he stuck to it like grim death. We gave him a hell of a rough time, needless to say, and at one time I felt pretty sure that he'd been to see some woman whose husband was on nights. But he denied it—seemed quite upset by the suggestion in fact—and in the end, as I say, the conclusion we came to was that he was none too bright but that he was absolutely truthful. He'd just been out for a walk to help him to sleep.'

'And that was as far as you got?'

'Yes, that was all. Apart from that, after months of work, zero.'

'No motive?'

'No. None that would bear any weight, anyway. You can always hypothesize a motive—you know, Meadows gets a girl pregnant, father kills him in revenge and kills the boy to keep him quiet, that sort of thing. But we never got very far with ideas like that . . . He was a curious man, the victim. Teacher at a little Church of England primary school across the river in Tallmead. He had a gammy leg, some sort of arthritic condition, and I think it had made him a bit sour. He wasn't a good mixer, but he wasn't a hermit, either. Lived outside the village, kept to himself, and looked after his lad on his own.'

'Any help in the house?'

'No. We looked for that, naturally. Cleaning woman whose husband felt Meadows was a bit too familiar or something like that. But there was no such animal.'

'Religious, I suppose, being a C of E school?'

'Yes, he went to church, but he wasn't a fanatic. His son sang in the choir.'

'And nothing was stolen from the house?'

'No, not that we ever discovered. And the murderer didn't have to break in, by the way. In those days hardly anyone in Tinley ever bothered to lock their doors. Though they did afterwards, by God. We had vigilante groups being organized till we stamped on it. And it was summer, of course, there were plenty of windows wide open.'

Spence was thoughtful. 'I see,' he said. 'So that's the context. Now let's get back to last night's phone-call for a minute. It was a woman, you say.'

'Yes.'

'With some local knowledge?'

'Yes. I tried to pump her but she was a bit too smart for that. But she did speak of changes in the village, which suggests she's been there for some time.'

'So she's a long-term resident, then?'

Booth hesitated. 'Well, maybe. She seemed to know a lot about the residents. Spoke of there still being half a dozen people in the village who'd been there at the time of the murder. But she didn't talk like any long-term resident of Tinley that I've ever met. Much too sophisticated and big city. More like someone from the new estate.'

'There must be a few *nouveaux riches* around though,' said Spence. 'People who've been there perhaps ten or twelve years. Commuters who moved there when it was still an unspoilt village?'

'Well, yes, I suppose so. I can't think of any, but it's a year or two since I've been back. I used to go back there regularly over the years, every eighteen months or so. I used to look at the place in different seasons, talk to different people. I never closed the file and I never will. Not in my own mind. Not until we catch him or I die, whichever comes first.'

'You say not until we catch *him*. So you're sure it was a man, then.'

'No. I'm not sure of anything.'

Spence looked at the transcript again. 'Why do you think your caller used a pay-phone?' he asked. 'Why not a private phone?'

'I'm not sure. Perhaps she was afraid that someone might overhear what she was saying. Perhaps she went out to be sure of privacy. Or perhaps she hasn't a phone of her own—though I find that hard to believe.'

'And what about this noise in the background— what would that have been?'

'I don't know. It was a regular sort of sound. Might have been a fault on the line. But you could have a look at all the call-boxes in Tinley—just to see if any of them stand beside an electricity sub-station or a water pump or something.'

'But who's to say the caller was ringing from Tinley?' asked Spence.

'Well, yes, that's true. But I got the impression she was, somehow.'

'And the other worrying thing is that your caller was going to blackmail the murderer.'

'Oh, yes, no doubt about that at all. I tried to put her off but failed. That could be very dangerous indeed.'

'Damn right it could,' said Spence. 'It takes a lot of nerve to slit people's throats in the middle of a dark night, and a lot more nerve to sit tight and not give yourself away for seventeen years. If your lady friend is right and the murderer is still around, she'd better be careful or she might end up on a marble slab.'

'My feelings exactly.' Booth shook his head uneasily. 'I gave her the gypsy's warning but it didn't seem to do much good. Let's just hope that our killer, if she really has found him, has grown old and feeble in the meantime.'

'I think we ought to do more than just hope,' said Spence firmly.

'What do you mean, we?' said Booth suspiciously.

Spence grinned at him. 'Well, what I suggest is that you and I pay a visit to Tinley this afternoon. From what you say it sounds as if your face is well known there. And if we show the flag, so to speak, we might scare the blackmailer off.'

'Or persuade her to send us the evidence.'

'Precisely . . . So what do you say?'

Booth didn't need much convincing. 'Well, it wouldn't do any harm, I suppose. When do you want to go?'

'Well, if I remember rightly my wife is going to be over at Tallmead this afternoon, watching a student of hers teaching physics. And I've also got a cousin who owns a farm about two miles from Tinley. So how would it be if you and I went over there in your car at about 3? We can poke around for a bit, and then end up at my cousin's place. My wife can join us there after she's finished at Tallmead, and I'm sure my cousin won't mind us inviting ourselves for supper.

After that you can go home on your own and I'll go home with my wife.'

Booth nodded cheerfully. 'That sounds all right. Gives me time to go home and put my feet up for a bit . . . I'll join you back here this afternoon then.'

6

The sun was shining brightly over their left shoulders as Booth and Spence drove north up the London Road soon after 3 o'clock that afternoon.

They were travelling in Booth's Rover 2000 but Spence was driving. Booth wasn't nervous about having another coronary—he'd decided some time ago that it was either going to happen or it wasn't, and there was no point in worrying about it—but equally there was no point in exposing yourself to the stresses and strains imposed by driving in today's traffic unless you had to.

They didn't talk much. Instead Booth spent most of the time thinking about Spence and how he would cope with his new job as head of the Southshire CID.

Spence was thirty-nine now, six feet tall like Booth but somewhat lighter; not so long ago he had been a dangerous centre-threequarter, but nowadays he stuck to gentler pursuits, such as cricket or sailing. He had dark brown hair, brown eyes and a face which bore impressive and strong features without being handsome. His expression was normally cheerful, but like a good actor he could change it at will; experience of amateur dramatics in his youth had proved very useful in his police career. Today, as usual, he was dressed in a medium-grey double-breasted suit, cut from top-quality cloth. He also had on a white shirt, blue tie and hand-made black Chelsea boots; three years on the beat had taught him the value of good footwear.

It was a twenty-mile drive from Wellbridge, the county town, to Tinley. The road was busy but the countryside was for the most part peaceful; it was good farming land with an occasional small town set astride the road.

The last place they passed through before reaching their destination was Tallmead, an old market town chiefly famous as the home of a leading public school. Spence knew Tallmead well, having first come there as a visiting schoolboy to play rugger.

Half a mile out of Tallmead they bumped over a level-crossing, crossed a long bridge over the river, and then turned right up a tree-lined road. After another half-mile they turned left up a slight hill, and almost immediately they came to Tinley village green.

Spence parked the car on the edge of the green and the two men sat for a moment enjoying the sunshine and the view. It was all very relaxing: green grass, old cottages, the church in the distance, groups of trees, and very few people. Booth lit his pipe before speaking.

'Well,' he said eventually, 'let's call on Mrs Amble at the post office. That way the jungle drums will ensure within minutes that all the old inhabitants know we're here. I expect most of them will have read in the paper that I've retired, but if it's all right with you I'll take the lead in the conversation. They're used to me and I think they'll open up more. OK?'

'Certainly,' said Spence. 'You're the expert as far as this place is concerned.'

The two men got out of the car and walked over to the village shop. An old-fashioned bell above the door rang loudly as they went in and Mrs Amble greeted Booth as if it were only yesterday that she had seen him last; in fact he had not been in Tinley for well over a year.

'Good afternoon, Mr Booth,' she said briskly. 'I've nothing for you I'm afraid, though never a day goes by when I don't think about it. I look at everyone who comes in here, strangers particularly—and you get some very queer people about nowadays, I can tell you—and I wonder if they could have done it. It makes you feel real funny at times, knowing that there's someone walking free that did a wicked murder like that. But no one's heard anything. Nothing new that is.'

Booth nodded and asked politely about Mrs Amble's health and that of her husband. He listened patiently to the lengthy and detailed reply. Then he steered the conversation round to the older inhabitants of the village.

'I don't suppose there's so many left now, though, are there?' he suggested. 'Seventeen years is a long time and nowadays people tend to move on.'

'Or die,' said Mrs Amble solemnly.

'Well, yes, there is that,' Booth agreed. 'But there can't be all that many people left now who were here when Mr Meadows and his boy were killed. After all, it was a very small village in those days. Let's see now. There'll be the Vicar, I suppose. Then the Colonel and his wife. . . .'

'Yes, they're still here,' said Mrs Amble. 'Though the Vicar was taken very queer yesterday, so Mrs Trayle tells me, and as for Mrs Host-Wall, well, in a very bad way so they say. Not fit to go out on her own.'

'Really?' said Booth. 'I'm sorry to hear that. Who

else now . . . Walter Underwood, he'll live to a ripe old age. And Mrs Cordwright's still here, of course, and her son's back again now, I gather.'

'Oh, yes. And Mr Read, I suppose, though he lived in Tallmead back in them days. Still teaching, he was, at that time, so he doesn't count. He's not an old inhabitant at all really . . . And then there's me and my Will.' Mrs Amble paused. 'And that's about all, really. Hundreds of newcomers, of course, on the new estate.'

Booth nodded. 'Yes,' he said, 'I know all about them. But not many old-timers. Just a small, select band . . .' Booth stuck a match and relit his pipe. 'Now then, Mrs Amble, I want a bit of information. Public phone-boxes in the village—where are they these days?'

'Well, there's one outside of course, and then two on the new estate. Not that you'll find them working—vandalized, they are, nine times out of ten. There'll be a nasty accident one day, you mark my words, I've complained time and again but no one ever listens to me . . .'

But Booth and Spence were forced to listen to Mrs Amble for another five minutes before they could easily get away. Then they went outside to the phone-box nearby to see if they could identify the source of the regular thumping noise which Booth had heard in the background during his call in the early hours of the morning. But there was no obvious source for the sound.

'Could it have been a car engine?' asked Spence. 'Perhaps your caller drove to a phone-box, and she may have left the engine running while she rang you.'

Booth shook his head. 'No, that doesn't feel right

at all. I feel as if I ought to be able to say what it was. It was something I've heard before but I can't just place it . . . Anyway, let's leave it for the moment. What do you want to do now?'

'You lead the way,' said Spence. 'You're the expert. You show me what you think I ought to see.'

They sat down on a bench on the green for a minute while Booth rekindled his pipe yet again.

'You'll have looked at the file, I suppose?' he asked.

'Yes,' said Spence. 'A nice summary.'

'I boiled it all down eventually. Got all the essentials into one thin folder so that if anything happened to me someone else could take it over . . . Seventeen years ago nearly all the people who lived here were farm labourers or they worked at the school over in Tallmead. A sprinkling of the upper middle-class, of course, but for the most part the villagers were quiet, uncomplicated people, about as honest as any you could find anywhere. They all knew each other intimately—perhaps too intimately. You couldn't walk across the village green without everyone else knowing about it—and they all leaned over backwards to co-operate with us. It should have been easy to tell who was lying, but it wasn't. We couldn't even identify the motive, though we could think of dozens of possible ones, of course . . .' Booth paused and blew a cloud of smoke high into the air. 'I don't know,' he continued. 'Two deaths. I felt very strongly about them at the time. But perhaps it doesn't matter very much. People get killed every day on the roads.'

'It matters all right,' Spence assured him. 'You were right to spend all that time on it, just as it's right that I should be here now. Murder is a deliberately evil act, not an accident, and you were fully justified in not letting it rest.'

Booth puffed on his pipe in silence for a few moments. 'What do you know of the history of Tinley?' he asked eventually.

'Not much.'

'Well you don't need to know much, except that 500 years ago it was a big place, an important market town. Hence the large church. And then in the mid-nineteenth century, for a variety of reasons, the balance shifted and it began to decline. Until, as I've said, when I first came here on business there were barely a hundred people. Now, of course, it's growing again. And that's what complicates matters—this big new housing estate behind us.'

'Commuters, I suppose.'

'Yes, God help them. Colonel Host-Wall sold some land a few years back and the developers got to work and now you've got a whole new population—hundreds of them. I don't know them, they don't know me, and most of them probably don't know each other.'

'Do you think one of them could have phoned you last night?'

'Possibly. I suppose a newcomer could have got to hear of the crime and then noticed something crucial. Perhaps something so obvious that the rest of us overlooked it.'

'What was the police strength here in those days?'

Booth gave a hollow laugh. 'Huh! There used to be two men over in Tallmead, and one of them used to visit the village once in a blue moon. He was a real old village bobby—retired to live in Coventry some years back. Funny place to go.'

'And what about this mysterious man in the trilby hat—the man with a pipe who was seen walking through the village on the night of the murder. Where was he seen?'

Booth indicated with the stem of his pipe. 'Over there, on the far edge of the green. About fifty yards beyond the post office. It was pretty well pitch-dark here in those days, but there was a lamp over there on the corner of the green, and that's where he was seen, walking this way. It was a fellow called Walter Underwood who saw him.'

'Yes, I know,' said Spence. 'It's in the file. I wouldn't mind a word with Walter some time.'

'Well, we can kill two birds with one stone, then,' said Booth. 'We can go and see the house where it all happened, and with any luck we'll see Walter at the same time.'

'Why so?'

'Walter lives there now,' said Booth.

They returned to the Rover and Spence drove past the garage, the pub, and the post office, and up a narrow lane which led north away from the village.

'This is the road to the Colonel's house,' Booth explained, 'a big mansion a mile and a half beyond the village. At the turn of the century the Host-Walls were a very rich and influential family. Got their money from banking. But they've come down in the world since then, no doubt about it. The place we want is only about halfway to the manor house, on the left. You'll miss it if you don't watch out.'

After three-quarters of a mile a sign-post marked a road to the left, and on the corner of the road, set well back behind unruly hedges, stood a small detached cottage with a thatched roof. An estate agent would not have been overwhelmed by it: it was a cramped and unattractive little house, faintly depressing to look at even if you knew nothing of its unhappy history.

'Do you want to hear something really far out?' asked Booth, as they sat in the car and looked across the road. 'Sometimes when I was feeling low because of the lack of progress, I used to feel that the solution to this case was really quite simple. My idea was this: somebody told a not-very-bright lad that if you came to Tinley and took the road to the north, you would come to a house where a very rich man lived.'

'Meaning the Colonel's house.'

'That's right. And what happened was this: the dim-witted bloke came to Tinley, took the road he'd been told to take, and came across this place, three-quarters of a mile up the road. It wasn't the house he'd been told about, not by a long chalk, but being a bit on the thick side he committed the murders, found nothing worth stealing, and went away again.'

'No,' said Spence. 'I'm not convinced by that. He would have wrecked the place, looking for something to steal, and you said there was very little disturbance.'

'True,' said Booth. 'True. Which is one reason why I don't go for that theory wholeheartedly myself. But it's still a possibility. Perhaps he got frightened and ran away after he'd done the killings.'

They got out of the car and went up the front path of the house together. The garden had not been touched for some years.

'You say the Colonel owns this house?' asked Spence.

'Yes. This one and a number of others round here.'

'And he rents it to Walter Underwood?'

'Not rents it, no. Lets it. No one would pay rent to live in a place with a history like this. Walter Underwood hasn't paid a penny in rent since he moved in.'

'Doesn't seem to have cleaned the windows since he moved in either,' said Spence. 'What's he do for a living?'

'Farm-hand,' said Booth.

The front door of the house had clearly not been opened for a decade, so the two men passed round the side of the building to approach the back door.

'Walter's health hasn't been too good for some years,' Booth continued, 'so he's not very hot on house-maintenance. He stops the place going completely to ruin, but that's about all . . . Let's see if he's in.'

7

It was many years since the back door of the house had been painted and when Booth banged on it loudly several flakes of brittle and faded blue crust drifted down to the ground.

After some moments the door creaked open a few inches and the suspicious face of a man about sixty appeared in the gap.

'Oh. 'Ullo, Mr. Booth,' said the man, and pulled the door wider open. 'Come on in, sir.'

'Thanks,' said Booth.

He and Spence stepped directly into the kitchen, which was small and already overcrowded with furniture, sacks of potatoes, and a dog kennel. The draining-board beside the cracked and dirt-encrusted sink was piled high with used pots and plates; a platoon of empty beer bottles stood in one corner. Overall there was a smell of drains and elderly dog, and the source of the latter staggered to its feet and pattered away as the newcomers entered.

Booth introduced his companion and Underwood nodded awkwardly. He was of average build, with the battered hands, red face, and old clothes of an aging farm-labourer.

'There's nothing new I can tell you, though, Mr Booth,' he said anxiously. 'No hard feelings and all that—I don't bear no grudges, as you know—but I've never seen no one who rang a bell. Never. And I think I'd remember, even after all this time.'

'Not to worry,' said Booth. 'I didn't think you'd have anything new to tell me. We'd just like to look upstairs, that's all—OK?'

Underwood nodded. 'All right. You know the way. I'll put the kettle on for you while you're up there.'

Booth and Spence passed through the gloomy hall and mounted the uncarpeted stairs to the main bedroom, which overlooked the front garden. Walter's single bed was still unmade.

'This was where the father slept,' said Booth. 'Patrick Meadows. There was a double bed over here, where the single one is now. Big Victorian dressing-table to the right of the window. And a carpet on the floor in those days . . . Walking-stick by the bedside because of his limp. A wardrobe over on the far side of the room—fishing rod propped up against it. Meadows apparently spent a lot of time fishing with his son. Wasn't very mobile, you see, but he enjoyed sitting by the river . . . And then there were books piled up on a small bedside table with a lamp. He was a voracious reader, apparently.'

'But nothing stolen, you said.'

'No. Didn't have much worth stealing, anyway. No, I don't think theft was the motive.'

'How old was he?'

'Thirty-eight. And the boy was ten.'

'How did he get over to his school in Tallmead?'

'He used to cycle. He had a bike specially adapted for his gammy leg. Only one pedal went round, a fixed gear type of thing.'

'And the boy? How did he travel to school?'

'He had a bike too. It was all right in those days,

very little traffic. And they could go across the fields part of the way, they didn't have to follow the road the long way round like we did.'

Spence and Booth moved on into what had been the boy's bedroom and Booth described the layout there as it had been seventeen years earlier.

'What sort of lad was he?' asked Spence.

'Peter? Oh, normal, physically and mentally. Lively, cheerful. He liked going fishing, collecting stamps, that sort of thing. He didn't deserve to die, that's quite certain. A wicked crime that was—miserable, wicked, and unforgivable.' Booth spoke with unusual force; normally he was quite objective.

'Was Meadows a good teacher?'

'Oh, yes, by all accounts. A regular church-goer, concerned for the kids. But the death of his wife had driven him in on himself a bit, so he wasn't very sociable. People respected him rather than liked him.'

'And what about the little girls?'

'What little girls?'

'The ones he taught at school. Any suggestion that he ever had a hand in their knickers, or hanky-panky with the cane?'

'No, no. Or at any rate, if there was we never heard about it, and we asked some very pointed questions.'

'I see . . . What about his past, before he came here?'

'Clean as a whistle, apparently.'

'Yes, as you say, apparently. But the fact is, someone had a reason for killing him.'

'Yes . . .'

Spence turned to look out of the window. 'I'm

interested in this man Underwood,' he said quietly.
'He was the one who saw the man with the hat and
the pipe on the night of the murder. He came to you
with that story, and you gave him the treatment and
he came out clean—'

'I wouldn't say he came out 100 per cent clean,'
said Booth. 'But we couldn't find any motive. Of
course if we'd kept him at the station for forty-eight
hours without regular meals and sleep, done an Evans
on him, we could probably have got a confession.
But the Yard man didn't work that way, thank God,
and I wouldn't have let him if he'd wanted to.'

'Nevertheless,' said Spence, 'it's a bit odd that a man
so closely involved in the case should end up living
in the murder house.'

'Not really,' said Booth. 'You've got to remember
that *everyone* in the village was intimately involved
in the case. Seventeen years ago it was that sort of
community. Walter is not really too bright, you'll see
that soon enough when you talk to him. So sleeping
in a room where a man was killed doesn't give him
nightmares the way it would you and me. He just
hasn't got enough imagination for it to worry him.
It's enough for him that the roof over his head is
rent-free.'

Spence ran a finger through the dust on a chair.
'He lives alone, I suppose?'

'Absolutely. Been a bachelor all his life. Fairly
solitary sort of chap.'

'And been a farm-labourer all his life too?'

'Until recently, yes. He was in the army during
the war, of course. But these last few years Walter's
been ill, and I don't think he's worked at all. I don't

know what it is. Some sort of progressive disease which weakens for years before it kills.'

Heart, thought Spence, but didn't like to say so. 'And you rule him out as a suspect,' he said aloud.

'Oh, no,' said Booth firmly. 'I don't rule him out at all. I didn't rule anyone out at the time, from the Vicar downwards, and I don't now. The murders that took place in this house were committed in the middle of the night—and in the middle of the night no one really has an alibi, not even the married ones. Plenty of wives can sleep through anything—mine for a start.'

Spence came away from the window. 'Let's go back to Colonel Host-Wall for a minute. If the man with the trilby hat and the pipe was really the murderer, and if he was going home when he was seen, then the Colonel would have been going the wrong way wouldn't he?'

'Correct,' said Booth. 'And Walter said it wasn't the Colonel, as it happens, though local gossip suspected him.'

'Why?'

'Oh, envy. Class prejudice, I suppose. The Host-Walls had thrown their weight about at one time.'

'And what was your view of the Colonel as a suspect?'

'I told you—I ruled out nobody.'

Spence grinned. 'Very wise,' he said.

From the floor below Walter Underwood called out, 'Tea up!' and Spence and Booth went back downstairs.

Underwood served them tea in chipped and stained mugs, and Spence felt as if he were risking food poisoning with every sip but did his best to look grateful. Underwood drank his own tea noisily, his dark eyes, deeply recessed in his weathered face, watching his visitors cautiously.

'Good brew that,' said Underwood happily when he had finished. 'I 'ad a winner last week and bought some of Mrs Amble's best.' He laughed hugely, displaying serious gaps in his teeth.

There was a knock at the back door, and when Underwood opened it Spence knew at once that the caller must be the Colonel. No one else in the village would be likely to be sporting a peaked Kangol cap, tweed suit, distinguished grey moustache, Viyella shirt, bow tie, chukka boots, and a walking-stick. The Squire had come calling and Underwood all but tugged his forelock.

'Come in, Colonel,' he urged heartily. 'Come in. Have some tea. You'll know these gentlemen, I expect.'

The Colonel didn't know Spence, but was soon introduced and skilfully argued his way out of partaking of tea. Clearly an old hand, thought Spence.

'Just came to tell you that the builder will be coming to do the roof on Friday, Walter,' said the Colonel briskly.

'Ah,' said Walter absorbing the information. 'High time, too.'

After a few further words about the roof the four of them then began to discuss the day's weather, yesterday's weather, and the weather likely to develop over the next month.

'Well,' said the Colonel, after this was exhausted as a topic, 'this is not a business call I trust, Mr Booth?' His hands moved nervously on the top of his

walking-stick, making Spence wonder what the man
had to hide.

'Yes and no,' said Booth. 'Just showing Mr Spence
here the scene of an old crime. The file was never
closed, you know.'

'Ah, yes,' said the Colonel. 'Ah, yes. A bad business,
that. Very bad.' He laid his walking-stick down,
took out a pipe, and began to fill it from a well-stocked
pouch. 'It's a year or two since you were here last,
though, isn't it? Came over to look at the Blue Bazaar
last time, I think.'

'Yes, that's right,' said Booth. 'Soon after it opened.'

'Local den of vice, you know,' said the Colonel to
Spence by way of explanation. 'The Blue Bazaar—
nightclub, you know.'

Spence nodded. 'Yes,' he said. 'I've heard of it.'

'I was opposed to it myself,' the Colonel continued,
putting away his tobacco pouch despite Underwood's
envious looks. 'Lowers the whole tone of the neigh-
bourhood 100 per cent. Always thought better of Mrs
Cordwright than that. She's gone right down in my
estimation over the last few years. Doesn't even go to
church now, you know.' He raised his eyebrows at
all present as if to emphasize the seriousness of that
situation.

'Who's Mrs Cordwright?' asked Spence.

The Colonel attempted to light his pipe, without
great success. 'Local widow-lady,' he said between
sucks. 'Lived here for donkey's years, pillar of the village and all that . . . But one day she inherited a bit
of money, and the next thing you know she's set her
son and his friend up in business with a brand-new
nightclub. Why she couldn't have made it a straight-

forward hotel, which is what the boy was trained for, I'll never know.' He continued puffing for a few moments. 'Have striptease there every week now, you know. Can't think what the world's coning to . . . Times are changing, there's no doubt about it. Times are changing.'

Everyone agreed that times were indeed changing, and then, as soon as they decently could, Booth and Spence left the Colonel to the company of Walter Underwood and went on their way.

8

'Well, what do you think of the Squire then?' asked Booth as Spence drove the two of them back down the road to the village.

'Seems a shifty sort of fellow to me,' said Spence. 'Farmer, is he?'

'Not in person, no. He owns a fair bit of land round here, or did at one time, but he lets it out to tenant farmers. He shoots a bit, plays golf, sits on the local council, and that's about it.'

'Hmm. Was he any good as a soldier?'

'Well, he was a professional before the war, not just a wartime man like most of us. I think he had a fair record.'

Spence steered round a stray cow in the road.

'Mrs Amble said something about his wife being ill.'

'Yes . . . It's something psychiatric, I don't know what. She's been a trifle eccentric for years, and they keep very much to themselves nowadays.'

'He must be worth a few bob, then, if he owns a few farms.'

'Well, yes. But I get the feeling that the Colonel's not as wealthy as he used to be.'

Spence laughed. 'It's called taxation,' he said.

'No, it's not just that, though the redistribution of wealth enters into it no doubt. There's more to it than that. They must have made some bad business decisions somewhere.'

Spence changed gear as they approached the village green again.

'Where to now?' he asked.

'Bear left,' said Booth. 'I want to go and see the Vicar. Seventeen years ago he was one of my two chief sources of information.'

'The other being Mrs Amble, I presume.'

'Correct. Or to be more precise, there were three main sources of information, because the Vicar's wife was alive in those days. Surprising what she knew that he didn't and vice versa . . . She was a very sick woman even when I knew her, and she died about a year later. Poor old Barndean's never been the same since.'

'Any children?'

'Yes, one, but for God's sake don't mention the subject. He has a son, James, but after the boy's mother died James went off the rails a bit. He left home, oh, three or four years later, I think, and the Vicar has never heard from him since.'

'Well, just one of the many thousands who do the same,' said Spence.

'That's what I tell him,' said Booth. 'But it's precious little comfort, I'm afraid. It's very much an open wound with the Vicar.'

'Lives alone, does he?'

'Yes. He has a housekeeper, Mrs Trayle, but she just comes in daily.'

'So he broods,' said Spence.

'Yes, I'm afraid you're right. He broods.'

Spence arrived at the vicarage by the simple expedient of aiming at the church spire. Once there,

Booth rang the doorbell and introduced himself to the stout, fiftyish woman who answered it. She was Mrs Trayle: a sensible country housewife with short brown hair, wearing a flowery blue dress with an apron over it.

'Ah, yes,' said Mrs Trayle. 'Mr Booth, I remember you.'

'Is the Vicar in?' asked Booth.

'Well, yes, he is . . .' Mrs Trayle hesitated, her hands thrust into her apron pockets.

'But what?' said Booth.

Mrs Trayle looked over her shoulder before answering, and then spoke quietly. 'Well, to tell you the truth, Mr Booth, he's not at all well. I'm quite worried about him. He went over to the church yesterday afternoon and came back looking simply awful. And I don't think he slept a wink last night. I did wonder whether he'd had some kind of a stroke, but he says he feels all right. And I've suggested he might like to see the doctor, but he won't hear of it.'

'Oh, dear,' said Booth sympathetically. 'I'm sorry he's not fit.'

'Now you're an old friend of his, Mr Booth,' Mrs Trayle continued. 'He speaks of you quite frequently. You have a word with him and see what you think. But I don't think you ought to stay long.'

'Right you are,' said Booth. 'I've spent a lot of time with doctors myself recently, so you just leave him to me, Mrs Trayle. I promise you we won't overstay our welcome.'

Booth led the way into the Vicar's study, where they found the Reverend Albert Barndean sitting in an easy chair with a rug over his knees; he had been reading a book about ancient Egypt. Barndean was of average height and build, with thinning hair brushed firmly backwards. When he rose to his feet he moved quite easily for a man in his mid-sixties, but his face was pale and his eyes were apprehensive behind brown-framed glasses. He looked like a man who had just awoken from a nightmare.

The Vicar greeted Booth warmly, obviously pleased to see him. Then he turned to Spence.

'Mr Spence,' he said thoughtfully as he shook hands. 'Let me see now, there's a George Spence who's a farmer not so very far from here.'

'My cousin,' said Spence with a grin.

'Ah, yes, yes. A splendid man is George, quite splendid.' The Vicar's face almost brightened for a moment, but then it resumed its previous haggard appearance. 'Not one of my parishioners really,' he continued, 'but he comes to church occasionally with his wife, and she's a member of the Women's Institute, of course. A most likeable couple altogether. Most likeable.'

The Vicar resumed his seat and asked the others to be seated too. He offered refreshment, which they politely declined.

'Well then please smoke instead if you wish. I often do.' He indicated a rack of pipes. 'Though my doctors told me years ago I shouldn't.'

'Mine too,' said Booth ruefully.

For some minutes Booth gently pumped the Vicar about recent developments in the village. Then he embarked on the serious business of the day.

'I want to tell you something in confidence,' he said.

The Vicar folded his hands in his lap. 'People usually do,' he said, with a shy, half-smile.

'I've had an anonymous telephone call, from a woman who claims to have new evidence about the murder of Patrick Meadows and his son.'

'My word—after all this time,' said the Vicar wonderingly.

'Yes . . . It was evidently someone who knew all about the murders, and quite a lot about the village as a whole. I definitely got the impression that she was here at the time of the original crime. Possibly as a child. And yet she didn't sound like a typical villager. Not one of the old school, anyway. A sophisticated sort of woman.'

'Southshire accent?'

'No, far from it. Sort of mid-Atlantic somehow. And she was none too honest, if that's any help. Quite ready to break the law herself.'

'And so you want to know who she is,' said the Vicar.

'Yes, I do.'

The Vicar sighed. The situation seemed to intensify his previous distress. He twisted his hands in his lap and sighed again.

'Well . . . Really—I don't know . . . It's so difficult to say who it might be. You know, at the time when Patrick Meadows and his son were murdered, there were barely a hundred people living in the village itself—more in the parish as a whole, of course . . . And of the ones that were here then, why, there're hardly any left now. Those that were children then have grown up and moved away. Those that were old, have died. And those in between, like you and me . . . Well, we're still here, I suppose, after a fashion.'

The Vicar fell silent again, and Booth felt guilty about pressing him. The man definitely looked ill.

'So you can't imagine who it might be then?' Booth said at last.

'Well . . . Of course, there's all the new estate to think about. But leaving that aside for the moment, the only one of the oldtimers that I can think it might be is Mrs Cordwright.'

'I see. Why her?'

'Well . . .' Again the fingers obsessively fought each other. 'You know how much I hate to think ill of anyone, Mr Booth, it's against all my instincts. And yet with the best will in the world, I cannot convince myself that over the last few years Mrs Cordwright has conducted herself in a Christian manner. I really can't. She may keep within the letter of the law, but that nightclub of hers is an affront to all decent people. And her son David and that friend of his live together in a manner which is barely tolerable. It's truly scandalous. Not even I am naïve enough to see it as anything but a homosexual relationship, and I don't like it. And so, all things considered, I can no longer believe that Mrs Cordwright's morals are of the highest standard. I really can't.'

The Vicar turned his head away from them and Booth decided that it would be unfair to take the matter any further. He indicated to Spence with a glance that they should go.

'I think perhaps I'm too old for active work any longer,' said the Vicar as they took their leave of him. 'I think perhaps I should retire.'

'Retire to bed with a bottle,' Booth told him, in an attempt to cheer him up.

'What kind of bottle?'

'Both kinds,' said Booth. 'Hot-water and whisky.'

The Vicar smiled, and with that small success behind them they left the vicarage and returned to the car.

Once out of earshot Booth confided to Spence that he thought it would take a lot more than a good night's sleep to restore his old friend to full health.

'Well, maybe,' said Spence, 'but it's not so long since you were under the weather yourself, and now look at you—fit as a fiddle.'

'Don't you believe it,' said Booth. 'I'm tired and I'm hungry. Let's head for your cousin's place and get him to feed us.'

'We will in a minute,' said Spence. 'But there're just a couple of things I want to look at first. The local phone-boxes for a start.'

They climbed back into Booth's Rover 2000 and drove off.

'Now tell me,' said Spence. 'Is there any connection, do you think, between the fact that your lady friend on the phone said she was about to blackmail a murderer, and the fact that the Vicar has suffered a nasty shock?'

Booth took his time about answering.

'No,' he said eventually. 'I don't think there is. Though it had crossed my mind, too. That's why I mentioned the phone call specifically, to see how he would take it.'

'And did his reaction fit in with your previous estimate of his character?'

'It did, yes. I always saw him as a sincere, non-violent sort of a man. And not as a murderer . . . Though one can never be entirely sure, of course.'

Spence spent the next few minutes driving round the new housing estate, which seemed tolerably well designed and quite peaceful in the late afternoon. He stopped the car beside each of the two public phone-boxes on the estate, but at neither site could he or Booth see anything which might have caused the regular thumping which Booth had heard as a background to his midnight telephone conversation.

'I shall know that noise if I hear it again,' said Booth. 'But at the moment I just can't place it.'

'Don't force it,' said Spence. 'It'll come to you some time when you're least expecting it . . . Now, which way to the Blue Bazaar?'

'Take the next right,' said Booth. 'That takes you on to the London Road. And then turn left after 200 yards . . . Why do you want to look at the Blue Bazaar, anyway?'

'Seems to be an interesting topic of conversation,' said Spence. 'I've heard a lot about it since it opened, but I've never been there. It's never been a source of trouble as far as I know.'

'No, nothing to speak of,' Booth agreed. 'I looked in on it a couple of years ago and thought it fairly respectable of its kind.'

Two hundred yards further on, a large sign by the side of the road invited Spence to turn left for the Blue Bazaar, which he duly did. Some fifty yards beyond that he found himself in a large car park in front of a late Victorian mansion with a recent one-storey addition at the left-hand side. Spence brought the car to a halt about halfway down the car park.

'Presumably that new bit on the left is the night-club,' he said.

'That's right. You go in at the front, through the main door of the old house, and that takes you to reception. Then you go left down a passage which leads to a restaurant and a bar, and beyond that you get to the new extension, which is quite a big cabaret room with another bar.'

'What are the prices like?'

'Oh, reasonable—I had a good steak there when I came, and it didn't cost me a fortune. This lad David Cordwright, Mrs Cordwright's son, he's had about ten years' experience in the hotel business, so he knows what he's at.'

'Isn't there a third partner?'

'There is, yes. A rather older bloke called Read, Lester Read. He's the one the Vicar was talking about, the one who lives with young Cordwright and causes a scandal—at least in some people's eyes. He used to be a teacher over at Tallmead years ago, but he gave it up to go in for writing. He never produced very much but he didn't need to, I don't think. He's another of these lucky devils with a private income.'

'I don't know that they are lucky really,' said Spence. 'Doesn't seem to make them very happy. And anyway, who are you to complain—you're a pensioner yourself now.'

Booth chuckled. 'Yes,' he said, 'that's right. But the pension doesn't go very far.'

'How old was David Cordwright at the time of the murder?'

'Sixteen.'

'Old enough, then.'

'Oh, yes. And he was here at the time, he wasn't away on holiday like some—it was August, you know. We looked at him very carefully, the Yard man and I, but his mother was very protective. Calm, and willing to help on the surface, but underneath it all she was very, very determined that we weren't going to be let loose on her David.'

'Why was that, do you think?'

'I'm not sure. I think she was just a well-educated, intelligent woman who had a lot of respect for the police but who knew well enough that when coppers interview young men, the young men sometimes get flustered and say silly things. And she just wasn't going to have that happen.'

'What about Read—did he live in the village then?'

'No, he lived in Tallmead. I didn't even know of his existence at that point, he wasn't a suspect we considered. Though I suppose he did live within easy reach.'

'How long have he and Cordwright lived together?'

'Oh, two or three years, I suppose. Since the Blue Bazaar opened. But Cordwright was educated over at Tallmead, as a day-boy, when Read was there as a teacher, so their liaison is no new thing. They're one of the oldest affairs in the county, so my camp friends tell me.'

'Didn't know you had any.'

'Oh, yes, it's not illegal now, you know.'

Spence laughed and nodded towards the night-club. 'I bet there's a pay-phone in there,' he said.

'Yes,' said Booth thoughtfully. 'I suppose you're right.'

'And the Vicar did suggest Mrs Cordwright as a possible caller.'

'Yes, so he did.'

'Why don't we all come out here for a drink tonight, and see what we can see?' Spence suggested. 'I'm sure George and his wife will fancy a drink, and I know Julia won't say no.'

'Suits me,' said Booth. 'I don't know who's in the cabaret this week but I gather they always have a top-class stripper.'

'In that case you'll have to baby-sit,' said Spence. 'Your heart isn't up to it.'

He started the car and began to head for his cousin's farm, where both his wife and a welcome hot supper would be waiting.

'It seems to me,' he said after a moment, 'that if your telephone lady is to be believed and the killer is still alive, he or she must have access to a considerable amount of money. Otherwise there's no point in your caller blackmailing the murderer. Now—who of the oldtimers we've seen this afternoon has money?'

'Well,' said Booth, 'not Mrs Amble and her husband, for a start. Not money that you'd call money, anyway. And not Walter Underwood.'

'No,' Spence agreed. 'But the Colonel clearly has. And he smokes a pipe, like the man who was seen late on the night of the murder.'

'Yes, for what that's worth. And the Vicar smokes a pipe as well, but he's not a man of means as far as I know.'

'What about the Cordwrights and Lester Read?'

'Well, they're well off, I suppose. You've heard people say this afternoon that Mrs Cordwright inherited money, and Lester Read always had private means. But you can never tell with a business like a nightclub. Could be on the verge of bankruptcy quite easily.'

'Yes . . . Anyone else we should consider?'

'Not that I can think of. We've just about covered the field.'

'What's your feeling, then?' Spence continued. 'Do

you think one of those long-term residents is really a cold-blooded killer?'

'Yes,' said Booth without hesitation. 'Yes, I do. I can't give you any logical reasoning to support that view, but if gut feelings are worth anything, I'd stake my pension on it.'

9

It was a mile and a half along a winding country lane to the farm which was owned by Spence's cousin George. It was 6.30 when Spence and Booth arrived there, and the evening sun gave a golden glow to the stone of the old farmhouse.

George Spence was chiefly a dairy farmer, and the smell and sound of the cows came into the car even before Spence brought it to a halt. Once he climbed out, he only had to close his eyes to imagine himself back in his childhood, when he had spent many a long holiday staying with his hospitable aunt and uncle. In the distance a church bell was ringing, and Spence had vague memories of learning a poem at school which described just such a scene, but he couldn't quite recall it.

Also parked in the farmyard was an elderly blue Mini which belonged to Spence's wife, Julia, and as Spence approached the kitchen door, Julia emerged to give him an affectionate kiss on the cheek.

'All well?' she asked with a smile.

'Yes, I think so,' he smiled back. 'And you?'

'Fine, thank you.' Julia turned to greet her husband's former boss, who was standing quietly in the background. 'Good evening, Mr Booth,' she said cheerfully. 'It's nice to see you looking so well again.'

'Ah, thank you, my dear,' said Booth amiably. He

was always pleased to see a pretty face. 'It's nice to be feeling better, I can assure you of that.'

At thirty-four, Julia Spence was five years younger than her husband. She had the firm, trim figure of a regular tennis player, shoulder-length brown hair, and exceptionally blue eyes, which constantly observed everyone and everything around her; this was a habit which she claimed to have picked up from her husband, but in fact it was a direct outcome of her academic interest in psychology. She and her husband had no children, and she worked full-time as a lecturer in education at the Southshire teacher-training college in Wellbridge.

Julia's work frequently took her into schools, and as a result she tended to dress conservatively; headmasters are an old-fashioned lot, by and large, and trouser suits do not go down well. Today, having visited a student of hers at Tallmead School which had a particularly stuffy head, she was wearing a light-grey two-piece suit with a white blouse; she had even considered borrowing one of her husband's ties to go with it but had eventually abandoned the idea. The tie would have made little difference in any case, for whatever she wore, Julia Spence was undeniably an attractive and elegant woman, a source of much greater interest to a class of fifteen-year-old public-schoolboys than the physics lesson which had nominally been demanding their attention.

Spence took Booth through the kitchen door and into the farmhouse proper, where they were greeted enthusiastically by his cousin's wife Dora.

The kitchen seemed full of children, but only three of them were Dora's, and she took the opportunity to shoo the rest away with an assurance that they could always return tomorrow. Then she slid a large apple pie into the oven and shook hands with Booth as Spence introduced them to each other.

'You're very welcome, Mr Booth,' Dora said warmly. 'Very welcome, I'm sure.' The fact that Dora Spence had spent her whole life in rural Southshire was readily apparent in her voice. 'Sit down at once,' she continued. 'You've had a busy afternoon I hear, going round to see all the old-timers. Take the weight off your feet.'

Spence winked at Booth, and they both did as they were told and sat down at the huge kitchen table, the top of it white from frequent scrubbing.

'Not much wrong with the village grapevine, you see,' said Spence ruefully.

'That's no surprise to me,' grunted Booth. 'I can never get within three miles of this place without the word going round that Booth is back in town.'

Dora opened two bottles of beer and poured them simultaneously into two ancient pewter mugs with glass bottoms. Now in her mid-thirties, she had the well-built, well-fed look of the archetypal farmer's wife, with blonde hair, blue eyes, and rosy cheeks to match. A passing advertising man, playing darts with her in the local pub, had once offered to use her in an ad for margarine. But the idea had not appealed; Dora preferred cows to advertising men, on the grounds that they talked more sense.

'George will be in before long,' Dora continued. 'In the meantime have a drink. I've got a duck in the oven—I hope that's all right for you?'

Everyone agreed that duck for supper would do splendidly.

'And apple pie for afters,' Dora added. 'Alice, you lay the table, please.'

Alice, the eldest child of the three left in the kitchen, began to bring out the knives and forks; Spence helped her. Before long Booth found himself reading a story to Dora's six-year-old son, while Julia talked to the middle child.

Half an hour later Spence's cousin George came in from the fields. He topped up the beer mugs, served large glasses of sweet sherry to his wife and Julia, and sent the two younger children up to get themselves ready for bed.

George Spence was a thick-set, burly man of slightly more than average height; at thirty-six he was three years younger than his cousin, and like his wife he bore visible signs of earning his living from the land. He had grown up in this house and he confidently expected to die in it, but the sense of well-being which radiated from him suggested that he had many years of life ahead of him yet.

At 7.30 the five adults, plus the thirteen-year-old Alice, all sat down to a huge meal which began with soup and ended with cheese and biscuits, with duck and apple pie in between. At the end of it even Spence, who was a sound trencherman, felt distinctly full, and Booth looked as relaxed and contented as Spence had ever seen him.

Over coffee Spence put forward the suggestion that perhaps they should finish off the evening wih a trip to the Blue Bazaar.

'Certainly,' said George immediately. 'Dora and I are both members so that's no problem—we'll sign you in.'

'I wasn't sure about the baby-sitting situation,' said Spence.

'Oh, don't you worry about that,' said George. 'They're old enough to be left on their own now. Alice will look after them, won't you, love?'

Alice turned slightly pink and agreed that she would.

'You can sit up and watch the telly till we get back,' George continued. 'Or until it finishes, anyway.' He turned to Booth. 'She's thirteen now, you know. Sits in the living-room with my shotgun on her knees when we go out. She knows how to use it, of course—taught her myself. And she goes to karate classes, too, over in Tallmead church hall. I pity any rapist who tries to get in here, I can tell you.'

With that question settled the women undertook to wash up while the men retired to a more comfortable room to digest their meal; in Southshire farming circles this division of labour was considered entirely proper. Alice was despatched to quell a minor riot upstairs.

After the men sat down nobody spoke for a few minutes. Booth lit his pipe, George lit a cigar, and Spence closed his eyes in peaceful repose. In due course it was George who broke the silence.

'You'll be here about the old business, then,' he suggested.

Booth nodded.

'I'm glad to hear it,' said George. 'It's a worry to us, you know. And we don't even live in the village, so you can imagine how the ones who do live there feel.'

Booth grunted: 'Hmm. Not many of them left now, though.'

'No, that's true. It just seems as if there are still a lot because of all the newcomers living there . . . I did wonder if the bloke who did it was dead by now, but since you're here I take it you don't think so?'

Booth shifted his position in his chair. 'I wish I knew,' he said. 'If I knew for sure, one way or the other, I'd feel a lot better about it than I do.'

'Yes, I suppose you would. Not that we've had much other trouble over the years. Bit of vandalism here and there, but that's all.'

Booth puffed thoughtfully on his pipe. 'Tell me,' he said, 'did you know Patrick Meadows yourself?'

'Well, I knew him by sight,' said George. 'Knew everybody in those days, more or less, even in Tallmead. But I wasn't here at the time of the murders. National Service, you know.'

'Oh yes. But you must have heard a lot of gossip over the years.'

'About the murder?'

'Yes.'

'I should say so. It's the only big thing that ever happened round here. That and the bomb that fell on the churchyard in 1943. For years people talked about nothing else. Then the murder came along.'

'All right,' said Booth. 'Now, when all that gossip was boiled down—years later, when the dust settled— who did people really think had done it?'

George sat well back in his chair and drew on his cigar before answering. 'Well, I think most of the old hands, say five years after the event, most of them would have settled for one of two people. Walter Underwood was the first.'

'Why him?'

'Well, I think chiefly because he went to live in the

house where it all happened. Not that I blame him for that personally, though I certainly wouldn't fancy it myself. But people seemed to feel that that gave him a motive.'

'Did you feel that way yourself?'

'No, not really. Though he'd been in some rough stuff in the war, had Walter. He knew what it was all about. He stuck his bayonet in a few Germans by all accounts, so if he had killed Meadows it wouldn't have been the first man he'd done for. But I never saw him as a murderer really.'

'Why not?'

'Well, for a start he's too stupid. Whoever did that job obviously planned it. They waited till the middle of the night, and then sneaked in and did it, and sneaked home again. That's not Walter's style at all. You might get him to lose his temper and have a go at you—though even that's not easy—but he wouldn't bear a grudge long enough to commit a crime like that. It's just not in him.'

Booth nodded. 'So, if it wasn't Walter, who was the second man people talked about?'

'Oh, it was a fellow called Datchett—you remember him?'

'Yes.'

'He's dead now. He was a little bit peculiar too, though in a different way from Walter. He used to think people were getting at him all the time. What's the word for that?'

'Paranoid.'

'Yes, that's right. He could be an awkward customer, no doubt about it. And I suppose people thought he could have developed a grudge against Meadows—or possibly against that poor little lad of his. Datchett never did like children . . . I suppose in some ways we should hope it *was* Datchett, because he's been dead these ten years at least.'

Booth took his pipe out of his mouth. 'Well, perhaps you're right, about how we'd be better off if Datchett were the murderer, I mean. But I don't think he was.'

'Why not?'

'Well, in confidence, because Mr Barndean once told me that when Datchett realized that he was going to die, he asked to see the Vicar. And they talked over quite a few things that Datchett was worried about, none of them very creditable I gather, though I don't know what they were. And then the Vicar, who'd heard the rumours just as you have, asked Datchett whether there was anything else he'd like to get off his conscience. And then Datchett became very distressed, and said that he knew what people were saying about him. He knew people were saying he'd killed Meadows and the boy, but none of it was true, he'd had nothing whatever to do with it. And he swore by a lot of things which he held very dear that he'd had no part in the murders at all.'

'And did Mr Barndean believe him?'

'He did.'

'Oh, well that settles that, then,' said George. 'I'd back the Vicar's judgement any day.'

There was silence for a few more minutes before something else occurred to George. 'Why are we going to the Blue Bazaar tonight?' he asked suddenly.

Booth grunted with amusement. 'Ask your cousin,' he said with a grin.

Spence opened one eye as his cousin prodded him.

'Well?' said George. 'Are we going to the Blue Bazaar tonight just because you fancy seeing a nice young stripper, or are you going for business reasons?'

'Both,' said Spence.

George was genuinely surprised. 'Do you mean to tell me,' he said, 'that after seventeen years you honestly expect to find the bloke who did those murders having a quiet drink at the Blue Bazaar?'

'You never know,' said Spence. 'That's just the problem, you see. You never know where he might be.'

George looked worried. 'Oh,' he said after a pause. 'Well it doesn't bother me, but for Christ's sake don't tell my missus or we'll never get there.'

10

By half-past 9 that evening everyone was ready to leave for the Blue Bazaar. George had put on an unexpectedly fashionable blue suit, together with a white shirt and a blue and white striped tie. Dora, meanwhile, had squeezed herself into a little black dress with a degree of cleavage which might not have met with the unanimous approval of the Women's Institute.

The five adults made sure that Alice was happily installed with a box of biscuits in front of a huge colour television set, with her father's shotgun on the floor beside her chair. Then they climbed into George Spence's capacious Ford Granada Estate car and drove off into the night.

To Spence, the car park at the Blue Bazaar seemed quite crowded for a Tuesday evening. However George and Dora, who were apparently fairly regular attenders, estimated that it was about average for a weekday; on Friday and Saturday nights it was often impossible to get in unless you came early.

The main entrance to the club was up a short flight of steps; then there were heavy double doors which opened into a well-lit hall with a cloakroom to the right and a flight of stairs to the left. At the end of the hall was a reception desk manned by a grey-haired lady wearing a green trouser suit; to Spence's eyes she seemed exceptionally fastidious in her choice of clothes, makeup, and accessories.

'Mrs Cordwright,' Booth muttered to Spence as George approached the desk to sign in his guests.

Spence nodded imperceptibly.

'Good evening, Mr Spence,' said Mrs Cordwright to George. The voice was both deep and affected, but the intonation was not unfriendly.

'Good evening, Mrs Cordwright,' said George, taking out his wallet. 'What's the cabaret like tonight?'

'Excellent, Mr Spence, as always.'

'Hmm, I see what you mean,' said George. He eyed a publicity photograph on the reception desk which showed a well-endowed young stripper who called herself Thana.

Mrs Cordwright glanced shrewdly at George's guests as he completed the formalities; she also exchanged a few comments with Dora on the state of the weather. Then she smoothly transferred her attentions to the next couple in the queue.

George led the way down a dimly-lit corridor to the cabaret room; after a few yards the wall on the left of the corridor gave way to a low rail behind which were a restaurant and bar. Then the corridor turned right and opened into the cabaret room.

'Did that voice ring any bells?' Spence asked Booth as they followed his cousin into the club.

'Whose voice, Mrs Cordwright's?'

'Yes.'

'No, I can't say it did. The right sort of accent, though. Or nearly right, anyway. But it's difficult to tell when you've only heard someone over the phone. Some people sound so different in the flesh.'

The cabaret room turned out to be about two-thirds full, but George found them a table without difficulty; it was deep in the darkness which surrounded the brightly-lit square, which served as both a dance-floor and a stage, not too far from the bar.

'This'll do,' said George. 'Not quite close enough to snap the stripper's G-string, but you can't have everything.'

'You don't know if you'll like her yet,' said Dora. She turned to Julia. 'He's very particular, is George.'

Booth rubbed his hands. 'Well,' he said, 'it's probably illegal for a non-member to do so, but I'm buying the first round.'

Nobody objected, and the next few minutes were passed in ordering, waiting for and tasting the first drinks of the evening. It was grudgingly agreed by both George and Booth that the best bitter was passable, if expensive; Spence was a draught Guinness man himself, while the two wives drank gin and orange.

Before long a trio of musicians appeared on stage: an organ, bass guitar, and drums. Fortunately one of them must have had a severe hangover, because they chose to play surprisingly quietly, allowing conversation to continue.

Spence, who was sitting beside his cousin's wife, took advantage of the situation to add to his knowledge of the village. George and Booth were already deeply engrossed in a discussion of Muhammad Ali.

'Now then, Dora,' Spence began, 'you're a local girl, lived here all your life—tell me a little bit about the people in the club tonight.'

'What do you want to know?' asked Dora.

'Well, let's start with the lady on the door.'

'Mrs Cordwright?'

'Yes. How long has she lived in Tinley?'

'Oh, ages—over twenty years, anyway. Came here after she was divorced, so they say.'

'And she brought her son with her?'

'Yes, that's right. That's David, over there, by the bar.' She indicated a tall, slim young man with a tanned and handsome face.

'Ah, yes,' said Spence. 'I've got him. And what does the village think of him?'

'Well, they think he's a right nancy, naturally. But we're used to him by now, otherwise it might be different. He's quite popular on the whole. He grew up here, you see. Went to Tallmead, like George.'

'As a day-boy?'

'Yes. After that he went away for a good few years. Got himself some sort of training and worked in some posh hotels. Went all over the world, so they say. And then about three or four years ago he came back here and opened this place with his mother and Lester Read. They're the ones with the money, his mother and Lester, and David has the know-how.'

'Lester Read is David's boy-friend I gather.'

'Well, sort of.' Dora laughed. 'I'd put it the other way round myself. I can't see Lester at the moment, but he's usually in here somewhere—over at the bar mostly, having a chat with someone. He loves to talk, does Lester, and to drink. But he can hold it as well as anyone.'

'I take it Lester's the older partner then?'

'Oh, yes. I suppose he's a good ten years older than David, if not more.'

'And the villagers don't mind the two of them living together?'

Dora considered the matter seriously. 'No,' she said.

'I don't think there's anyone who minds, except perhaps the Vicar. And possibly the Colonel. Most people are too innocent, you know, even in this day and age. They wouldn't recognize a homosexual if you painted him green. And I suppose that most of those who are on the ball just feel that it's a case of live and let live. And David and Lester are discreet, of course—they don't have drag parties or anything like that. And we've known them both for years and years—so, like I say, everyone seems to take it in their stride.'

'I see,' said Spence. He saw his wife listening to his conversation with Dora and winked at her, knowing that sooner or later what was said would probably serve as the basis for a learned paper on 'Changing Social Mores in a Southshire Village'.

'There was one thing, though,' Dora added thoughtfully. 'David very nearly did blot his copy-book on one occasion. He got had up for soliciting, or accosting or whatever it is, in a public lav. Now that would have put people off in a big way if they'd known about it, but I don't think many of them do.'

'Why not?' said Spence.

'Well, I suppose chiefly because he got off. His mother got a private detective on to it, and it didn't happen round here anyway, it was in Surrey. And this private detective found some sort of mistake in the police evidence, so David was found not guilty. Some friend of George's told us.'

Spence nodded. 'I see. You say his mother helped him to get off?'

'Yes. His mother's always fought tooth and nail for him. I remember once, soon after they came here, he was being bullied at school and his mother got a solicitor on to it even then. No messing about and seeing the headmaster first, like most people would do. Just a solicitor's letter, bang.'

'Hmm, interesting,' said Spence. 'What's Mrs Cordwright's attitude to the relationship between David and Lester?'

'Oh, well, to hear her talk you'd think they were just good friends. She talks about David not having found the right woman to share his life yet, and all that sort of rubbish. Makes you sick really. The fact is, she's put him off women for good, poor lad.'

'And what does the Women's Institute think about her?'

'Oh, we think she's all right. But only just. She tries hard, I'll give her that.'

'Tries in what way?'

'Well, she's a fearful snob, if the truth were known. You can tell, when you talk to her. But she tries not to let it show. She'll have a long chat in the village post office, just like the rest of us, but she does it so we won't think she's stuck-up, not because she really wants to. And she's a chronic name-dropper, she loves having all the big stars here. I think that's the main reason why she opened this place, to hobnob with all the big names in show-business. They only come for one night, mind you, the really big people, but they do get them here, there's no doubt about it.'

'What, like Frank Sinatra, you mean,' said Spence.

'Yes, that's right,' said Dora. 'He's here next Monday, or would be, if Jennifer Cordwright could have her way . . . Oh, look, there's Lester now.'

She pointed out a plumpish, middle-aged man with dark hair and slightly flushed features. He was expensively but unobtrusively dressed in a well-cut blue blazer, light-grey flannels, and black shoes with small gold buckles. He had a glass of whisky in one hand and a pipe in the other, and was talking earnestly to a young couple at the bar.

'He was a teacher once, wasn't he?' said Spence.

'Yes, he taught over at Tallmead for a good few years,' said Dora. 'Then he gave it up to write books. That was when he came over here to live—the house he and David live in belongs to him really.'

'Fair enough,' said Spence. 'So who else is there in the club tonight who's lived in Tinley for a long time?'

Dora looked around carefully. 'Well,' she said, 'there's not many here who've lived here *very* long. The population is that much more mobile now, you know. Everyone moves except farmers, and even we have to move sometimes . . . One of the lads in the trio was born in Tallmead. And that barmaid over there has lived in Tinley for about ten years I should say—but there aren't many in the room who could match her. If it comes to that, there aren't many people left in the whole village who were here when I was a child. There's the Colonel and his wife, of course . . .'

'And the Vicar.'

'Yes . . . Mrs Cordwright and David . . . Mrs Amble at the post office, and her husband . . .'

'And Walter Underwood.'

'Yes, he's still about, though you don't see much of him. And that's about all I can think of.'

George broke off his conversation with Booth and interrupted. 'Now then,' he said briskly. 'Let's get another round bought before the cabaret starts.'

11

The drummer rattled a roll on his snare-drum, and the organist, who was wearing dark glasses, turned on his stool to face the audience. He pressed a microphone tight against his lips.

'And now, ladies and gentlemen, it's 10 o'clock and cabaret time at the Blue Bazaar.'

The lights over the ringside tables dimmed even further and two spotlights came on to focus attention on the clear space in the centre of the room.

'We have two acts for you tonight,' the organist continued, 'both of them absolutely out of the top drawer. The boys in the band here'—he indicated his mates, one of whom sniggered cheerfully at this description—'the boys in the band here beside me, we watched these acts work here for the first time last night, and believe you me, we were absolutely astounded. I can tell you quite definitely that you've never seen anything like either of these acts in your life. First of all, ladies and gentlemen, I want you to put your hands together and welcome our beautiful exotic dancer for this week—the lovely . . . Thana!'

There was a burst of enthusiastic applause. Then the deceptively quiet opening bars of Jimmy Smith's recording of 'A Walk on the Wild Side' began to echo through the club. A few moments later the room was filled with sound as the full band began to play; then a curtain at the side of the stage was swept dramatically to one side, and out stepped a glittering creature in a long snow-white gown trimmed with fur and sequins.

Thana's legs snaked out on silver high-heeled shoes, and as she moved across the stage her dress shimmered and sparkled rhythmically. Her blonde hair was piled high on her head and held in place by a tiara which scattered light like a Catherine-wheel. The face was compellingly pale, and the eyes were emphasized with an expert make-up; Thana's gaze swept swiftly around the room as she began to dance.

The overall effect was sensational, and even the most hardened show-business pro would have been forced to admire Thana's style. Spence grinned at his cousin George, whose gleeful expression indicated that he thoroughly approved of what he had seen so far.

Out of the corner of his eye Spence noticed something else. A young chef, dressed in a white coat and tall hat, had emerged from a door marked 'Staff Only' and had approached the stage area in order to watch the act. The chef fingered his right ear and Spence caught a glimpse of a hearing-aid before the long black hair fell back and covered it.

Spence returned his attention to the stripper. One striptease act is inevitably very much like another, but in the next ten minutes Thana gave as sophisticated and erotic a performance as Spence had ever seen. The dress gave way to contrasting black underwear, and the underwear, slowly but surely, gave way to almost nothing at all.

Thana's figure was near-perfect and she was clearly exceptionally proud of it. So much so, in fact, that with the final chords of her accompanying music, she took off the last few square inches of covering altogether.

Blackout and noisy applause. The audience clearly thought that Thana was a winner of her kind, and Spence was inclined to agree with them. He noticed the chef moving unobtrusively back to his kitchen.

'Cor,' said George loudly, just audible over the clapping. 'That was a bit of all right!'

His wife smiled and made a comment in Julia's ear which made her laugh.

'Thank you very much, ladies and gentlemen,' said the organist. 'Thank you very much indeed. I told you that Thana was something special and I think you'll agree that I wasn't kidding . . . And now for an act which is really going to leave you open-mouthed. I can safely say that this is one of the most amazing acts we've ever had here at the Blue Bazaar, and that's saying a very great deal. I want you to welcome—the great Deceivo!'

The organist punched out a few swift bars of introductory music to allow a good-looking man in his thirties to walk relaxedly on to the stage. He came into the centre of the open space, stood to attention, bowed low, and smiled at the audience in response to their greeting. He was wearing a beautiful white dinner jacket over black trousers; his black shoes rippled with light.

'Thank you, ladies and gentlemen,' said Deceivo, 'thank you very much indeed. And now, to begin with, I'd like to show you a pack of cards. Just an ordinary pack of cards, nothing special about it at all. And it's a new pack, so perhaps you'd be kind enough to open it for me, sir, and check that there's nothing unusual about it, nothing to distinguish it from a thousand others . . .'

The great Deceivo advanced on a man at a ringside table and after a few preliminaries embarked on a series of card-tricks, most of them demanding an exceptional degree of manual dexterity and skill. Once or twice Spence thought he could guess how a trick was done, but the great Deceivo anticipated that reaction in the audience and promptly demonstrated that that was not the way it was done after all.

Following the card-tricks Deceivo did a little elementary 'mind-reading'. Then he embarked on a rapid succession of other illusions, most of them involving small items of equipment brought on to the stage by his assistant, an attractive but silent blonde girl in a black leotard. The climax of the act, however, involved both equipment and the girl.

Deceivo announced that he would end his performance by demonstrating a power that many had often longed for, but which very few actually possessed—the power to make a woman disappear at will.

From one side of the stage an upright, coffin-shaped box on wheels was pushed into the spotlights. At the front of the box were two doors which opened to reveal an empty upper half and an empty lower half respectively.

'And now,' said Deceivo, 'we shall attempt the impossible. My assistant, the lovely Sue, will step inside this box, and with just a wave of my magic wand, she will disappear before your very eyes.'

It was all extremely corny, Spence reflected, and yet Deceivo had the audience's complete attention. Everyone present had heard this build-up before, or something very like it, but the fact that it was all happening before their very eyes, as Deceivo put it, seemed to mesmerize them. That plus the fact that Deceivo delivered his lines with a twinkle in his eye, as if acknowledging that he too knew that his patter was hackneyed and banal.

The lovely Sue, as Deceivo called her, did an elegant twirl and then squeezed herself into the upright coffin. The bottom door of the box was slammed shut, leaving only her smiling upper half visible. Then the top door was shut, and bolted. A member of the audience was invited to assure himself that there were no trap-doors in the stage, the cabinet was turned round three times, and finally the magic wand was waved and the appropriate words spoken.

Deceivo opened the top door of the box to reveal an empty space.

Aha, he accused the audience of saying, she's in the bottom half.

But lo and behold, he opened the bottom half of the box, and she wasn't there either. He spun the box round to demonstrate its emptiness to all quarters of the nightclub. Then, to complete the illusion, he called for the barmaid to collect the lovely Sue from the restaurant down the corridor. And sure enough, after a few tense moments, the barmaid returned with Sue following her.

If anything, the audience was even more impressed by the great Deceivo than it had been by Thana. He and Sue, together with their magic box, left the stage to loud cries of approval.

'Bloody clever, that,' said George, shaking his head in admiration after the cabaret was over. 'It would be worth a quid or two to know how he does that.'

Spence was forced to agree. The box on stage had certainly looked empty, and how the lovely Sue had transferred herself from the box to the restaurant at least fifty feet away, without anyone in the audience seeing her, was a complete mystery to him. At least, it was a mystery for half an hour, after which he had worked out how it was done.

Whatever else anyone might say about the Blue Bazaar, no one could deny that the management provided a first-class cabaret.

'Is it as good as this every week?' Spence asked.

'Near enough,' said George. 'Some acts you like more than others, naturally.'

'Are any of those performers local?' asked Spence.

'What, you mean do they live round here?'

'Yes.'

'Good God no.'

'Why are you so surprised? Strippers and conjurors have to live somewhere.'

'Yes, but not round here, surely. I mean, this is just not the place for producing strippers and conjurors, is it? More sort of dairy-maid and tractor-driver country.'

Spence grinned. 'Just wanted to be sure,' he said.

'Mind you, that stripper does remind me of someone, though,' George added. 'Can't think who for the moment.'

'Probably Raquel Welch,' said Spence.

With the cabaret over the trio of musicians left the stage and the juke-box started up. Spence and Booth took advantage of the change of mood to visit the gents and then examine the pay-phone in the entrance hall.

Booth stepped inside the cubicle and closed the door. Sure enough, most of the music from the cabaret room was lost when the door was shut, but the deep vibrations of the rhythmical bass notes seemed to penetrate the wood and glass and produce a booming effect. Booth emerged and nodded at Spence.

'Could well be it,' he said. 'And I imagine that with the band playing live the effect is even more pronounced. That's a bass guitar that lad who needs a haircut is twanging.'

'All right,' said Spence thoughtfully. 'So we'll assume for the moment that this is where your midnight caller was ringing from.'

'Which leaves us the problem,' continued Booth, 'of who made it.'

'Well, you said it was a sophisticated woman with a deep voice.'

'And not a local accent.'

'No.' Spence sighed. 'Trouble is we've got a roomful of sophisticates out there, almost none of whom were born round here, what with today's mobile society. Or if they were born here they don't talk very Southshire any longer. The telly seems to have ironed out most of that, among this class of people at any rate.'

They returned to their table and sought inspiration in their drinks. After a few moments Spence nodded towards one of the joint owners of the club, Lester Read, who was standing by the bar.

'Tell me, Charlie, was there ever any connection between the murder victim and Mr Read over there?'

Booth glanced towards the middle-aged Read before answering. 'At the time we didn't know of any, no. And I've no reason to believe that Patrick Meadows and Lester Read ever met. But they might easily have known each other by sight. They both worked over at Tallmead and they were both teachers.'

'Though in different schools.'

'Oh, yes. Different worlds. Meadows taught at a C of

E state primary school, and Read taught at *the* school
—Tallmead public school for boys aged thirteen to
eighteen. But they did have some other things in common.'

'Oh? Such as?'

'Well, they both did a bit of writing, or reckoned
to. People are a bit sarcastic about Lester Read as a
writer, but the truth is he did publish a novel a few
years back, and I gather it was tolerably well reviewed.'

'And what about Patrick Meadows?'

'Well, he was a poet in a modest sort of way. He
belonged to a little postal club which circulated members' work. Nothing very successful, but he dabbled.'

'I see,' said Spence.

'Of course,' Booth continued, 'if you really want to
link up Meadows and Lester Read it's easy to do it
now, with hindsight. Patrick Meadows knew Mrs
Cordwright very well, and now Read and Mrs Cordwright and her son are all big buddies.'

'And did Read know the Cordwrights seventeen
years ago?'

'I'm not sure, but we could find out. David Cordwright was a day-boy at Tallmead, but whether he
was actually taught by Read or not I don't know. I'm
pretty sure he was, though—it's my belief their relationship started when David was pretty young.'

'And how old did you say David was when the
murders were committed—sixteen?'

'Yes.'

'Hmm.' Spence was silent for a few moments. Then
he continued. 'Did David know Meadows's young son,
Peter?'

'Yes,' said Booth, 'in a general sort of way. Everyone
in the village knew everyone else. But Peter was only

ten, so they weren't close friends or anything like that.'

'Yes, I see. And you say Mrs Cordwright and Meadows had some sort of connection?'

'Yes. They were more or less the same age, fortyish, and both single, both with children. There were one or two kind souls in the village who had ideas about bringing the two of them together.'

'Never came to anything, I suppose?'

'No. Most people agreed it would never have worked. But they did have one other thing in common, too—they both took part in amateur dramatics, mostly over in Tallmead.'

'I see . . . The Colonel called her a widow but she's not really, is she?'

'No. Divorced, but doesn't object if you think she's the other thing.'

'Yes, I thought as much. She looks pretty hard-nosed. Was she upset about Meadows's death?'

'Oh, yes, but no more than anyone else. I questioned her on one occasion and it ended in tears.'

'Hmm. How did young David feel about Meadows? Did he see him as any kind of a threat do you think?'

'What, do you mean was he afraid of the bloke as a potential stepfather?'

'Yes.'

'No, it would be unfair to say that. His mother had never been even remotely interested in Meadows as a potential husband, or indeed anyone else either. She devoted herself entirely to looking after her son.'

'Always had enough private income to manage on her own, then?'

'Apparently, yes. And in recent years, with a good deal to spare.'

'Ah, well,' said Spence, 'let's forget about all that for a few minutes and have another drink.'

Which they duly did.

Towards midnight George and Dora decided to call it a day, in view of their need to be up and about well before most other people in the club, and George drove everyone back to the farm.

Once there Dora offered to make some cocoa but she met with polite refusals all round. Booth, looking tired, climbed into his Rover 2000 and headed for home, and Spence and his wife did the same in Julia's Mini.

It was after 1 o'clock in the morning when Spence turned his bedside light out, but he lay awake for some time, thinking over what he had learnt in Tinley that day.

There weren't many facts he could be certain of: only that a particularly nasty double murder had been committed seventeen years earlier; that a man wearing a hat and smoking a pipe had been seen in the village on the night of the murder; that the killer had never been caught; and that Booth was still passionately interested in solving the crime.

Then there was the fact that a woman had rung Booth up in the early hours of Tuesday morning. She seemed convinced that she possessed evidence to identify the murderer; and apparently she intended to use that evidence for blackmail. The impression she had conveyed to Booth was that the murderer was someone still living in the village, one of the few who were still there after seventeen years—and there weren't many of them.

Spence sifted through the old inhabitants in his mind. Mrs Amble and her husband; the Colonel and his lady; Mrs Cordwright and her son; Walter Underwood; the Vicar; and Lester Read in a sense, though strictly speaking he had been living in Tallmead seventeen years ago.

Spence sighed and turned over restlessly. He didn't like the feel of the situation at all. It was claustrophobic and in-bred and worrying. He had the uncomfortable feeling that somebody, somewhere was going to come to a sticky end.

12

The following day, Wednesday, was relatively un-
eventful. It was Thursday when all the trouble started.

At 9.30 in the morning Ben Spence was sitting
quietly in his office on the first floor of the Southshire
police headquarters building in Wellbridge. He was
just beginning to think about the possibility of a cup
of coffee, which was not unreasonable for a Detective
Chief Superintendent who had been at his desk since
8 o'clock, when the phone rang.

The telephone call turned out to be tedious but
innocuous, involving a long discussion of the problem
of pickpockets in Shireport, a resort on the Southshire
coast. However, after the conversation had been going
on for some ten minutes, a Detective Sergeant called
Wilberforce entered the office with a piece of paper in
his hand; he began waving it at Spence and making
peculiar faces.

Wilberforce was a potentially ridiculous figure at
the best of times. He was fortyish, with a military
moustache, ramrod posture, an immaculate crease in
his trousers, and a brisk manner. His current attempts
at sign language threatened to make him look totally
absurd so Spence cut short the telephone conversation
and put the man out of his misery.

'Yes, Sergeant?'

'Urgent phone call, sir. Put through to me since you

were engaged. There's been a murder over at Tall-mead.'

'Damn,' said Spence bitterly. 'And double damn. Where precisely in Tallmead?'

'At a nightclub called the Blue Bazaar.'

'That's in Tinley, not Tallmead.'

'Oh, well, I'm sorry, sir, but it was a Tallmead man who came through to me.'

Spence sighed deeply. 'Very well, then, tell me the worst. Who's dead?'

'A woman, sir.'

'Mrs Cordwright?'

'I don't think so, sir, but I wasn't given the sur-name. It's the stripper who's in the cabaret there this week. Name of Thana.'

'Is it, indeed?' said Spence. 'That's very interesting. Extremely regrettable, but interesting.' He leaned back in his chair and thought about it.

Wilberforce looked at Spence through narrowed eyes; he thought it made him look shrewd. 'You were over there on Tuesday, weren't you, sir?'

'I was, yes.'

'Get some sort of a whisper?'

'Some sort, yes. We had a hint of trouble but I had hoped we might have staved it off.'

'You don't think this is a coincidence, then?'

'Unfortunately, no.' Spence came forward in his chair. 'Any details?'

Wilberforce consulted the piece of paper in his hand. 'Not many. Apparently she was found in her bedroom, tied to a chair. She'd been gagged and then stabbed. Sounds messy.'

Spence grunted. 'Yes, I've no doubt it is. Could be a

simple sex killing, or a robbery I suppose, and in some ways I hope it is. But I have a nasty feeling it's a lot more complicated than that.'

'There was a double murder over at Tinley, years ago.'

'Yes,' said Spence. 'I know.'

'Mr Booth never closed the file on that. Used to brood over it. Think there's any connection?'

'Probably', said Spence. 'But we'll keep that strictly to ourselves for the time being. The press have got long memories too, not to mention the villagers, and they'll pick up the possibility of a connection soon enough. But no help from us in the meantime. OK?'

'Yes, sir.'

Spence rose to his feet. 'Well, we'd better get moving, I suppose. Who's on the scene?'

'Detective Sergeant Lindhurst.'

'Oh, yes,' said Spence. 'Well, tell him I'm on my way.'

'Right, sir.'

'You know the rest of the drill by now, I trust, so get things rolling. Get hold of Mr Laurel—I think he's in Downsea this morning—and ask him to meet me at the Blue Bazaar as soon as he can.'

'Right, sir.' Wilberforce began scribbling fiercely on his piece of paper.

'Ring my wife and tell her the usual story. And I've got a cousin who lives near Tinley—get his number from my wife and find out if I can stay the night there.'

'Right, sir.'

'There's a big car park at the Blue Bazaar so the mobile office can go there for the time being. Oh, and ring Mr Booth and let him know what's going on.

Tell him I'd be glad to see him a little later on if he can spare the time. And bring the file on the earlier murders with you.'

'Right, sir. Anything else?'

'No, I think that's all for the moment.'

Spence dismissed the Detective Sergeant and hurried out to his car. He reflected, not for the first time, that Wilberforce was never happier than when working on a good juicy murder. And in many respects this one seemed likely to be even juicier than most.

13

Spence drove a dark-blue Ford Cortina 2000 GT which allowed him to weave his way quickly and safely past a long succession of lorries on the London road; it was ten-past 10 when he drew up outside the front door of the Blue Bazaar.

Immediately on arrival Spence went into the night-club and looked at the body; that was the first essential step in any murder inquiry. Later he would examine the room in which Thana had died, and the body, in much more detail; but before doing anything else Spence always made sure that he gave himself a preliminary impression of what the crime was all about. And having spent five minutes on his own upstairs he came outside to the car park again and began to fill in the background.

There were four other cars in the car park in addition to Spence's Ford; in one of them a detective in civilian clothes was sitting in the front seat with the door open, talking into the radio. One uniformed constable stood at the front door of the nightclub and another was stationed at the entrance to the car park.

After a moment the detective finished his radio call and came over to where Spence was standing. He was thirty years old and sandy-haired.

'All right, Mr Lindhurst,' said Spence briskly. 'Let's hear what you've found out.'

'Well, sir, the nightclub operates until the early

hours of the morning, as you can imagine. And at 9 o'clock this morning a cleaner arrived—Mrs Young.'

'Local, I suppose.'

'Yes, sir, off the new estate.'

'OK, go on.'

'She's been given a key for convenience—the people on the premises tend to sleep late—so she let herself in.'

'Is there only one cleaner?'

'Yes, sir, only one in the morning. There's a man who comes in the afternoons, I gather.'

'I see. And how many people sleep on the premises?'

'Two this week—the chef and the murdered woman. She's a cabaret artist, a stripper.'

'What about the other half of this week's cabaret, the conjuror and his assistant?'

'I'm sorry, sir, I know nothing about them.'

'All right. So Mrs Young set about cleaning, I suppose. What then?'

'Well, after a bit she says she smelt something funny. Couldn't identify it, but she went upstairs. She saw a bedroom door ajar—'

'The stripper's?'

'Yes. And every other morning this week it's been shut. And that's where the bad smell was coming from, so she looked inside.'

'What then?'

'Well, she panicked a bit—not surprisingly in view of the mess the body's in. Then she came downstairs and helped herself to a brandy. After that she rang one of the owners, Mrs Cordwright.'

'And what did Mrs Cordwright do?'

'She rang her son and he came up here with Mr Read. Those three are the joint owners of the club.'

'Yes,' said Spence, 'I know. Who got in touch with you?'

'Mr Cordwright. He took one look at the body and dialled 999. I was over at Tallmead when the call came through so I came straight here. All three of the owners were here when I arrived.'

Spence looked up at the first-floor windows: most of the curtains were tightly closed, shutting out the sunshine. 'And have all three of them been tramping around upstairs?' he asked.

'No, sir. I gather Mr Cordwright's the only one who's been and had a look. It seems to have upset him a good deal.'

'But they all know that it's the stripper who's dead, and that she's been murdered?'

'Oh, yes, sir. No doubt about that.'

'All right. And where are the owners now?'

'They're all in the cabaret room, sir, waiting for you. I thought it best to sit them all down and I've got a man in there keeping a discreet eye on them.'

'Good . . .' Spence was developing a liking for Lindhurst. He seemed to be competent and unruffled, taking it all in his stride. 'What did you do when you got here?'

'Well, I checked the body to make sure the woman was dead.'

'Have you had a doctor to confirm that?'

'No, sir,' said Lindhurst. But he didn't sound worried about it and Spence let it pass.

'Now think before you answer this one,' said Spence. 'Did you touch anything in the murder room?'

Lindhurst thought. 'No, sir,' he said eventually.

'All right. Did you search the premises?'

'Superficially, sir, yes. I got my men to carry out a

brief search just to make sure that no one was lurking in the kitchens or anything. But the only people here are the cleaner, the three owners, and the chef.'

'Ah, yes,' said Spence, 'the chef. Is he downstairs too?'

'No, sir, he's still asleep in his room.'

'Bloody hell!' said Spence. 'Stoned out of his mind, is he?'

'I don't think so, sir. I gather he's deaf.'

'Ah, so he is,' said Spence, 'so he is.' He remembered now: on Tuesday night the chef had come out of the kitchen specially to watch Thana perform, and he had adjusted his hearing-aid as he stood by the bandstand.

'Yes,' said Spence again. 'The chef is deaf all right. So he's still sleeping, is he? Bedroom door locked?'

'No, sir, it's open. I've looked in on him but I didn't disturb him because he's such an obvious suspect and I thought you might want to see for yourself that he's genuinely asleep. My man in the corridor can actually see the chef while he's standing outside the door where the body is.'

Spence looked surprised. 'He didn't tell me that when I went upstairs just now,' he said. 'Perhaps he thought I knew. Anyway, I suppose it's all right. It's bizarre, to say the least, but it's no problem. Any sign of a break-in anywhere?'

'No, sir, but you wouldn't need to break in. When we searched the premises we found two windows open on the ground floor alone. You could take your pick and climb in either of them without any difficulty at all.'

Spence shook his head. 'Bloody marvellous,' he said. 'Every sex freak from here to John O'Groats has probably been in—and out . . . Still, it's no good grumbling now.'

From the road there was the sudden roar of a powerful car engine changing down. Spence turned towards the source of the noise and saw a Lotus Europa turn in through the car park entrance. It was closely followed by a more sedate Ford Escort. The Escort was driven by Detective Inspector David Laurel and the Europa by Dr Oscar Dunbar, the pathologist appointed to the Southshire police by the Home Office.

Spence wandered over to greet them; he spoke to Laurel first.

'Didn't take you long to get here,' he said. 'You can't have come all the way from Downsea, surely?'

'No, sir. I was nearly in Wellbridge when your message reached me so I came straight through.'

'Oh. Well, I'm pleased you got here so soon, anyway.'

Detective Inspector Laurel was Spence's second-in-command. He was thirty-five, with gingery-red hair and a crooked nose which had been badly set after a break some years earlier. He had been a widower for some years, and tended to wear off-the-peg suits with baggy knees; his teenaged daughter had just about got the knack of looking after her younger brother but could not yet cope with her father as well. Laurel was a reliable, hard-working officer, and on a previous murder investigation* Spence had found him an unobtrusive but helpful assistant.

Spence turned to Dr Dunbar, who was just climbing out of his low-slung Europa. Dunbar was ten years older than Laurel, dressed in a fawn trench coat and wearing a brown, narrow-brimmed hat. Spence wished him good morning.

*See *Spence and the Holiday Murders.*

'Morning, Ben,' said Dunbar cheerfully. Close proximity to death never seemed to diminish his good humour.

Spence pointed towards the upper floor of the Blue Bazaar. 'It's slightly messy upstairs, Oscar. I've had a quick look already but we'll go up together in a moment.'

'Very well,' said Dunbar. 'It's a young woman, isn't it?'

'Yes. I'll just sort out a few details and I'll be right with you.'

Laurel and Dunbar wandered off towards the front door and Spence turned to Lindhurst again. 'Right, then, here's the drill. I've got a mobile office on its way here with Detective Sergeant Wilberforce in charge. He'll want some guidance on where to put it. The Forensic people will also be here before long so they'll need to be shown the way upstairs. And I'm also going to need at least twenty men, preferably with local knowledge, to do the door-to-door work this afternoon in the houses round about. So you can start setting all that up now. I'm going to go upstairs now, and after that I'll come back down to see the owners and the cleaner in the cabaret room. But in the meantime they're to stay where they are. OK?'

'Yes, sir.'

'And keep the press at a distance.'

'Yes, sir.'

Spence walked over to join Laurel and Dunbar by the steps to the front door.

'Right, gentlemen,' he said. 'Let's go and view the body.'

14

Spence followed the procedure he had used earlier and opened the front door of the Blue Bazaar very carefully. He held it open with a pencil while Laurel and Dunbar stepped inside; there was no point in spreading any more fingerprints around than was absolutely necessary. Then he led the way up the broad and thickly-carpeted flight of stairs which was just to the left of the doorway.

At the top of the stairs there was a long corridor with a uniformed constable at the end of it, standing beside an open door. As Spence approached him the constable saluted, and Spence peered past him into the bedroom beyond. After a moment he saw the figure of a young man in pyjamas stretched out under the sheets on a single bed on the far side of the room.

'Hmm,' said Spence. 'So there's the sleeping beauty.' He turned to Laurel and Dunbar. 'Damn me if the chef who works here isn't still asleep!' he said. 'I'll have a word with him in a minute—but the body's in here.' He indicated the half-open door to the constable's right, and then pushed it fully open with his foot. He noticed that the door was fitted with a mortise lock but that there was no key in the hole on either side; the deadbolt was not extended.

The curtains at the one window in the room were drawn shut, but the light in the ceiling was on, illuminating an extremely unpleasant scene. Spence stepped to one side to allow Laurel and Dunbar to enter.

'Take a look,' he said. 'I'll be with you in a moment, but I just want to wake that young man up first.'

'Right you are,' said Dunbar. His attention was already fully focused on the corpse.

Spence went back into the chef's room and stared down at the figure in the bed. The young man was breathing evenly and deeply, and it took Spence only a few moments' examination to confirm that he was not putting on an act.

Spence shook the young chef by the shoulder and then restrained him when he started to react with surprise. 'Gently, gently,' he said.

When he was sure that the chef was not going to make any further sudden movements, Spence left him rubbing the sleep out of his eyes and crossed to the window to draw the curtains.

The chef squinted against the light when Spence returned to his bedside. He groped for his hearing-aid and slotted it into his right ear.

'What's going on?' he asked. 'And who the hell are you?'

Spence took care to speak clearly, raising his voice slightly to make sure that the chef could hear him. 'Detective Chief Superintendent Spence,' he said. 'And what's your name?'

The young man's face changed from wearing a puzzled expression to a worried one.

'Um—Colin,' he said almost inaudibly. 'Colin Marples.' He pressed the hearing-aid further into his ear, as if to give himself reassurance. His wide eyes looked past Spence at the constable in the corridor and panic seemed about to set in.

'What's going on?' he said breathlessly. 'Why's that copper here?'

'It's all right,' said Spence firmly, 'there's nothing to worry about. I just want you to get dressed and then come downstairs for a chat with me. OK?'

Marples continued to look extremely worried but the panic faded from his eyes. 'Well, um, yes, I suppose so,' he said. He sat up in the bed and scratched his head. He was a slim, frail-looking young man, with long black hair surrounding a pale, slightly spotty face. The fingers of his left hand clutched the top sheet so hard that the knuckles showed white.

'Just put your clothes on,' Spence repeated, 'and do as you're told and you'll come to no harm.'

He crossed to a chair at the foot of the bed and examined the clothes on it: a T-shirt, jeans, underpants, and socks. They all seemed clean enough: certainly there was no sign of blood on them. He turned to go.

'Just a minute,' said Marples. His voice was squeaky with fright. 'Who did you say you were?'

'Spence. Southshire CID.'

There was a pause and then Marples nodded; the answer seemed to reassure him a little. 'Oh. Right, then. I'll get dressed.'

Spence left him to it but paused to have a quiet word with the constable in the corridor outside. 'Wait until he's ready and then take him downstairs. Don't let him see into the murder room and don't under any circumstances talk to him. And keep him away from the others. Find an empty office or something and keep him isolated until I get there—OK?'

'Yes, sir.'

Spence then rejoined Laurel and Dunbar in the

room where Thana had died. After examining the curtains carefully, the two others had drawn them back to let the daylight in.

Spence now crossed to the window and paused to register the layout of the scene in his mind.

The room was a spacious oblong, with the door on a short side opposite Spence and the large window behind him. The bed was positioned against the longer wall to Spence's right, its head against the far wall, and nearer the window was a fireplace with a gas fire. Positioned against the other long wall were a Victorian dressing-table and a wardrobe. The floor was carpeted.

The bed had been ripped apart, the sheets and blankets thrown on to the floor, the mattress slashed. Everything had been emptied out of the wardrobe and out of the drawers of the dressing-table. Even the seat of an easy chair had been gutted, and where possible the edges of the carpet had been pulled up to look underneath.

In the centre of the room was an upright chair. Tied to it was the naked and very dead body of Thana, whom Spence had seen performing less than forty-eight hours earlier. At that time Thana had been a vital and beautiful girl; she wasn't very beautiful any longer.

Spence came forward into the centre of the room and began to jot down some notes. Dunbar was technologically further advanced: he pulled out a pocket tape-recorder and began to dictate into it.

Thana's body, without any trace of clothing, was tied to the wooden chair with three pieces of new-looking rope which had been cleanly cut with a knife: two pieces bound each ankle to the chair legs, and a

longer piece tied the victim's wrists and arms tightly
to the back of the chair. A length of sheet, torn from
one of those on the bed, was knotted savagely round
Thana's head as a gag. The head itself lolled gro-
tesquely forward, the long blonde hair covering the
once-perfect breasts.

Thana's arms and thighs were covered with blistered
red marks which Spence took to be burns. There was
blood matting the hair on the back of her head, vomit
running down from her mouth and pooling in her
lap, and a mixture of urine and excrement lay on
the floor beneath the chair. Spence could well understand that the cleaner had 'smelt something funny'.

On the front of the body were a number of marks
which had bled, though not copiously; Spence suspected that they were stab wounds, and their number and location suggested a frenzied determination
to kill.

Spence noted down the time, date, and place, details of the lighting and heating, and a rough plan of
the room. Then, with Dunbar's agreement, he opened
the window a few inches at the top. As he turned
away from the window he noticed a piece of angle-
iron on the floor by the door; its dark colour made it
blend in with the carpet and he hadn't seen it before.

'Take a look at this, Oscar,' he said as he bent over
it. A dark patch of blood was visible at one end.

'Oh, yes,' said Dunbar, without much interest. 'Used
to bash her over the head with, I suppose.'

'Is that what killed her?'

Dunbar shrugged. 'God knows. Whoever did this
seems to have been willing to use anything and everything. She's been burnt, and stabbed as well.'

'Yes,' said Spence. 'So I see. What do you think—a plain unvarnished sex maniac?'

Dunbar sighed. 'Well,' he said, 'one never knows, but it's hard to come to any other conclusion from the evidence we have here. This job has got all the earmarks of a sadist who lost control. Possibly he saw the cabaret act and got all stoked up over it, and hid in the bog or something till everyone had gone.'

'Maybe.' said Spence. 'Maybe. Anyway, let's try and reconstruct a little. First of all we've got the naked body of what I can assure you from personal experience was once a very beautiful girl.'

'Saw her while she was alive, did you?' asked Dunbar thoughtfully.

'Yes.'

'Hmm. I gather she was working here as a stripper.'

'That's right.'

'And you saw her dance?'

'Yes.'

'I see. Well, lucky you. She must have looked a bit better than she does now. How old would you say she was—twenty-five?'

'Something like that.'

'Do we know who she was?'

'Not really. Not yet, anyway. She worked under the name of Thana.'

'Thana?' said Dunbar curiously. 'Really—now that's interesting. Thanatos is Greek for death, you know. I wonder if she knew that.'

'I doubt it,' said Spence. 'But perhaps she does now. . . . Anyway, here she is, as dead as a doornail, and the question is, what can we make of it? The clothes have been cut off the body with scissors or a knife, so

far as one can tell. And dumped in a heap over here.'
He indicated a pile of clothes by the bed. 'That suggests that the clothes were removed after the victim
was tied up, which suggests, though by no means
proves, that she wasn't tied up willingly.'

'As part of some fun and games, you mean.'

'Yes.'

'Well, I won't argue with you on that,' said Dunbar.
'In my experience truly masochistic women are very
rare. And while she might have been agreeable to a
bit of bondage, she was hardly likely to want to be
burnt.'

'Agreed. It would present a few problems to someone working as a stripper. Now, we've no idea at
present when that bang on the head was delivered, but
let's suppose for the moment that it was delivered as
she came into the bedroom. Then, unconscious, she
was tied up and gagged. After that the clothes were
cut off, and the burns were applied. And finally, by
the look of it, she was stabbed.'

'Repeatedly.'

'Yes. Though there's no sign of a knife in here at
present. . . .'

'It might turn up.'

Spence looked around him. 'God, what a mess,' he
said. He glanced at Laurel. 'Well, Mr Laurel—what
do you think caused those burns?'

Laurel paused before replying. 'Well, sir, I've been
looking at the shape of some of them, and they're
sort of wedge-shaped.' He pointed out one or two
examples. 'It's my guess that the blade of a knife
was heated on the gas fire and then applied to the
body.'

Spence grunted. 'Yes, you're probably right. There's

a box of matches in the hearth there, so let's just hope
that it's covered with fingerprints. . . . Looks distinctly premeditated then, doesn't it? Whoever did this
came equipped wih an iron bar, a rope, and a knife.'

'And possibly matches,' said Laurel.

'Yes . . .'

Spence jotted down details of the scene for several
more minutes before putting his notebook away.

'Well, we'll clear out of your way now, Oscar,' he
said. 'Let me know the time and place of the post-
mortem, please.'

'I can tell you now,' said Dunbar, 'Four o'clock,
Wellbridge Hospital.' He began to unbutton the
sleeves of his jacket, which were made with real but-
tonholes for that purpose, in order to begin his work
in earnest.

Spence went out into the corridor, where the team
from the Regional Forensic Laboratory was beginning
to arrive. He spoke to the team leader who was clutch-
ing a huge roll of polythene.

'I've seen all I want to,' he said, 'so I'd be glad if
you'd send in your men.'

The man from Forensic nodded placidly. 'Right you
are.'

Over the next hour or two the team from Forensic
would apply their specialized knowledge to the scene
of the crime to see what they could discover; other
police officers would search the room for fingerprints.
The iron bar on the floor would be carefully examined,
the chef's room would be minutely searched, and a
videotape of the scene would be recorded; other
specialists would make drawings, take photographs
and measurements. The result would be a mass of
data.

Spence leaned back inside the room and spoke to Dunbar. 'The body can go when it's been photographed. I've seen enough.'

Dunbar nodded absently, reading a thermometer.

'Time of death?' asked Spence.

'Oh—between 3 and 5 a.m.' said Dunbar. 'So long as you don't hold me to it.'

The man from Forensic looked past Spence at the scene within. 'I hope you catch this bloke quick,' he said earnestly. 'Lunatic sadists are a menace.'

Spence paused before going downstairs. 'So they are,' he said. 'But it's my belief that this particular murderer is not a lunatic, and not a sadist either, not in the sense you mean. He's just deliberate, callous, and brutal.'

The man from Forensic looked surprised. 'Oh. Well in that case, the very best of luck to you. It's not going to be easy.'

15

Spence went back downstairs, followed by Laurel; he found Detective Sergeant Lindhurst in the front hall.

'Your mobile office unit has arrived, sir,' said Lindhurst. 'Sergeant Wilberforce is setting it up at the side of the building furthest from the road.'

Spence nodded. 'Good. It'll do there for the moment. Now—let's have a look at these open windows you told me about. Round the back are they?'

'At the side, sir, actually. The side nearest the road.'

Spence grunted angrily. Nothing like making it easy, he thought.

Lindhurst led the way down a long, dark corridor, past the deserted restaurant off to the left, and through the nightclub's kitchens. He was about to enter a storeroom beyond when another door into the kitchen swung open and Mrs Cordwright entered.

Spence remembered her clearly from Tuesday evening. She was wearing brown slacks with a loose fawn coat on top; her hands were deep in its pockets. Her short grey hair was neatly brushed back at the sides.

'Excuse me,' she said. The tone of voice was well judged, Spence noticed. Polite, but authoritative; concerned, but not outraged. 'Excuse me,' Mrs Cordwright continued, 'but are you the officer in charge of this operation?' She addressed her remarks to Spence.

'I am.'

'I see. Well, allow me to introduce myself. I'm Jennifer Cordwright, one of the directors.' She approached Spence and stood close to him, looking up into his face; she made no attempt to shake hands. 'Now, I know that what has happened here is extremely serious, and that we're all under suspicion. That's reasonable enough—I don't argue with that at all. But I am very concerned about my son. He's the one who actually saw the body, and being the sort of boy he is he naturally wouldn't let anyone else see it. But the experience has done him no good at all. He's most upset, and he ought to be allowed to go home at once.'

Spence felt tempted to smile, but didn't. 'Mrs Cordwright,' he said, 'a number of us have seen the body, and none of us has enjoyed it. Now I promise you that you and your son will both be allowed to go home just as soon as possible. But if you'd be kind enough to go back to the cabaret room for the time being I'll join you as soon as I can.'

Mrs Cordwright hesitated and then accepted his statement. 'Oh, very well,' she said, and retired the way she had come.

Spence nodded to Lindhurst to continue and they moved on into a large store-room adjacent to the kitchen; Lindhurst indicated the two offending windows, either one of which could easily have admitted a very stout burglar.

'Just look at that,' said Spence in disgust. 'Anyone could have got in there. These people need a good hour's lecture from the Crime Prevention Officer.'

'Too late now,' said Laurel.

'Yes indeed. But it would serve the buggers right

if they'd been robbed blind. As it is, someone's been murdered instead . . . Ah, well.'

He returned through the kitchen, pausing only to look at a selection of broad-bladed knives hanging from a row of hooks; one of the hooks was empty.

'I'm beginning to get a bit cross with the owners of this place,' he told Laurel irritatedly. 'There's a knife missing from that rack and I'd like to place a bet on what it's been used for. They really couldn't have made it any easier for the killer if they'd tried.'

He walked on and turned left down a short corridor which led to the cabaret room. Once there he paused and took in the scene.

The room was lit partly by daylight streaming in from a large expanse of glass forming most of one wall to the right, and partly by the ceiling lights which illuminated the darker corners. Seated round a large table on the edge of the cabaret area were the three joint owners of the Blue Bazaar: Mrs Cordwright, her son David, and Lester Read.

Also present, but sitting at a separate table, were a middle-aged woman whom Spence took to be the cleaner who had found the body, and a uniformed constable. Spence indicated with a glance and a nod of his head that the constable could withdraw; then he and Laurel drew up chairs and sat down where they could see the anxious faces of all four of the others present.

Spence rested his forearms on the table in front of him and paused before speaking. David Cordwright shifted uneasily in his chair and his mother glanced at him sharply. Laurel quietly took out a notebook.

'Now then,' said Spence, 'perhaps I ought to begin

by introducing myself. I'm Detective Chief Superintendent Spence, and I'm the head of the Southshire CID. This is my colleague, Detective Inspector Laurel . . . As you may have gathered from Mrs Cordwright, I'm in charge of this murder investigation—and murder is very definitely what it is, if you're in any doubt.'

'We weren't,' said Cordwright tautly. He seemed to be fighting hard to keep a grip on himself and Spence looked at him very carefully for some moments.

'I see,' Spence continued. 'Well, then, I take it that you know that the victim is the girl who was working here this week—Thana.'

Lester Read took his pipe out of his mouth and nodded gravely. 'Yes,' he said, 'we knew that. Perhaps you'll allow me to introduce us too. I'm Lester Read, and I'm a joint owner of this nightclub together with my good friend David Cordwright here, and his mother. This other lady is Mrs Young, who does some cleaning for us.'

Mrs Young looked down at the floor and said nothing.

'I'm afraid David is not feeling too well,' Read continued. 'Come to that none of us are, but David particularly is feeling rather queasy.'

'Don't wait if you want to be sick,' said Spence curtly. 'You know where the toilets are, I expect.'

Mrs Cordwright looked daggers at him but Spence was still annoyed about the windows.

'I'd like to ask you a few questions,' he went on. 'A few preliminary questions at any rate—there'll no doubt be plenty more later on. First of all I'd like to know why there are two windows wide open in the store-room off the kitchen.'

Read acted as spokesman. 'It's part of the chef's duties to make a final check on windows and doors, Superintendent. It's allowed for in his terms of employment. If there's something amiss it's basically his fault.'

'I see,' said Spence. 'Well we'll come back to the chef later on. But I'd like to start with Mrs Young if I may. Do you live in the village, Mrs Young?'

The cleaner sat up straight with a start. Her cheeks turned pink. 'Oh. Yes, sir. Forty-two Hover Hill.'

Mrs Young was about fifty, Spence judged, of average build and plain appearance; her face was probably paler now than usual. Her glasses constantly slid half an inch down her nose, and she constantly pushed them back. She was wearing a striped butcher's apron over a black skirt and a green blouse.

'What time did you arrive here this morning?'

'Oh, 9 o'clock, sir, on the dot.' She glanced anxiously at the steely-jawed Mrs Cordwright.

'And you let yourself in?'

'Yes, sir. There's usually only the chef here and he sleeps late, naturally.'

'Yes . . . And what made you think anything was wrong?'

'Well, sir, it was the smell, you see. As soon as I came in the door it hit me—well it does, doesn't it? I thought it must be a cat or a dog, so I looked around—'

'Did you see anyone on the premises?'

'Oh, no, sir.'

'And what made you look in Thana's bedroom?'

'Well, the door was ajar, sir. All the others were shut, so I thought a cat might have crept in.'

'Yes, I see. Was the light on when you looked in?'

'Yes, sir, it was. And in the corridor, of course, that light's always left on.'

'You didn't switch on the bedroom light yourself?'

Mrs Young shook her head. 'No, sir.'

'All right. So you were probably a bit shocked—'

Mrs Young nodded affirmatively. 'I was that, sir. Shook me to the core it did. I almost fell over myself, I came down the stairs that fast. And I phoned Mrs Cordwright naturally. Told her something terrible had happened.'

'Yes, I see. You've got your own key, you say?'

'Yes, sir.'

'Ever lend it to anyone?'

Mrs Young looked horrified. 'Oh, no, sir, certainly not. It's a matter of trust. Mrs Cordwright trusts me to do the right thing and I wouldn't let her down.'

Mrs Cordwright smiled without warmth.

'Hmm,' said Spence. 'How long have you been working here?'

'Since the club opened. Before, come to think of it.'

Spence placed his hands flat on the table in front of him. 'Right,' he said. 'Well that'll do for the moment, Mrs Young. Do you live far away?'

'Oh, no, sir. A short walk.'

'Well, I think you'd better go home for now. I shall send someone round to see you a little later on. He'll ask you the same sort of questions as I have and he'll write down what you say, and then he'll ask you to sign a statement. There's no need to worry about it, it's just something we ask everyone to do when they come across a crime that's been committed. OK?'

'Yes, sir.'

'Thank you, Mrs Young.'

With a nervous glance at her employers Mrs Young hesitantly rose to her feet and then left the room. Lester Read refilled his pipe in stolid silence. David Cordwright twisted his hands in anguish. Mrs Cordwright sat very still, apparently taking a close interest in the carpet.

'Now then,' said Spence. 'What I've just said to Mrs Young applies to you, too. I shan't keep you here for very much longer, but later on this morning I shall send someone round to take a detailed statement. I expect I shall also visit you myself at some stage, just to fill in the background for me. But in the meantime there are one or two questions which won't wait . . . First of all, can you tell me the stripper's full name?'

He looked at Lester Read, who in turn glanced expectantly at Mrs Cordwright. She shook her head.

'No, I'm sorry, Superintendent,' said Mrs Cordwright, 'but I can't help you at all. She was booked under the name of Thana, and if she had any other name she never used it in front of me.'

'What about her contract?'

'Well, not every artiste insists on a contract, Superintendent. So long as they get their money at the end of the week they're quite happy. And some of them come at very short notice, you know.'

'In other words you didn't sign a contract.'

'No.'

'I see. Have you got an address for her?'

'Well, not a personal address, no, but she was booked through an agent, of course, and he might know. I can get you his address from the office.'

'In a minute will do,' said Spence. 'Tell me, who decides which acts to book here?'

'It's a joint decision,' said Mrs Cordwright firmly, raising her chin as she spoke. 'Though I suppose I put up most of the suggestions. I like to think that I'm the expert on show-business amongst us. My son, of course, is an expert on the catering side, and Mr Read is our legal and financial specialist.'

'You have a stripper every week, I believe.'

'Yes, that's right.'

'Booked through the same agent?'

'Usually, yes.'

'And when did Thana arrive?'

'On Sunday.'

'How did she get here?'

'By train, I believe.'

'I see. And did anyone meet her at the station?'

'No, but my son came along to show her the bedroom she would be using and all that sort of thing.'

'Well, Mr Cordwright?' said Spence.

Cordwright looked up. His face was lined with tension. 'Well what?' he said.

'What can you tell us about Thana's arrival?'

With an effort Cordwright sat up straighter; he took several deep breaths. 'Well,' he said, 'she arrived on Sunday just like any other cabaret performer. She rang up on the Saturday night from Newcastle, where she was working last week, so I told her where to come and what to do. And shortly after she arrived the chef gave me a ring and I came down to show her round and settle her in.'

'The chef let her in, I suppose?'

'He did on Sunday afternoon, yes. After that I gave her a key, of course.'

'That's usual is it?'

Lester Read broke in, obviously anxious to take the pressure off his friend. 'Yes, it is,' he said. 'You see, Superintendent, despite what you say about open windows, we do try to keep the place reasonably secure. We tend to keep the premises locked when we're not here, but the chef lives in, so he has a key, and so do Mrs Young and Mr Smith, who cleans in the afternoons. And of course, the cabaret artists who choose to stay here are given a key also. Since there are literally hundreds of people in and out of here every evening, with ample opportunity to steal things, we've always felt that the precautions I've described were quite adequate.'

'Do you get much pinched?'

'Not a lot, no. Ashtrays and cutlery, of course. We lose a few bottles of spirits now and then, especially at Christmas, but the cash is carefully guarded. And if I may say so, Superintendent, I think your concern with keys is misplaced. It seems to me that either Miss Thana had a friend who stayed on after we closed, or else she went down and let someone in.'

'Possibly,' said Spence. 'Possibly. I take it you three owners all have keys, though?'

Read nodded. 'We do, yes.'

'And what about the other half of this week's cabaret, our conjuring friend, Deceivo—where's he staying?'

'Over in Tallmead,' said Read. 'At the Royal Hotel.'

'What name is he registered under?'

'Um—Counter, Ray Counter. And his assistant's there too.'

'I see. So I take it he did sign a contract then?'

'Oh, yes. Insisted on it.'

'Right. Now then, let's briefly go over Thana's movements this week. She arrived on Sunday, you say —what time?'

Cordwright provided the answer. 'Oh, about 5 o'clock.'

'Any idea what she did with the rest of the day?'

Cordwright shook his head.

'All right. What about Monday?'

'She went for a walk on Monday afternoon,' said Mrs Cordwright. 'We discussed it briefly. She caused a bit of a stir, as a matter of fact. She wore a see-through blouse, which was very silly. She also spoke to Colonel Host-Wall outside the post office, which apparently embarrassed the poor man a good deal. All in all she did not make friends and influence people, and I asked her to watch her step. We have to be very careful in the village, even now.'

'Did she know Colonel Host-Wall?' asked Spence.

'I shouldn't think so for one moment. No, I imagine it was just a few idle words about the weather. But in a relatively small community these things are noticed.'

'Yes, I see. Any rehearsals before the show?'

'Yes,' said Mrs Cordwright, 'there were. She worked to a tape, of course, but she set everything up at about 8 o'clock on Monday night just to make sure it was all in working order.'

'Anything unusual happen that night?'

'No, nothing at all,' Mrs Cordwright continued. 'She worked well—she had a good act, very professional. We were very pleased with her.'

'Was it a big crowd?'

'Reasonable. Our prices are lower on a Monday to encourage people to come in.'

'All right. Now what about Tuesday?'

'Ah, now, on Tuesday she went to London to do some shopping. We exchanged a brief word about some of her purchases on Tuesday evening. That was the night you and Mr Booth were in, of course.'

'Yes,' said Spence. 'So it was.'

'So nice to see Mr Booth again after all these years,' Mrs Cordwright continued. 'Such a *good* man. We really admire him round here, you know. Those of us who remember, that is. He's retired now, I believe?'

'Yes,' said Spence, 'he is. Let's move on to Wednesday. Any idea of Thana's movements yesterday?'

'She went to the pictures in the afternoon,' said Cordwright. 'Over in Tallmead. She mentioned it last night.'

'Alone?'

Cordwright shrugged uninterestedly. 'Never thought to ask, I'm afraid.'

'Do you know whether she did anything else in Tallmead?'

'No idea. Sorry.'

'Did Thana ever give any of you any reason to suppose that she was frightened—that she was expecting trouble?' He looked from face to face but received no response.

'Not at all,' said Read. 'Far from it. I'd say she was one of the least worried people I've ever met. Almost continuously euphoric in fact. Always seemed to be enjoying some sort of private joke. I assumed she was taking something, of course.'

'Of course,' said Spence. 'But whatever it was, it produced a permanent high?'

Read nodded. 'I could do with a little of that myself,' he said, and chuckled.

'Now then,' said Spence. 'Last few questions. Apart from Thana, the chef is the only person who slept here overnight, I take it?'

'Oh, my God!' said Cordwright. His hand went to his mouth and his eyes bulged.

'What's the matter?' said Spence.

'The chef!' said Cordwright. 'Young Colin. With all these terrible things happening I forgot all about him— he's still in bed!'

'No, he's not,' said Spence firmly. 'No need to alarm yourself. I've woken him up and had him brought downstairs.'

'It's all right, David,' said Lester Read soothingly. 'It's quite all right. I told the first policeman who got here all about him and it's all taken care of. I'm sorry, I should have told you, but you weren't feeling too good at that stage.'

Cordwright's shoulders sagged with relief and he put a hand to his forehead.

'How long has the chef worked for you?' Spence asked.

'Oh. Six months or so,' said Read. 'There's a big turnover in kitchen staff, you know. But he's better than most, quite a pleasant lad. Comes from Wellbridge, I believe. He's deaf, of course, that's why he slept through it all . . . You don't suspect him, surely?'

'I suspect everyone,' said Spence flatly.

There was a moment's silence. No one had anything to say in reply.

'Well now,' Spence continued, 'you'll have to arrange for the club to be closed for tonight at least, until we've finished our work. We shall need to search the premises very thoroughly, and the grounds, and I'll see that there are men at the gate to turn people away. Before you go I'd like one of you to leave your names and addresses with Mr Laurel here, plus Mrs Young's address. And later on I shall want full lists of all your staff and club members and so on—but that can wait. In the meantime I'd like your permission to park a mobile office unit nearby, at least for today. Will that be in order?'

Lester Read spoke for the three owners. 'It will. And you may use the telephones and other facilities here if you wish—provided, of course, that we shall be suitably reimbursed.'

'Very well,' said Spence. 'I'll get my administrative officer to discuss it with you later. Oh—and one last thing, Mrs Cordwright. That agent's name and address—I shall want to get in touch with him to find out who Thana really was.'

Five minutes later the three owners of the Blue Bazaar, with obvious relief, made their way home. Mrs Cordwright travelled in a brand-new, Mini, while David Cordwright and Lester Read departed in a Jaguar XJ6.

Spence and Laurel were soon busy with something else: the men from Forensic had made two interesting discoveries in the chef's bedroom. One was a packet of photographs and the other was a broad-bladed kitchen-knife; it was stained with blood.

Spence glanced at his watch: it was 11 o'clock. 'Right,' he said. 'Let's have a look at this knife.'

The Forensic Science Laboratory team leader led Spence and Laurel back to the chef's bedroom and pointed out where the knife had been found: under the removable seat of an easy chair near the door, resting on the broad bands of elastic material which criss-crossed the frame.

'This is the chair his clothes were on,' Spence remarked. 'Funny place to hide a knife. Anyway, there it is.'

'Looks like the one missing from the set in the kitchen,' said Laurel.

'Yes,' said Spence heavily. 'It does.' He turned to the man from Forensic. 'Well, I'm going to talk to the chef now, and at some stage I'd like to get his reaction to that knife. Could you leave it with the constable outside the door of the room where I'm interviewing him?'

The Forensic team leader nodded. 'Certainly.'

'I'll return it to you later on,' said Spence. 'And I'll also see if I can persuade young Marples to agree to a body check and so forth. Now then—you said you'd found two things—what's the other one?'

The team leader advanced on the chef's wardrobe. 'Over here. In a jacket pocket.' He reached into the inside wallet pocket of a dark-green sports jacket hanging from a rail in the wardrobe, and produced a brown envelope about six inches by four.

'What's this?' said Spence. 'Dirty pictures?'

The man from Forensic nodded. 'Very—and sadistic too.'

Spence slid out one or two of the postcard-sized black and white prints and then grunted. 'Hmm, yes, I see what you mean. Have you tagged them?'

'Yes.'

'Well, I think I'll take these downstairs too. Things are beginning to look a bit black for this young man.'

Spence and Laurel returned to the ground floor and located Colin Marples, the chef. He was sitting in what was evidently the owners' office, carefully watched by a stony-faced uniformed constable.

The chef looked frightened: his face was white, his eyes were wide and staring, and his mouth dropped open with shock as Spence and Laurel came into the room.

'Wait outside,' Spence told the constable. 'One of the Forensic team will bring something down for me in a few minutes. Hold it outside until I ask for it.'

'Yes, sir.'

The constable left the office and closed the door behind him. Spence sat down in the swivel chair behind the desk and Laurel took a chair in front of it. The chef stayed where he was, sitting on a straight-backed chair by the wall; he still looked terrified.

'Now then, Colin,' said Spence, raising his voice as before. 'Do you remember my name?'

The chef bit his lower lip and shook his head. His eyes were glassy with tears, which were not quite overflowing on to his cheeks.

'It's Spence. Detective Chief Superintendent Spence.

This is my colleague, Mr Laurel, and we're going to ask you a few questions. You're not obliged to say anything unless you wish to do so, but what you do say may be put in writing and given in evidence. Do you understand?'

A nod. 'Yes.'

'All right. Now, first of all, why are we here?'

Marples tilted his head to one side. 'What's that?'

'I said,' Spence repeated distinctly, 'why are we here? Mr Laurel and me, and half the Southshire police force—why are we here?'

Marples looked bewildered. 'I dunno . . . Something up, I suppose.'

'What, for instance?'

'Well . . .' Marples's eyes roamed wildly around the room, seeking inspiration. 'Well—something's been pinched?'

Spence said nothing in reply to that but moved on. 'How old are you, Colin?'

'Twenty-two.'

'And where were you born?'

'Wellbridge.'

'Lived there all your life, have you?'

Even the simplest question now looked like a trap. Marples's hands rubbed the knees of his jeans to remove the sweat from his palms. 'Well, yes,' he said hesitantly. 'Until I came here, that is. Lived with me Mum.'

'And how long have you worked at the Blue Bazaar?'

'Oh—about six months.'

'I see. OK. Now, on Tuesday night this week I came to the Blue Bazaar with some friends. Did you see me?'

Marples looked at Spence reluctantly in order to check his memory. Then he shook his head. 'No, I can't say I did. But then I wouldn't, would I? Being in the kitchen all night.'

'You didn't stay in the kitchens all the time,' said Spence firmly. 'You came out to watch the stripper . . . Thana. Didn't you?' He stared at Marples hard and the young man's cheeks turned dark red, but this time he held Spence's gaze.

'Well, yes. I did. But so what? You watched her too!"

Spence smiled. 'Good for you, lad. So I did. Do you always come out and watch the stripper?'

'Sometimes. If she's any good.'

'And was Thana any good?'

'One of the best.'

Spence's use of the past tense in relation to Thana had made no apparent impact on Marples. Spence scratched the back of his head and changed tack. 'What time did you get to bed last night? Or rather this morning.'

'Oh, about 3 o'clock.'

'Is that the usual time?'

'Yes. The last meals get ordered at midnight, they're usually finished by 1, and then we've just got to wash up and clear up.'

'What time does the club close?'

'Oh, well, the bars close at 1. That's when the last cabaret starts. And the club's usually empty by 2.'

'What time did Thana go to bed last night?'

Marples thought about it. 'Well, I dunno, really. I didn't see her after the second show.'

'I see. Now I believe you're supposed to lock the windows up last thing at night.'

Marples nodded. 'Yes.'

'Is there a burglar alarm system?'

'No, no, nothing like that. Just ordinary locks.'

'Why didn't you close the windows in the store-room last night?'

Marples gazed at the ceiling for a moment, trying to recall. 'Well—I didn't know I hadn't.'

'Take it from me,' said Spence, 'you didn't. Why not?'

'Well—I must have forgot.'

'Perhaps you had your mind on other things. Like a date upstairs with Thana.'

Marples laughed. The idea was so patently absurd to him that he had to laugh, despite his predicament. 'That'll be the day,' he said.

'Alternatively,' said Spence, who wasn't laughing, 'perhaps you left the windows open so that your mates could come in.'

Marples was offended by that; his jaw jutted forward in self-justification. 'No, I never,' he said petulantly.

'Tell me, did you hear any strange noises during the night?'

'Course not. How the 'ell could I? At least . . .'

'At least what?'

Marples became thoughtful. 'Well, I didn't *hear* anything exactly . . . But I did wake up in the night.'

'What time?'

'Oh, I dunno. Not long after I went to sleep.'

'How do you know that?'

'Well, I don't really, but it was still dark.'

'You looked out of the window, did you?'

'Yes. I thought I heard something funny. I couldn't

be sure, mind you, but anything that wakes me up
has got to be something unusual. So I got up and had
a look out.'

'What did you think it might be?'

'Well, I thought it might be some drunks in the car
park or something like that. You get some odd things
happening now and then.'

'And what was happening last night?'

'Well—nothing. Only one bloke out there, walking
away.'

'Had he been trying to get in, do you think?'

'I dunno. He was leaving then, anyway.'

'Describe this man.'

Marples scratched his nose. 'Well, I couldn't see
him, really. I was looking down on him for a start—
my room is just above the entrance. And he had a
hat on.'

'What else was he wearing?'

'Oh, I dunno. I only saw him for a minute. Then I
went back to bed.'

'Was he stark naked?'

Marples grinned. 'Course not.'

'Well then did he have jeans on?'

'No.'

'What then? Sports jacket?'

'No—a suit, I suppose.'

'OK, so he had a suit and a hat on. Light-coloured
suit or dark?'

'Well—dark.'

'And you didn't see his face?'

'No.'

'What sort of hat?'

'Oh, greyish. Trilby, I think you call them.'

'Anything else you can tell me about him?'

'No.' Marples thought for a moment. 'Well, only that he was smoking a pipe.'

Spence leaned back in his chair and folded his hands on his chest. 'Was he, now,' he said.

He looked at Marples very carefully for some moments. Then he went to the door and returned with the blood-stained knife in a transparent polythene bag. He put it on the desk together with the packet of pornographic photographs which had been found in the chef's sports jacket. Marples's eyes widened in alarm at the display in front of him.

'Got any girl-friends, Colin?' asked Spence disarmingly.

Marples fidgeted. 'One or two, yeah.'

'What sort of a relationship do you have with them?'

'What sort of a what?'

'Relationship,' said Spence louder. 'Go to bed with them, do you?'

No answer.

'Or do you just beat them up?'

Marples's face began to turn red again. Spence took out a selection of the photographs and laid them in a row on the desk.

'You know where we found these, don't you, Colin?'

Marples nodded miserably.

'Bought them in London, did you?'

Another nod.

'All right, then. Now I want you to listen to me very carefully, Colin. Here on the desk we have photographs of a number of girls. Young girls, very young some of them, bending over, being whipped. Tied up. Gagged. Men in masks doing nasty things to them. Now then . . . Upstairs we have another young lady. Name of Thana. And do you know what's happened to her, Colin?'

Marples's eyes bulged out of a guilt-stricken face. He shook his head.

'Well, then, I'll tell you. She's been murdered, Colin, that's what's happened to her. Someone tied her up. Gagged her. Tortured her. And then stabbed her . . . Like to go upstairs to take a look?'

'God, no!'

Marples turned his face away from Spence and the pictures, his features screwed up in revulsion.

Spence sighed. 'No, I don't suppose you would. Turn round and face me, lad, we've nearly finished.'

Slowly, encouraged by a more friendly note in Spence's voice, the chef turned back to look at his inquisitor again.

'Take a look at this knife,' said Spence, holding up the polythene bag by one corner. 'Recognize it, do you?'

'Well—yeah,' said Marples slowly. 'It's out of the kitchen.'

'Sure?'

'Well—yes. I know the marks on the handle.'

'Do you know where we found it?'

Marples looked bewildered again. 'No, where?'

'Under the seat of a chair in your room.'

Marples shrugged. 'Well, I didn't put it there.'

'Who did, then?'

Marples earnestly did his best to be helpful. 'Whoever killed her, I suppose.'

Spence was silent for some moments while he thought what to do. Then he looked up.

'Colin, I'm going to send you over to Tallmead police station. You're not the brightest lad I've ever met, and you're deaf, which doesn't help, but you're not a fool. Now just think about the situation you're in. Here you are, you sleep in the Blue Bazaar overnight, and when you wake up the only other person who slept in the building has been murdered. Stabbed with a knife from your kitchen. Which is found in your room. And what's more, the murdered girl has been tied up and tortured, and we find dirty pictures in your room which suggest that you like looking at girls being tied up and tortured . . . Can you imagine how the case against you could be made to look any blacker?'

The chef shook his head glumly. He stared at Spence with all the horrified concentration of a mouse backed into a corner and faced with an angry tom-cat.

'Well neither can I,' said Spence, 'short of finding someone who actually saw you do it. So I'm going to send you over to Tallmead, and I'm going to get some scientists to do tests on your clothes, take your fingerprints, take samples of your hair and all that sort of thing. And with a bit of luck we'll be able to prove it wasn't you who did it. Do you understand me?'

The chef nodded. 'Yes,' he whispered.

'And you're willing to co-operate fully in those tests?'

'Yes.'

'Right, Mr Laurel, take this young man away and organize everything I've just told him about, and then come back here for a chat with me.'

17

Fifteen minutes later Laurel returned to the owners' office in the Blue Bazaar and found Spence scribbling furiously.

'All well?' asked Spence, looking up.

'Yes, sir. I've arranged for young Marples to be taken over to Tallmead—discreetly, of course. I get the feeling that you don't want the press boys getting wind of the fact that a man is "helping us with our inquiries".'

'Not at this stage I don't, no.'

'I thought so,' said Laurel. 'Though I'm bound to say that I fail to understand why.'

'Why what?'

'Why you're keeping it quiet. And why you haven't charged him.'

'Well, I'll explain all that in a minute,' said Spence. 'In the meantime I assume that the Forensic people know where to find him, do they?'

'Yes, sir. They're going to go over his room, his clothes, his body, take his prints, the lot. I've explained to Marples that he'll be kept at the police station for several hours but he didn't seem too worried.'

'No,' said Spence, 'I don't suppose he'd complain.'

'What are we going to do if we find his fingerprints on that knife? And what if it proves to be the murder weapon?'

'It almost certainly is the murder weapon,' said Spence. 'And it's probably got his prints on it too. He must have used it often enough. But I wouldn't regard either of those things as sufficient reason for holding him.'

There was a pause while Laurel chose his words carefully. 'Would you mind telling me why we're doing the exact opposite of what seems appropriate?' he said at last.

Spence chuckled cheerfully. 'Certainly. Thought you'd never ask.'

He leaned back in his chair, his hands linked behind his head, and began to tell Laurel about the phone call which the retired Detective Chief Superintendent Booth had received in the early hours of Tuesday morning. Then he went on to recall the details of the seventeen-year-old murder of the schoolteacher, Patrick Meadows, and his young son, Peter. As it happened Laurel remembered that case very clearly; he had had an aunt living in the village at that time, and she had talked of little else until her death.

'Let me just get this straight,' said Laurel after a few minutes. 'I've got the drift of the telephone call and I'd like to read the transcript later on—but what you're saying is that both you and Mr Booth think that the woman on the phone knew who the old murderer was, and that he's still in the village?'

'That's our working hypothesis, yes.'

'And what you're saying now is that the person who made the call must have been Thana, the stripper.'

'Well, not "must have been",' said Spence, 'that's too strong. But the odds must surely lie in that direction, very heavily. Charlie Booth and I came here on Tuesday night, and the old man was reasonably sure that the phone call to him was made from that pay-phone just down the corridor.'

'All right. So we assume so far that the stripper came here for the week. Either she knew the village from way back, or she talked to someone who did. Anyway, somehow or other she stumbled across some information which told her who had committed the old murder. And having found that out, she decided to blackmail the person who'd done it.'

'Correct.'

'How on earth would she come across evidence like that?'

'God knows. But the caller claimed to have it.'

'All right, we'll skip that for a minute. But assuming Thana came across the evidence somewhere, presumably the reason why she was tortured was so that the murderer could find out what evidence she had, and where it was hidden. And once she'd revealed that, she was killed.'

'Exactly.'

'And since the chef is only twenty-two years old, he could hardly have committed the first murder, seventeen years ago at the tender age of four, so he's not likely to have killed Thana.'

'Exactly again. And that's why I'm proceeding on the basic assumption that Marples is innocent . . . Mind you, if Forensic find so much as a pinhead of blood on him I'll put him through the wringer till he's only half an inch thick. But at the moment I'm inclined to think that come tonight he'll be tucked up in bed by his Mum.'

'Yes,' said Laurel, 'I follow your reasoning now. So you think the chef was telling the truth when he says he saw a man with a hat on, walking away from the Blue Bazaar this morning.'

'Yes, I do. And don't forget the pipe too. That's the same description as the one we were given seventeen years ago.'

'So it's the same man who committed both murders?'

'Can't see any reason why not. He doesn't want us to think so, of course—that's why he planted the knife in the chef's bedroom. But that was going a bit too far. I find it rather hard to believe that anyone, even a deaf chef, would be quite as stupid as that.'

'No . . . Have you any idea how many people living round here now were also here seventeen years ago?'

'Yes, a pretty good idea as it happens. Counting only those who are old enough to have committed the earlier murder, there are about half a dozen.'

Laurel raised his eyebrows. 'Hmm, as few as that? Well now, that should help a bit. Do you think the murderer knows about the phone call that Thana made to Mr Booth?'

'I hope not,' said Spence earnestly. 'That's our one advantage. If the murderer doesn't know about it that will give him confidence, because he'll assume that we'll be looking for a sex murderer rather than for anyone connected with the old killing. But who knows what Thana may have told him under pressure?'

'Yes . . . But I can't think how she told anyone anything with that gag on,' said Laurel. 'It was so tight it practically cut her head off.'

'He probably freed a hand for her to write with. Quieter that way.'

'Yes, maybe . . .' Laurel sighed. 'Well, I suppose we set the wheels in motion and just carry on. But for a minute or two there I was hoping it would be all over by dinner-time.'

'Yes, it's always a nice feeling while it lasts. Now then, let me bring you right up to date. Percy Wilberforce is round the side in the mobile office, as usual— I've had a word with him and told him what to be getting on with. I've also got that DS from Tallmead —what's his name, Lindhurst—assembling a group of men for the door-to-door work. You and I can use this office for today, I dare say—there's a bit more room here than in the mobile. And we'll follow the same drill as in the Petal Park case, OK?'

Laurel nodded. 'Yes, that's fine.'

'In other words you and I do the job cards to decide what work will be done, and Wilberforce sets it all up. Afterwards he collates the reports and passes them on to you and me for signature.'

Another nod.

'And when we interview people, I do most of the talking, unless you especially want to chip in, and you just jot down a few of the key points.'

'Yes, that suits me.'

'That's agreed, then,' said Spence. 'Now then—the usual questionnaire will do for the door-to-door work. And for the time being you and I keep two things strictly to ourselves. One, the phone call to Booth. And two, the man the chef saw leaving the premises last night, or rather early this morning.'

'Understood,' said Laurel.

'The press would make a meal of either of those if they knew about them. Which they'll have to in time, no doubt, but not yet.'

Spence pulled a pile of numbered forms towards him across the desk.

'Now, let's do a few job cards. First off, I want to make sure that the other half of this week's cabaret is in his hotel room this afternoon. I want to talk to him . . . Then we shall want the names and addresses of all the staff, barmaids and waiters and so on—they'll all have to be interviewed. Then the members of the club, of course—they're all in this card-index system over here. Wilberforce will just love going through that.'

'Search the house and the grounds,' suggested Laurel.

'Yes . . . And I must get Wilberforce to come to some arrangement with the owners of this place about the use of their facilities.' Spence scribbled for some moments. Then he looked up. 'I suppose I ought to ring up this agent and find out what Thana's real name is. Let's do that now.'

He referred to the piece of paper on which Mrs Cordwright had jotted down the details of Thana's show-business agent and then dialled a London number. When he got through to the man he wanted he explained succinctly that the agency was now one performer short, and why. Pained expressions of dismay came crackling over the telephone line at such a volume that even Laurel could hear them. After a minute or two Spence lost patience.

'Look, just calm down, man, and listen to me for a change,' he said sharply. 'Just answer a few straight questions and save the eulogy for later. Now, what was Thana's real name?'

'Melody McFee,' said the agent, suddenly subdued.

'Melody McFee?' repeated Spence incredulously.

'Don't blame me, Superintendent, I didn't invent it.'

'No,' said Spence, 'but she did. You don't seriously expect me to believe that Melody McFee was her real name, do you?'

'Believe what you like,' said the agent crossly. 'That's the name she gave me—Melody McFee, Flat 21, Warmingly Mansions, Roehampton.'

Spence grunted. 'Huh. Well, all right. And how long had she been on your books?'

'A year, give or take a little.'

'Who was she with before that?'

'Abroad, so she said. For what it's worth. Though it could be true. She seemed to have worked in a lot of places—Germany, Sweden, Japan . . . They're very unreliable these girls, you know. They change their name like changing a hair-style, and they move from country to country to dodge the taxes.'

'I see. And how often did she work?'

'Not as often as I would like. Would have liked. She was a lovely girl. I could book her in anywhere. International class. All my acts are, of course—'

'Of course,' said Spence hastily. 'How did you come to book her into the Blue Bazaar?'

'Well now—there's a strange thing. There's a story to that.'

'Make it short.'

The agent was upset. 'All right, all right already. So this is the story. She came in here, about ten days ago, said she'd seen a reference in *The Stage* to a night-club down in Tinley. What did I know about it? So, naturally I told her it was a nice place, books good acts, she could go a lot further and do a lot worse. So, she said could I get her in there. She'd work there a little cheaper for old times' sake.'

'For old times' sake?'

'That's what she said. So I rang up Mrs Cordwright and told her I had this really sexy top-class international stripper with a spare week, at an absolutely bargain rate, just back from a continental tour, and naturally she took her on. Why not? She knows I can give her satisfaction.'

'Yes,' said Spence thoughtfully, as an image of the agent giving Mrs Cordwright satisfaction passed through his mind. 'I may need to speak to you again later on. But that's all for now.' He put the phone down. 'You got the drift of that, I take it?' he asked Laurel.

'Most of it, yes.'

'Well, let's draft a brief note for the press. I've an idea that this case is going to need careful news management—otherwise we shan't be able to move for men with notebooks and pencils.'

18

Towards half-past 11 a dark-blue Rover 2000 was allowed into the car park of the Blue Bazaar by the constable on duty at the gate. Charlie Booth was no longer a serving officer on the county force, but the constable never had a second's doubt about letting him in.

Booth made his way at a relaxed pace to the office in the Blue Bazaar, where Spence and Laurel greeted him warmly. After Laurel had made three cups of coffee in the restaurant's kitchen they all sat down for a serious discussion.

'I've had a message from my cousin George to say that we're welcome for lunch at half-past 12,' said Spence. 'Shall I tell him there'll be three of us there, or just two?'

'Two,' said Booth. 'Thanks very much for the offer, but the Vicar rang me up earlier on. He'd heard about the murder, of course, probably before you did, and he invited me over for a bite to eat if I was going to be here.'

'Fine,' said Spence. He made the appropriate brief phone call to his cousin and then returned his attention to Booth. 'Well now,' he said, 'let me fill you in on what's been happening.'

Swiftly Spence described his arrival at the Blue Bazaar, what he had found there and the steps he had taken. He also gave a brief summary of his theorizing about the case so far.

Booth listened without comment for the most part, but he winced when Spence told him that the chef claimed to have seen a man with a hat and a pipe walking away from the club in the early hours of the morning.

'Hmm,' said Booth slowly when Spence had finished. 'Well, I accept most of your arguments without question. But one thing we ought to ask ourselves is this: is the chef an exceptionally clever liar as well as a brutal murderer? After all, he *could* have murdered the stripper so easily. Motive, lust. Means, the knife. Opportunity, alone in the nightclub with her. It's practically an open and shut case. He could have decided to throw suspicion away from himself by leaving the weapon in his room—which looks so stupid that we won't believe he did it—and by telling us this story about the man with the hat and the pipe, which he knows will make us think of the earlier murders. Seventeen years ago we kept the fact that such a man had been seen fairly quiet, but it got out later on, of course. So the chef could have heard about it. And therefore my first question to you, Ben, is whether the chef has enough brains to do all that? Could he be deliberately bluffing us?'

'No,' said Spence firmly. 'He couldn't.'

Booth accepted the answer immediately. 'All right. Well that means that the murder was in all probability committed by the man the chef saw walking away. And from what you tell me I gather you've decided that it's the same man who killed Patrick Meadows seventeen years ago.'

'Yes.'

'And that his motive was to cut off a blackmail threat almost before it got started.'

'Yes again . . . You see, if you hadn't received that phone call on Tuesday morning then at this precise moment in time Mr Laurel and I would probably be banging that chef's head against the wall, metaphorically speaking of course, until he owned up and told us he'd done it. We wouldn't have believed that story about the man walking away at all. But because of that phone call to you I've virtually ruled out the chef already, unless Forensic come up with something dramatic. And I'm also assuming that it was Thana who phoned you.'

'On what evidence?'

'Well, you thought yourself that the call came from here because of the bass guitar. And she called you darling, remember? That's show-business talk.'

'Well, not exclusively,' said Booth. 'But I'm prepared to accept that the balance of probability lies in that direction. You must be careful not to close your mind to other possibilities though.'

'Point taken,' said Spence. 'All right, so two things follow. First, Mr Laurel does a job card to see that all known sex criminals in the county are checked out thoroughly, just so we don't miss anything from that angle. It's possible, though unlikely in my view, that the man walking away is unconnected with the earlier crime and that he killed Thana out of sheer lust. And secondly, following our main line of reasoning, we take a close look at the fairly small number of men who were in the village all those years ago and of an age to have been physically able to kill Patrick Meadows at the time.'

'Yes,' said Booth slowly. 'I'll come back to that in

a minute. But there's still one thing bothering me. You say it's unlikely that Thana's death is a sex killing, and that it's much more likely that she was killed by her blackmail victim. But doesn't that assume that Thana revealed to her victim that she was the one doing the blackmailing? And isn't that a dangerous assumption?'

'You mean you think the blackmailing could have been done anonymously?' asked Laurel.

'Yes. Much safer that way.'

'Yes, but not so much fun,' said Spence. 'Half the satisfaction of blackmail, if not more, is not the money, it's seeing your victim crawl.'

'That's all very well if the victim is a pathetic little queer,' said Booth. 'Or a Sunday-school teacher caught with his pants down—someone you can dominate without any difficulty. But if you're blackmailing a murderer, it seems just plain foolhardy to me to let him know who's putting the squeeze on.'

'Well, all right,' Spence persisted. 'But judging by the transcript of that phone call, I'm inclined to think that Thana had some sort of tangible proof of who the murderer was, which gave her the confidence to apply the blackmail face to face. But let's assume she did it anonymously. You look at that transcript again. What does Thana herself say about the murderer? That he is clever, cool, and totally ruthless. That means he's clever enough to find out very quickly, or guess, who was applying the pressure, and ruthless enough to torture the girl until she revealed just where the evidence was.'

'Well, maybe,' said Booth, who clearly wasn't happy. 'Time will tell. But if you're right, and Thana *was* persuaded to cough up the evidence, then we shan't find it in her room or anywhere else. Which means that we shall, in effect, have to solve the old murder all over again. So let's go back to your earlier point, and remind ourselves who these few men in the village are.'

'Right,' said Spence. 'First of all, the Colonel—what's his name, Host-Wall.'

'Yes,' said Booth. 'You'll have to read the file, Mr Laurel, to bone up on who all these people are. Colonel Host-Wall certainly had some contact with Patrick Meadows—Meadows coached the Colonel's son in the holidays. But there wasn't any motive there. Host-Wall's wife had a number of lovers but Meadows wasn't one of them—I asked the butler.'

Spence chuckled. 'All right. Now the Vicar—the Reverend Barndean.'

'Well, I'm no longer suitably qualified to talk about him,' said Booth. 'I've got to know him well over the years and I'll have to leave an objective assessment to you.'

'Fair enough.'

'Both the men you've mentioned so far are pipe-smokers by the way,' added Booth. 'And anyone can wear a hat.'

'True,' said Spence. 'And anyone can smoke a pipe, too. Now then, what about Walter Underwood?'

'Well, I couldn't pin it on him seventeen years ago, though I tried. His position then was much the same as the chef's today. And I also find it hard to believe that Walter is capable of doing what you've described upstairs.'

'Hmm. OK. So that only leaves the owners of this place, Lester Read and David Cordwright.'

'There *are* one or two others,' said Booth. 'There's

Mr Amble, the post-mistress's husband, but the Vicar tells me he's in hospital at the moment with a hernia. And then there are assorted youngsters who were only children seventeen years ago. Four and five years of age.'

'Yes,' said Spence. 'Well, doesn't it begin to look as if it was one of the people we've mentioned? It's as if he were laughing at us. He did it seventeen years ago and got away with it, and so now he just walks away again, casually smoking his pipe. And no doubt wearing his hat at a jaunty angle.'

Booth sighed. 'Yes, I agree that the laws of probability suggest that. But don't ask me to plump for any of those people you've mentioned because none of them feel right. I know them all and I can't honestly say that any of them fit the mould.'

'But you agree that the killer is an exceptionally cool customer?'

'Well, I suppose I must. All murderers are very peculiar people, to put it mildly.'

'I'm puzzled about this stripper,' said Laurel. 'How did she come to know anything about a murder which most people have long since forgotten? Was she a local girl?'

'My cousin said not,' Spence replied. 'Though he did admit that she reminded him of someone. The fact is, she could have been living here ten years ago, and then run away from her family or something, dyed her hair, had her nose bobbed and her tits lifted, and after all that even her own mother wouldn't recognize her. We'll just have to hope that her real name can be found from her papers at home—I'm quite sure she wasn't christened Melody McFee. Either that or her prints may betray her—she might have a criminal record.'

Booth rose to his feet. 'Well,' he said, 'I'll leave all that to you. I'm going to go and see my friend the Vicar.'

'Take a thought with you,' said Spence. 'We must assume for the moment that Thana had enough local knowledge to know about the murder of Patrick Meadows and his young son. We also know, from her agent, that she specially asked him to get her a booking here. And almost as soon as she got here, she saw something, or heard something, or maybe even read something, which in some mysterious way gave her certain knowledge of who had committed the old murders. Now—what I want to know is this: what was it that gave her enough evidence to be able to think of blackmail? Was it a face she saw? Or the fact that someone had money—or didn't have money? Or the fact that someone was married—or not married?'

'God knows,' said Booth glumly.

'Yes, He does,' said Spence. 'The point is, I want to know too.'

19

At 12 o'clock Spence drove the two miles to Tallmead police station. The late April sunshine glinted off the surface of the river as he drove over the long stone bridge and up the hill. Two women in head-scarves were walking their dogs along the river bank.

Tallmead was an ancient market town with a tall church spire which dominated the surrounding countryside. The police station was a solid Victorian building at the far end of the High Street. It was half-day closing in the town and the streets were almost deserted.

Pausing only to check that the chef from the Blue Bazaar, Colin Marples, was quite happy with the way he was being treated, Spence proceeded to a large briefing-room at the back of the police station. There a group of some twenty-odd men were patiently awaiting his instructions for the house-to-house inquiries which were to be made in the afternoon. Spence gave them his usual crisp summary of what had happened and what he wanted them to do, his eyes moving from face to face as he spoke.

'You'll see from the questionnaire what details are required,' he said. 'The main thing to establish is who lives in each house—but I want you to find that out discreetly, not by being heavy-handed and antagonizing everyone. I also want to know whether anyone saw the victim in the village, and if so at what time and which day. She didn't exactly blend in with the land-scape, so those who saw her shouldn't have any diffi-culty in remembering. I'm also interested in any man over the age of about thirty who wears a hat and/or smokes a pipe. So keep your eyes open.'

After the briefing Spence and Laurel retired to George Spence's farm, to the east of Tinley, for lunch. They were offered a massive meal of chicken and fruit salad, plus a detailed dialogue on the murder from George and his wife, Dora. Spence came away con-vinced that the information he received from and about the long-term residents of Tinley was going to be the key to this case.

'Just one thing,' Spence said to George as he was leaving. 'Are you quite sure that that stripper you saw on Tuesday evening never lived in the village?'

'Absolutely certain,' said George. 'I'd remember a face like that, now wouldn't I?'

'Not to mention the figure,' said Dora. 'And I'd never seen her before either, though I must say she did remind me of someone.'

'You too?' said Spence. 'George said that on Tuesday night. Try to remember who she reminded you of, will you please? It would help!'

Former Detective Chief Superintendent Booth had a rather smaller lunch than was served at the farm. Until the last moment the Vicar had neglected to tell his housekeeper, Mrs Trayle, that he had invited a guest, and the result was that an already frugal meal was re-quired to stretch for two. But Booth didn't mind; his doctor was still anxious for him to lose a little more weight.

Booth had enjoyed the short drive from the Blue

Bazaar to the vicarage. In fact he had parked his car on the far side of the village green and walked the last few hundred yards in the sunshine, just for the pleasure of it.

Over the years he had grown fond of Tinley, and he particularly liked the old cottages grouped around the open space in the centre of the village. They seemed so civilized and peaceful, and yet he knew from experience that not all was so peaceful within: that in a few of those houses, just as in the new estate behind him and in the darkest slums of far-off cities, there was jealousy, rage, wife-beating, and the occasional case of incest. Now that he was retired he was trying hard to forget about the darker side of life, but it was, he supposed, an occupational disease of policemen that they habitually saw the worst in everybody.

The Vicar was delighted to see him. 'Mr Booth, Mr Booth,' he said warmly, shaking him by the hand. 'Come along in.'

They drank a good dry sherry, and after a brief reference to the murder agreed to discuss it further after they had eaten. The Vicar opened a bottle of hock to accompany the small helpings of fish, and it was only after coffee that their thoughts returned to the fate of Thana rather than the fate of the world in general.

'You know,' said the Vicar, 'I've been thinking about this girl, and the reason I asked you to call is that I think I must have seen her myself.'

'Oh?'

'Yes . . . Of course, Mrs Trayle is quite convinced that the shameful hussy, as she calls her, came to an end that she fully deserved. But I really can't agree with that. "Thou shalt not kill", you know. It's quite

plain what that means, at least in this context, so I
feel I must do what I can to help. And perhaps my
thoughts might just conceivably be of some value.'

'I'm sure they will be,' said Booth. 'What day do
you think you may have seen her?'

The Vicar hesitated for a moment before answering.
'It was . . . on Monday,' he said. 'I was in the church,
during the afternoon—about 3 o'clock I think it was.
Anyway, I came out of the darkness of the church into
the sunlight, and I saw this figure on the far side of
the churchyard. I was blinking a bit, because of the
sunlight—and for one horrible moment . . .'

He paused, blinking frequently even now. Then he
continued.

'Well, there was this young woman standing among
the gravestones, as I've said. She was very . . . well,
tarty I suppose. Quite unlike any of the villagers
More like a pin-up girl, a film star. She was dressed in
a black skirt and a white top, and a cardigan, I think.
She smiled at me, and I really think that smile was one
of the most upsetting things I've ever seen in my entire
life. It was as if she somehow personified everything
that was loathsome and evil. Now, perhaps that's quite
unfair. Perhaps in real life she was quite a moral person, quite good—though as she earned her living as a
stripper I suppose that's unlikely. Anyway, there she
was.'

The Vicar reached for a pipe from a rack nearby and
carefully lit it before going on. Booth waited patiently.

'Well, after a few moments the woman walked away.
Perhaps it was coincidence, I don't know—but in any
case I felt terribly ill. I wondered for a minute if I was
going to have a heart attack, my heart pounded so
fiercely. I'm not afraid of death, you know, far from it,

and I just leaned against the church door and waited. And after a few minutes I felt a little better, so I went inside and prayed . . . And then I came home. And I must have looked rather ill even then, because Mrs Trayle wanted to call a doctor. I didn't let her, of course. However, let's forget about me and get back to this girl.'

The Vicar puffed on his pipe while he collected his thoughts.

'Well now, I knew instinctively that this young woman was from the nightclub. One look at her was enough—that's the only place she could have come from. People who live in Tinley just don't dress like that, not even on the new estate. And that's what I found so disturbing, I think. This young woman represented change—and it's not what I consider change for the better.'

'There's always change,' said Booth gently.

'So there is,' said the Vicar. 'But it's our job—mine, particularly—to see that it's the right sort of change. And that's where I feel I've failed. I think that's what upset me—the consciousness of failure. You see, Mrs Cordwright, who owns the Blue Bazaar—she was once a regular attender at my church. But over the years she gradually drifted away, until now, of course, she never comes at all. And that's failure with a capital F.'

'I think you said once that you tried to dissuade her from opening the Blue Bazaar.'

The Vicar nodded. 'So I did. And you can see what success I had with that.'

'How did she behave when you tackled her?'

The Vicar grimaced. 'Oh—it's painful to recall, even now. Let's just say that she was exceptionally rude and told me to mind my own business.'

'I know how hard you find it to pass on what you feel is gossip,' said Booth. 'But just remember that we are dealing with a murder case, and that the only way to combat murder is with information. Now—what kind of a person is Mrs Cordwright?'

The Vicar sighed. 'Well, of course she never did have quite the background she claimed, you know. It sounds cruel to say so, but although she inherited money from somewhere, it's my belief that she wasn't brought up to be a lady—it was something she adopted later on in life, purely as a surface veneer. At least, that's my impression. Underneath I think she's as common as muck.'

'And she's not really a widow, either, is she?'

'No, and not many people know the truth of that. When she first came here she claimed that the whole matter of her status was so distressing to her that she refused to discuss it. And she certainly gave the impression that she was a widow, even if she didn't tell barefaced lies about it. But the fact is, she and her husband were divorced, many, many years ago now. A colleague of mine who knew the family well told me that her husband was gentleman enough to let her institute the divorce proceedings and he also gave her custody of the child, despite the fact that she was the guilty party.'

'Adultery?'

The Vicar nodded sadly. 'With more than one partner, I regret to say. Though I've heard no scandal on that front since she came here.'

'Would you say she's a snob?'

'Oh, yes.'

'To use an old-fashioned term, has she an inferiority complex?'

'Yes, I think that's a very fair description. She has always sought the company of the wealthy and the well-placed—and I suppose in her misguided way she feels that running a nightclub will bring her into association with such people.'

Booth seemed satisfied. 'Good. Now, what about her son, David.'

The Vicar pursed his lips. 'Well, in my view he lets her down, though she will never admit it. He's an only child, of course, and he's never really broken free of her. Even I know that he is a homosexual, but his mother would never admit it for one second. She talks about him not having found the right woman to share his life and all that sort of thing. And what a good idea it is for two bachelors to share a house so that they can keep each other company and reduce costs.'

'Speaking of that household,' said Booth, 'what do you make of Lester Read?'

The Vicar's expression lightened. 'Oh, Lester's all right. Quite a gentleman, in fact. One of the old school. An Oxford man. Loves cricket, you know. Travels miles to see a good match, and you certainly won't see him in the village when there's a Test match on.'

Booth suppressed a smile.

'Yes, I've got a lot of time for Lester,' the Vicar continued. 'Never comes to church, mind you, but he's a good organizer and he'll always lend a hand at a fête or whatever—never a moment's hesitation. If you ask him about church he'll say he doesn't come because he can't stand the music—that he's tone deaf. But the truth is he has very well-developed taste in opera, so that's just an excuse. I think he's an agnostic myself—

but he wouldn't offend anybody by forcing his opinions on them.'

'And what about the Colonel—what's your assessment of him?'

The Vicar puffed on his pipe before answering. 'Well,' he said, 'a few years ago I would have given him a spotless reference. But now—now I'm not so sure.'

'Why not?'

The pipe was waved in the air. 'Well, I don't think I can refer to anything specific. It's just that my instinct—for what it's worth—tells me that with the passing of time he has become shifty and unreliable.'

'Hmm. I see.'

There was silence for two or three minutes. Booth finished his coffee. Then the Vicar knocked out his pipe into a wastepaper basket and spoke again,

'You know,' he said, 'it's just occurred to me that you've asked me for my assessment of practically everyone who lives in the village now who was here seventeen years ago.'

'Yes,' said Booth. 'I thought I'd covered most of them.'

20

After lunch at the farm Spence and Laurel drove back to Tinley. They were using Laurel's car, a green Ford Escort 1100L; Laurel was driving and Spence was keeping his eyes open.

They crossed the river again, passed the Blue Bazaar on their left, and continued for another three-quarters of a mile along the London Road until they came to a modern detached house set back some thirty yards from the highway. The name of the house was 'Nightingales' and it was the home of Lester Read and David Cordwright.

As Laurel parked his car safely off the road Spence took note of the house: it had been built in red brick, presumably some thirty or forty years earlier, and to Spence's eyes it looked singularly unattractive. It was not at all the house he would have pictured Read and Cordwright living in; but then, he reminded himself, not all homosexuals have exquisite taste, and the house did have the virtue of being close to its owners' place of work.

A ring at the door was answered by a shirt-sleeved Lester Read, who had an extremely ancient pipe clenched in his teeth; without his well-tailored jacket he looked distinctly tubby and more middle-aged than ever.

'Oh,' he said, apparently rather surprised. 'It's you—Superintendent Spence, isn't it?'

'That's right,' said Spence. 'We did say we'd be calling.'

'Oh. Well, you'd better come in.'

Read led the way into the front room of the house, where he offered his visitors two easy chairs. The furniture was just as undistinguished as the house itself—orthodox in design and far from new; the pictures on the wall were traditional landscapes.

'Take a seat,' said Read. 'David will be with us in a minute. He's just finishing washing up.'

Read crossed the room ahead of his visitors to pick up a dark-grey lounge suit from one of the chairs; he suspended it by a hanger from the picture-rail on the wall. 'Mustn't let you sit on that,' he said. 'Just been pressed for tonight.'

'Oh? Going somewhere special?' asked Spence.

Read laughed shortly. 'No, not really. But I'm in a play. *Private Lives,* you know.'

'Really?' said Spence. 'Who's putting it on?'

'Oh, the Tallmead Players—it's an amateur production over in Tallmead. Mrs Cordwright press-ganged me into it, and I didn't have the strength of character to say no.'

'I thought writing was more your line than acting,' said Spence.

Read brushed invisible specks of dust off the lapels of the suit. 'Well, not entirely. Years ago I had visions of being an actor. Even tried it professionally for a couple of years. But I got so bored with "resting" as they call it that I went into teaching, just to give myself something to do. After that I did do a spot of writing, it's true, but since we opened the Blue Bazaar I haven't put pen to paper, except to sign cheques.' He chuckled heartily, leaving Spence with the impression that unlike most mortals Read did not suffer pain when he signed a cheque.

'What part is Mrs Cordwright playing?' Spence asked.

'Oh, she's not actually doing any acting. She's a backroom boy, so to speak. Does the costumes, helps build the sets, that sort of thing. It's our first night to-night, curiously enough, but the show must go on. It should have been all over in March, but half the cast had the flu, so we postponed it.'

'I see . . . You say Mr Cordwright's washing up?'

Read seated himself comfortably on a settee. 'Yes, that's right. He won't be a minute.'

'How's he feeling now? He was a bit queasy earlier on.'

Read's face showed concern; he took the pipe out of his mouth. 'He's still pretty shaken, I must say. This murder business seems to have hit him pretty badly. I think he sees everything we've worked for over the last few years going up in smoke as a result. But I don't see it like that at all. On the contrary, I'm afraid human nature being what it is, I think the club will do record business once it re-opens. In our game I don't think there's any such thing as unfavourable publicity.'

At that point David Cordwright entered the room with a pot of tea on a tray. Lester Read hastened to put a small table into position for him, and the next two minutes were taken up with Cordwright asking whether everyone liked his tea weak or strong and with or without milk and sugar. The tea, when it was finally delivered, tasted indistinguishable from that served in police canteens.

While Cordwright was busy with the cups and

saucers Spence used the time to take a careful look at him. He was wearing black polyester trousers with flared cuffs and a dark green polo-necked shirt. He looked a good five years younger than the thirty-three years old which Spence knew him to me. His features were handsome, in an old-fashioned, Michael Wilding sort of way, but his face was drawn with strain and there were beads of sweat at his hairline; his hand shook as he lifted the teapot.

'Well now,' said Spence when everyone was settled. 'Let's get down to brass tacks. What I'm after at this stage is a bit more background information. Some of it may seem irrelevant to you, but it all helps me to build up a picture in my mind. Now—first of all I'd like you to tell me how long the Blue Bazaar has been open.'

David Cordwright glanced at his friend and they tacitly agreed that Read would answer.

'Three years, Superintendent. Very nearly, anyway.'

'And what's the arrangement, a limited company with the three of you as directors?'

Read puffed on his pipe and nodded. 'We've all known each other for many years, Superintendent. We'd often discussed the possibility of doing something together—possibly opening a hotel or whatever. But then about four years ago we decided that the time was ripe for a nightclub, right here in Tinley. And how right we were.'

'I've been told that what finally tipped the balance was that Mrs Cordwright inherited some money.'

Read blinked. 'Well, I don't know who told you that, Superintendent, but I suppose that was one of the factors, yes. I'd often offered to put some capital behind David's training and ability myself, but Mrs

Cordwright—and David too, I think—preferred to wait until they were able to take on some of the risk themselves.'

'Yes, I see. You said earlier that you didn't think the publicity would do any harm—I take it you've arranged for the club to be closed tonight?'

'I have, yes. I phoned the evening paper about an advert as soon as we got back here. But we'll open again on Friday and Saturday, if that's all right with you.'

'Yes. We'll be finished by then.'

'We've still got half a cabaret act, and I dare say we can get a replacement stripper easily enough if we try. May not be necessary, though. I think the crowds will come anyway.'

'Tell me about the other half of your cabaret,' said Spence. 'The great Deceivo, I believe he calls himself. And his assistant, the lovely Sue. Is he a local act?'

'Good God, no,' said Read firmly. 'He's an international. He could work anywhere in the world with an act like that, and I believe he does.'

'Did he or Sue have much contact with Thana?'

Read shook his head. 'No, not that I saw. What about you, David?'

David Cordwright also shook his head negatively. 'Kept themselves very much to themselves,' he said quietly. 'Just turned up each evening, did their act, and left again afterwards. And don't ask me how he makes the girl disappear from that cabinet, because I just don't know.'

'Trade secret no doubt,' said Spence. 'Now then, I'd like a brief rundown on the sort of people who attend your nightclub. Give me a cross-section of your clientèle.'

Read pursed his lips. 'Oh, we get a very wide variety of people. People from all walks of life, from working-class to the nobility.'

'What about Colonel Host-Wall, for instance—does he come?'

Read laughed. 'Oh, Lord, no. No. If you're talking about individuals, of course, we can tell you yes or no. But the Colonel doesn't come, no. I think he goes to London to pursue his interests.'

'What makes you say that?'

Read's eyes twinkled. 'Oh, a little bird told me. I don't think it would be fair to say more than that.'

'Do you ever have any trouble in the club—people getting drunk or fighting?'

'Well, we have our share of heavy drinkers. And there's the occasional voice raised in anger, or a slight scuffle. But nothing we've ever had to call the police about.'

'I'll be getting one of my officers to go through your membership files before long,' said Spence. 'You never know, the name of someone convicted of various sex offenses may leap out at us. But if we contact any of your members we'll do it discreetly.'

'We'd certainly appreciate that.'

'In the meantime,' Spence continued, 'I want the two of you and Mrs Cordwright to make a list for me of the names of as many people as you can remember who were in the club on Wednesday night. You won't have known them all, of course, but do your best. And, of course, I want to know about any suspicious characters you can think of—people who've given you trouble by pestering the strippers, that sort of thing.'

Read nodded. 'I wasn't in the club on Wednesday

night myself, Superintendent, but I'm sure David and his mother will do as you ask.'

'Good. I'd like the list by tomorrow morning, please. Now, next I want to go over yesterday in a bit more detail—we spoke about it briefly this morning. How did you and Mr Cordwright spend your day, for instance?'

'Well, let's see . . . Yesterday was Wednesday. Well, David and I got up about 11, which is our usual time. We had a bite to eat, and then we all three went to London to do some shopping.'

'You mean Mrs Cordwright went as well?'

'Yes. She joined us at the last minute. Changed her mind as women do, you know.'

'Did you go by road?'

'No, we went on the train.'

Spence looked at Cordwright. 'And you say Thana went to the pictures over in Tallmead?'

'So she said, yes,' replied Cordwright hesitantly. 'We had a brief word about it in the evening.'

'But she didn't say what she'd seen?'

'No. But there's only the one cinema there. It's a pre-war place divided into two, like most of them nowadays. The cinema is in the old balcony and the bottom floor is a bingo hall.'

Spence looked back at Read. 'What did you do in London?'

'Who, me personally?'

'The three of you.'

Read looked surprised. 'Well, for what it's worth we all went our separate ways. I went to see my dentist and did a bit of shopping. David ordered a new suit, and as for his mother—well, I've no doubt she put the fear of God into half the staff of Harrods, as usual.'

He laughed heartily. David Cordwright managed a sickly smile, his eyes downcast.

'What time did you get back?'

'Well, David and I caught the 5.30, so we were back here at 6.30. I went to a dress rehearsal of *Private Lives* after that, and David was on duty at the club.'

'What time did Mrs Cordwright come back?'

Read rubbed the side of his nose. 'Well, I'm not sure, but she was around after the dress rehearsal ended, doing things to the costumes.'

'I see,' Spence turned to Cordwright. 'And what happened after the second cabaret?'

Cordwright seemed puzzled. 'Well, nothing special. The staff and I just cleared up as usual, and then went home. It was no different from a hundred other nights.'

'Not at that point,' Spence agreed. 'Now then, there was a piece of angle-iron in Thana's bedroom this morning, about two feet long. Was that usually there?'

Cordwright and Read looked at each other with blank faces.

'Good heavens, no,' said Read. 'Who would want a thing like that in a bedroom?'

'Any idea where it came from?'

More blank looks.

'No, none at all.'

'All right. And there was a box of matches in the hearth—are they a standard fixture?'

'Ah,' said Cordwright, 'now I gave Thana those myself on Sunday. It's still a bit chilly in the mornings and I thought she might want to use the gas fire.'

Spence nodded and continued to speak to Cordwright. 'OK. Tell me, what was your opinion of Thana?'

Cordwright paused before answering. 'Well, I don't

know, really. She was a good professional act. Apart from that I haven't got any opinion. I didn't spend a lot of time talking to her, I've got other things to do.'

And she wasn't your type, thought Spence. 'Had she worked for you before?' he said aloud.

'No. She said we'd met before—kidded me a bit because I couldn't remember where. But she'd never worked here before, no.'

'Did she take any customers upstairs?'

'Not that I saw, no.'

'But it happens occasionally?'

'Well, perhaps I ought to explain why we have cabaret artists staying in the club at all,' said Cordwright. 'We never intended to run the place as a hotel, but it does no harm to have some people sleeping in overnight, and for a variety of reasons we don't live in ourselves.'

'I understand all that,' said Spence. 'But to repeat my question, occasionally your overnight guests take people up to bed, do they?'

'Occasionally, yes,' said Cordwright. 'If someone is very indiscreet, then they have to move into a hotel. But normally they use common sense.'

'Yes, I see. Now, you gave Thana a key to the front door—but did you give her a key to the bedroom door as well?'

'No. No, I didn't. You see, let's get one thing straight.' Cordwright was speaking with more confidence now. 'Strippers aren't prostitutes, Superintendent, at least, not in my experience. But they're not saints, either—and by and large they don't seem to want to lock people out of their bedrooms.'

'That's fair comment,' said Spence. 'But what I'm getting at is this. If someone went upstairs at say half-past 2 in the morning, and knocked on Thana's door, would she have opened up to them?'

'I imagine she would,' said Cordwright. 'This is Tinley, you know, not New York City.'

'Perhaps so,' said Spence. 'But she's dead, just the same.'

Spence left it at that, and he and Laurel returned to their car.

'Well,' said Spence as he settled into his seat, 'what do you make of that pair, then?'

Laurel took his hand away from the ignition key, as Spence obviously wanted to talk before moving off. 'Well, for what it's worth, the older one—Lester Read—smokes a pipe.'

'So I noticed,' said Spence drily. 'But if it had been him walking away from the Blue Bazaar in the early hours of this morning the chef would have recognized him, surely to God. He's not short-sighted as well as deaf, or he would have worn glasses to watch the stripper.'

'Contact lenses?' said Laurel.

'Well, it's a fair point, but he saw the pipe and the hat, and if he could see those clearly enough, then I'm certain he would have recognized Read . . . Well, fairly certain.'

'I quite liked old Lester,' said Laurel. 'It's hard to think of him being a poofter. Young David's a bit of a pansy though—he was almost in tears at one point.'

Spence chuckled. 'I think you're jumping to conclusions, Mr Laurel. Colin Marples was nearly in tears this morning, but you didn't think he was queer.'

'That was different,' said Laurel.

'You're also making a false assumption,' said Spence.

Laurel glanced at him sideways. 'What do you mean by that, sir?'

'Well, just that superficially Read appears to take the masculine role and Cordwright the feminine. But in homosexual relationships, as in everything else, things are not always what they seem.'

21

'Where to now?' asked Laurel as he started the car.

'Mrs Cordwright's house. It's on the edge of the village green—I'll show you where.'

Laurel drove off down the London Road, and in due course turned left through the new housing estate towards the heart of the old village. As they approached Mrs Amble's post office on the corner opposite the green, Spence noticed a familiar figure standing by the side of the road; it was Colonel Brian Host-Wall, sometime Squire and Lord of the Manor of Tinley, but now just another elderly man out for a walk with his dog. He was wearing a battered tweed sports jacket with knobbly brown buttons, cavalry-twill trousers, and brown brogues; the dog was an untidy-looking spaniel.

Spence asked Laurel to bring the car to a halt at the appropriate point and then wound the car window down. 'Good afternoon, Colonel,' he said.

The Colonel looked startled for a moment until he realized who was addressing him. 'Oh—afternoon. Let's see now—you're a colleague of Mr Booth's, aren't you? Met you last Tuesday, isn't that right?'

'It is.'

'Ah, yes, well, good, good. Just the chap I want to see.' The Colonel came closer to the car; he looked distinctly nervous. 'Is it true what everyone's telling

me?' he asked. 'Has there really been a murder at that
dreadful nightclub?'

'Yes, I'm afraid that's correct, Colonel.'

'Good Lord!' The Colonel's moustache almost flut-
tered with indignation. 'And it was the striptease
lassie who was the victim, is that right too?'

Spence nodded.

'Well I'm blessed. Well I'm blessed. What a dreadful thing. Dreadful!'

'Did she strike you as being a likely murder victim?'
asked Spence.

The Colonel stepped back a foot and his hand rose
to straighten his tie. 'What—er—what's that? Didn't
quite follow you—I mean, strike me as being what do
you say?'

'The girl who got killed,' Spence repeated calmly.
'You were talking to her on Monday afternoon outside
the post office.'

'Oh? Really? Was I?' The Colonel's gaze drifted
sideways distractedly; the ruddiness in his cheeks faded
to a pale grey. 'You mean—you mean, that was the
girl who got killed—the one who spoke to me on
Monday afternoon?'

'It was.'

'Well. Well I'm blowed. Well now—yes, come to
think of it—there was a young lady who had a word
with me on Monday. Thought she was a stranger at
the time . . . Rather flamboyantly dressed, you know.
Never realized she was from the Blue Bazaar though.
Was she really? Fancy that. Terrible thing, isn't it?
So young. Quite attractive too. Was she, um—was
she . . .'

'Raped?' suggested Spence.

'No, no.' The Colonel's cheeks rapidly turned red

again, and he looked thoroughly discomfited. 'No, no. Wasn't going to ask that at all. I meant was she local, was she from round here?'

'Did anything make you think she was?'

'No, no, not at all, not at all. Quite the opposite really—never saw her before in my life. But the papers have been ringing me up, you know. Asking me about her. Reporters and so forth . . .'

'Why should they do that?'

'Well, I don't know really, but a couple of them have. I suppose one or two of 'em looked up Tinley in their records and found the Host-Wall family name cropping up, that sort of thing. Snatching at straws as these press chappies always do.'

'Yes,' said Spence, 'I see. Well, if I were you, Colonel, I should tell them as little as possible. In the meantime you might think over that conversation you had with the victim very carefully. At some stage I shall be coming round to see you about it.'

'Oh? Really? Oh. Well—just as you wish—er . . .'

Spence began to wind up the car window again. 'Good-bye for now, Colonel.'

'Oh. Good-bye, Mr, um, er—Superintendent . . .'

The Colonel's face dissolved into something approaching panic as Spence and Laurel moved on. Laurel waited until they were a tactful ten yards down the road before allowing himself to laugh.

'Well!' he said cheerfully. 'If looking guilty's any guide, he's our man.'

'Couldn't agree more,' said Spence, who was also amused. 'He's guilty of something, that's for sure. Unfortunately I have the feeling that our real murderer will not be quite so easy to spot.'

* * *

Spence directed Laurel to Mrs Cordwright's house, an olde-worlde thatched cottage which had all the style and individuality, both without and within, which Spence had found so noticeably lacking in her son's residence. Mrs Cordwright was at home, and instantly invited them in.

'You'll have to excuse the mess,' she said, waving an arm over an immaculately clean and tidy living-room. 'But I'm without a home-help at the moment. Unbelievably hard to come by, even in these days of high unemployment. You'd hardly credit it, would you?'

Spence and Laurel agreed politely that the short-age of domestic assistance was indeed one of life's most pressing problems. Then they seated themselves in the offered chairs and declined the suggestion of further tea. Eventually Mrs Cordwright was persuaded to sit down opposite them.

'You live alone I take it?' said Spence.

'Oh, yes.' Mrs Cordwright crossed her trouser-suited legs and interlocked the fingers of her hands round the topmost knee. 'Yes, I've lived alone for many years now, ever since David got his degree. That's—oh —twelve years ago now.'

'He went to University?' asked Spence.

'Well, a polytechnic actually, but in many ways that's far superior, of course. He took a course in catering and the hotel trade, tourism, that sort of thing, really first-class. It was the only course of its kind in those days, though I believe some univer-sities have started them up since then. He did ex-tremely well, although I suppose I shouldn't say so myself.'

Spence smiled indulgently. 'And I see you do some

sewing,' he said, indicating a twenties-style dress and a sewing-box on a nearby chair. 'Is that for tonight's play?'

'Why, yes, it is, as a matter of fact. How did you know about that?'

'Ah—we have our sources.'

Mrs Cordwright dimpled her cheeks to indicate pleased surprise; she was no mean actress herself, Spence decided.

'Well, yes, Superintendent, as you say, it is for the play. It's a Tallmead Players' production. They're an extremely good company. Well, if the truth were known they're better than many professionals, really, and dear Lester you know actually *was* a professional earlier on in his career, and why he gave it up I'll never know, but that's the Tallmead Players' good fortune, I suppose. We're doing *Private Lives*, you know—an absolutely *super* play, it really is—Thursday, Friday, and Saturday. It seems a bit heartless to go on with it in some ways, but it is only Lester and me who're involved, from the village that is, and it is over in Tallmead, so it's not quite like being sacrilegious, is it? Or do I mean profane? Anyway, it doesn't seem entirely improper, in the circumstances. After all, we hardly knew the girl, any of us, even if she was killed on our property.'

'Yes, it seems reasonable enough that the show should go on. You're not acting in the play yourself, then?'

'No, not on this occasion. I have done, many a time, but not for quite a while. To tell you the truth, Superintendent, amateur acting is awfully bitchy you know, and anyone with even a little talent has to take an awful lot of criticism. So in the end I decided to play my part backstage. It's just as interesting and you get much less catty talk.'

'Yes, I see . . . So you're leaving the acting to Lester?'

Mrs Cordwright patted her short and beautifully-cut grey hair. 'Oh, yes. He's such a talented man. Acting, producing, writing, he can do it all.'

'Though I gather he hasn't had time to write much lately.'

'No, but he will again, I'm quite sure.'

'And what about David—has he any theatrical talents?'

'Well, he *had* as a boy, undoubtedly. He was in all the school plays at Tallmead. That was how we met Lester, as a matter of fact—he used to produce them. But in recent years he seems to have been too busy.'

Spence changed gear. 'Well now, Mrs Cordwright, as you can imagine, my main reason for calling round this afternoon is to ask you a few questions about this unfortunate business at the Blue Bazaar. But as you're one of the long-term residents here, so to speak, perhaps you could also give me a bit of background information about the village as a whole.'

Mrs Cordwright put on her helpful smile. 'I'll do my best.'

'You've lived here over twenty years, I believe.'

'Yes, that's right. It doesn't seem as long ago as that, but I suppose it must be. We came here when David was eleven.'

'Could I ask what attracted you to Tinley in the first place?'

'Well, it was the school, really. Tallmead, I mean. I was determined that David should get a good education, and by moving here I was just able to afford it.

He went to Tallmead as a day-boy. It was an awful struggle, needless to say.'

'What, a struggle to get him in, or a struggle to pay the fees?'

'Well, both, really. They swore by everything holy that they had no vacancies. But'—Mrs Cordwright's jaw momentarily closed in an expression of implacable determination—'I managed it in the end. And as for the fees—well, we did without any luxuries.'

'Was it worth all the sacrifice?'

'Oh, yes, worth every penny. It's a question of tradition, you know—and standards. Some of the most eminent men in the land were educated at Tallmead.'

Spence could think of at least one resident of HM Prison Wormwood Scrubs who had also been educated there, but he made no comment.

'Well, let's see now,' Spence continued, 'I suppose you'd have been here about five years when Patrick Meadows and his son were murdered?'

'Oh, my goodness, yes, how right you are. This latest business brings it all back. I don't believe the police ever solved that crime, did they? No . . . Do you know, I can remember to this day first hearing about that. David came home as white as a sheet—one Monday afternoon it was, in summer—he'd heard about it from someone in Mrs Amble's shop.'

'How old was David then?'

'Oh, sixteen or so. But he was a very sensitive boy—it really upset him, and of course he's upset again today, as you've seen for yourself.'

'Did you know Patrick Meadows?'

'Oh, yes. Slightly. Everyone in the village knew everyone else in those days. But we didn't have much in common, you know. He was a socialist—quite fierce about it. Surprisingly so for a teacher. We didn't really get on at all.'

'Did David know the boy?'

'What, young Peter Meadows?'

'Yes.'

'No, not really. They were in quite different age groups, you know. Peter was only about ten.'

'Yes, I see.'

'It was a very unhappy time for Tinley, now I come to think about it. Everyone in the village was terrified —really appalled to think that innocent citizens could be slaughtered in their beds like that. There were vigilante groups set up at first, you know—until Mr Booth got them quietened down. He inspired great confidence, did Mr Booth. And of course all the women were very suspicious of all the men—particularly those who wore hats or smoked a pipe. We weren't supposed to know that a man had been seen walking about on the night of the murder, but word got out, of course.'

Spence smiled. 'Yes, it would do . . . But I suppose there aren't many of that generation left now?'

'No, very few. Very few.'

'We passed the Colonel in the road on our way to see you. I couldn't help thinking that seventeen years ago he must have been a much more dominant figure in the village than he is today.'

Mrs Cordwright leaned forward to emphasize her reply. 'Oh, yes, infinitely, infinitely. Poor man, his fortunes have taken a real turn for the worse over the last few years. Yes, he's really had his problems, has the Colonel.'

'I gather his wife's not too well,' said Spence. 'Is it a physical thing?'

'Oh, no.' Mrs Cordwright pursed her lips. 'No, it's some form of mental illness, but don't ask me what, because they've refused all offers of help. Just withdrawn into themselves. Emily Host-Wall is never seen out nowadays. Hasn't been seen for years.'

Spence paused briefly and then continued. 'Tell me how you came to open a nightclub, Mrs Cordwright.'

Mrs Cordwright smiled; the opportunity pleased her. 'Oh, we'd had many a pipe-dream, David and I, about what we'd do when our ship came in. But then the day came when we did inherit a little money, and it was dear Lester who galvanized us into action. He told us bluntly that it was about time we put our money where our mouth was, and that he'd come in with us fifty-fifty if we did. We'd been talking about setting up some sort of a business for years.'

'And it's worked out pretty well?'

'Oh, yes. Yes, better than we could possibly have hoped. It was really all my idea, you know, though I suppose I say so as shouldn't. We live in a changing world, Superintendent, and I saw the possibilities for a nightclub in this area long before anyone else. I really had to work on David and Lester to convince them that that was the thing to go for, rather than a hotel or a health farm or something, but convince them I did, and I was right, too. And I love it, I really do. I love meeting so many different people, every night of the week. That's why I work on reception.'

'Yes,' said Spence, 'so I noticed. And I can see that David supplies all the necessary professional expertise, you can tell that from the way the place is run. But what about Mr Read—does he take an active part or is he a sleeping partner?'

'Oh, he's our financial genius,' said Mrs Cordwright.

'David looks after the day-to-day staff management and Lester keeps an eye on the long-term financial trends, pays the bills and so on. It's a very effective partnership, all things considered.'

'Yes,' said Spence. 'And I suppose it's made all the more effective by the fact that Mr Read and your son live together.'

Mrs Cordwright's smile became a little frosty. 'Well, they share a house, Superintendent, and have done since we opened the club. It's a very convenient arrangement, as you say, and I think it's best for a boy to get away from his mother. One of these days I suppose he'll find the right girl and get married, and we shall all have to rethink. But for the moment it all works very well.'

'They tell me,' said Spence thoughtfully, 'that the Vicar wasn't too keen on the idea of a nightclub in Tinley.'

Mrs Cordwright brushed aside all consideration of the Vicar with an imperious wave of her left hand; the wedding ring on her third finger glinted in the sunlight through the window.

'Oh, well, really,' she said, 'the Reverend Barndean is so totally out of touch with the world these days that it's really quite pitiful to talk to him. In fact I haven't talked to him for some time, the experience is so painful. He hasn't even been to London for six years, can you imagine? Still, I suppose it's not his fault, poor man. He's never really recovered from the death of his wife—oh, a long time ago now. And then there was all that awful trouble with his son . . .'

'Oh?'

'Yes. I mean normally I wouldn't talk about it, but

since you have asked for a background briefing as it were . . .'

'Yes,' said Spence, 'I think it would be useful to know.'

'Well, the fact is that the Vicar's son, who was also a day-boy at Tallmead, and about three years younger than David—I know all about it because it happened when David was a prefect—well, the fact is, not to put too fine a point on it, that the boy was very nearly thrown out for stealing. And of course poor Mr Barndean had to be told, and I gather he positively begged and pleaded for another chance for the boy, on the grounds that his mother's death had badly upset him. Which was absolute nonsense, of course, because he'd been a real little villain long before that, but never mind.'

'I see,' said Spence. 'And then, if I remember rightly, the boy left home altogether, didn't he?'

'Oh, so you've heard about that, have you? Well, yes, it's quite true, he did. He was eighteen at the time, so he was quite old enough to do exactly as he pleased, though most people's sons don't go rushing off into the blue without so much as a word of good-bye, thank goodness. Anyway, you're quite right, the boy did leave home, taking a good deal of his father's money with him, so I'm told, and I don't believe the poor man's heard a word from him since.'

'How long ago would that be, then?'

'Oh, goodness knows. A long time. Ten years, at least. Twelve, probably. Anyway, that was the beginning of the end for the Vicar, I'm afraid. He's never been the same man since. And once upon a time he had a really marvellous sense of humour. Could take a joke with the best of them.'

Spence glanced at his watch. Time was getting on and he was beginning to find Mrs Cordwright a little tedious. He decided to ask a few more questions about the events of the past week and then leave.

'Well now, Mrs Cordwright, I'd like to find out just exactly how much you saw of Thana yourself. I gather you didn't see her at all on the Sunday.'

'No, that's right.'

'What about Monday?'

'Well, I spoke to her early on in the evening, while she was rehearsing. And then I saw the 10 o'clock cabaret, which went very well—and then I went home.'

'All right. Now what about Tuesday?'

'Well, I understand she went to London during the day. We had a brief chat about some clothes she'd bought in the evening.'

'I see. And yesterday—Wednesday?'

'Well, yesterday was a bad day for me. I woke up feeling extremely unwell, but I recovered quite quickly, and in the end I went to London myself. There were a number of things I'd been meaning to do for some time, and I knew that David and Lester were going up for the afternoon, so I travelled up with them. And then in the evening there was the dress rehearsal of *Private Lives,* of course.'

'Yes, so there was . . . Now you say you'd never met Thana before she turned up for this week's engagement?'

Mrs Cordwright looked surprised. 'No, never. Why?'

'Oh, just a thought. So she wasn't a local girl, then?'

'Certainly not. My knowledge of Tinley girls is absolutely encyclopaedic, and I can assure you she wasn't from round here.'

'Fair enough. What sort of person would you say she was then?'

'Oh—well . . .' Mrs Cordwright fingered her necklace thoughtfully. 'Very much a show-business type of person, you know. Cheerful, friendly, quite happy to sit around chatting all day. She seemed . . . well, slightly unreal, somehow. Slightly out of touch with reality.'

'Do you think she was taking drugs?'

'Probably. Most of them do . . .' Mrs Cordwright paused, and then plunged on. 'As a matter of fact, Superintendent, far from feeling sorry for the wretched girl, I feel very angry with her.'

'Oh. Why?'

'Well, for getting herself killed the way she did. And for all the bad publicity it'll bring us. I know Lester says there's no such thing as bad publicity, but I don't altogether agree with him. As far as I can see, from what I've been told, the truth about Thana is that she was just a nasty little masochist whose boy-friend got carried away, that's all. And I very much wish he'd got carried away somewhere else.'

Soon afterwards Spence and Laurel took their leave of Mrs Cordwright, and on their way to Tallmead they conducted their usual post-mortem on the interview.

'Do you think she really believes all that guff about her son looking for Miss Right?' asked Laurel.

'Not for a minute,' said Spence. 'But I can tell you one thing—if Mrs Cordwright ever does decide that the time is ripe for young David to get married, he'll have a hard time avoiding it.'

Laurel laughed. 'What became of her husband then?'

'She was divorced. Though given half a chance I gather she gives the impression that she's a widow. Probably a dark secret there somewhere, but I doubt if it's relevant. Mrs Amble might know. Which reminds me—I must do a job card to get Mrs Amble interviewed. You never know what village gossip may have thrown up, and she's a natural clearing-house for it.'

Laurel slowed down to negotiate the level-crossing on the outskirts of Tallmead. 'By the way,' he asked, 'where do you want to go in Tallmead?'

'Oh, the Royal Hotel,' said Spence. 'I want to see the other half of this week's cabaret. He's a magician called Deceivo, and if he's half as astute as I think he is, he should be able to tell us quite a lot about Miss Thana.'

Spence introduced himself to the young red-headed receptionist at the Royal Hotel. 'I've called to see Mr Counter,' he said.

'Ah, yes, Mr Spence. Mr Counter said you would be calling.'

'And he has an assistant, I believe—I think she's staying here too.'

'Yes, that's right—Miss Harlowe, she has the room next door to his. He said you'd want to see her as well.'

'Yes,' said Spence. 'I do. And I think you've got another lady staying here as well, but I'm afraid I don't remember her name. I can describe her, though. She's a good ten years older than Miss Harlowe, has dark hair and wears glasses. And she dresses rather plainly. Can you think who she is?'

'Oh, yes,' said the receptionist at once. 'You must mean Miss Brown, in room 401—would you like me to tell her you're here?'

'No, not at the moment, thank you. I might have a word with her later on.'

Spence led a slightly bewildered Laurel up the stairs to rooms 201 and 202 where the great Deceivo—otherwise Mr Ray Counter—and his assistant were staying.

'Who's this Miss Brown then?' Laurel asked.

'I'm not sure—yet.'

'Well then, how did you know she was staying here?'

'I didn't, until I asked.'

Laurel reminded himself what happens to those who ask stupid questions and subsided into silence.

'It was what you might call a piece of deduction,' Spence told him as they reached the first-floor landing. 'I believe that's what detectives are supposed to do— deduce things. But you didn't see Deceivo's cabaret act, and I did. He had this rather beautiful young blonde assistant that he put into a box—and after being put into the box, she disappeared. And having seen that, I deduced that a rather plain girl with dark hair and glasses would be staying at the Royal Hotel this week.'

Laurel raised his eyebrows and said nothing. Spence paused outside the door of room 201 and then, following the reply to his knock, went inside.

Deceivo rose from the chair where he had been reading an Agatha Christie novel and gave Spence a surprisingly friendly greeting. He was a fit-looking man in his mid-thirties, of average height and build, with dark hair and brown eyes. His face wore a permanently amused expression, as if he considered life a long-running comedy. He was wearing expensive-looking brown and green checked trousers and a pale-gold shirt with an open neck. On his left wrist he wore the thinnest watch that Spence had ever seen. The pipe which he had been smoking until Spence and Laurel came into the room now lay in an ashtray beside his chair.

Spence gave Deceivo his usual introductory chat and the magician asked a number of polite questions about 'the unpleasantness' as he called it, including the number of nights the Blue Bazaar was expected to be shut.

'Only one,' said Spence. 'You won't be working there tonight but I think you'll find it'll be business as usual from then on.'

Deceivo nodded.

'Well now,' said Spence, 'before we go any further, perhaps you'd be kind enough to ask the rest of your act to join us.'

'Of course,' said Deceivo.

He left the room and returned a few moments later with 'the lovely Sue', whom Spence clearly remembered from the previous Tuesday night. Sue was young, blonde, and very attractive, smartly dressed in dark-green slacks and a white sweater which clung tightly to her slim figure.

When the four of them were settled back in their chairs Spence resumed his questioning.

'Mr Counter, I hope you won't think I've been playing games with you—though of course you're an expert at playing games with people yourself—but I phrased my last question to you quite deliberately.'

Deceivo raised a querying eyebrow.

'I asked you if you would be kind enough to bring the rest of your act in here to join us, and you returned with Miss Harlowe.'

'Yes?'

'Well now, last Tuesday night I saw your act for myself. Miss Harlowe here stepped into a sort of upright coffin, and you waved your magic wand, and she disappeared—and then a minute or two later she returned from the restaurant some distance away, without anyone in the audience seeing how she got there.'

'Yes, that's quite correct.'

'Now there's only one way that a trick like that

could have been done,' said Spence. 'So perhaps you'd ask Miss Brown to join us as well.'

Deceivo turned to his assistant. 'This man,' he said, 'is not as dumb as he looks.' Then he roared with laughter. When he had finished laughing he said, 'Go on, Sue. Go and fetch her.'

Two minutes later Miss Brown stood beside Miss Harlowe in Deceivo's room. The two women appeared to be much the same height and weight, but while Miss Harlowe was blonde, Miss Brown was a brunette. Miss Harlowe was beautiful, Miss Brown was plain, and wore badly-chosen glasses. Miss Harlowe was attractively dressed, but Miss Brown was dowdy; she wore an ugly, chocolate-coloured two-piece suit which made her look forty.

Spence stood in front of the two girls and addressed Laurel, who was just beginning to get an inkling of what was going on.

'You know, Mr Laurel,' said Spence, 'if I were an intellectual—which, thank God, I'm not—I'd say that what we have here is a sort of metaphor of what our role as detectives is all about. On Tuesday night I saw something happen, and I tried to work out *how* it happened. And this is how it was done. Excuse me . . .'

He approached Miss Brown and removed her glasses. Then he reached up to her hairline and carefully peeled back her wig. When it was removed the girl laughed and shook out her neatly-cropped blonde hair.

'You see?' said Spence.

'Of course,' said Laurel, with barely concealed irritation. Any fool could see now that the two girls were twin sisters.

'And what I've done there,' said Spence, 'is, I suppose, what I'm trying to do in a murder case. I'm try-

ing to find out the truth about what happened. And
what really happened is by no means always what
appears to have happened.'

Having assured Deceivo and his professional associates
that their trade secrets were safe with the police,
Spence returned reluctantly to the serious business in
hand.

'What time did you arrive at the hotel?' he asked.

'Well, Sue and I came on Sunday,' said Deceivo.
'Sandie came on Monday. The girls take it in turns
to be the odd one out each week, and we live entirely
separate existences, in public at any rate.'

'But you stay at the same hotels?'

'Yes.'

'All right. And when did you first go to the Blue
Bazaar?'

'On Monday afternoon.'

'So that would be the first time you saw Thana?'

'Yes.'

'Had you worked with her before?'

'No.'

'And did you have any long conversations with her?'

'Not really, no,' said Deceivo, filling his pipe. 'We
saw her every night before and after each show, but
in the nature of things we don't spend a lot of time
in the clubs where we work. It's best not to.'

'What was your impression of Thana?'

Deceivo paused to think before answering. 'Well, let
me put it this way, Superintendent . . . There are
some people for whom show-business is a way of life—
they have stars in their eyes till the day they die. And
then there are others for whom it is a way of earning
a living. Now, as far as the girls and I are concerned,

show-business is the latter. We earn a good living from our act, but as a way of life it has many disadvantages. In particular we are always on the move, always living out of suitcases, always sleeping in strange beds. For us it is not something we will do for ever and ever. But there are other people for whom the cabaret circuit is a highway through paradise—and Thana was one of those. It was meat and drink to her, Superintendent—she loved every minute of it. She was a genuine exhibitionist—she derived great satisfaction from being the centre of attention, from having her body admired. When she came off that stage after stripping, her whole being was lit up with pleasure.'

Spence nodded. 'I've also heard it said that in her ordinary day-to-day life she was euphoric.'

Deceivo nodded. 'Yes, that's a good assessment.'

'And what caused that euphoria, do you think? Drugs?'

Deceivo shook his head. 'I saw no evidence of it. No, I would say it was just the euphoria of life itself. To put it crudely, Superintendent, she got a big kick out of waving her tits in everyone's face.'

'Yes,' said Spence with a grin. 'I see . . . Tell me, do you think she was a masochist?'

'No. In fact I doubt if you'll find that Thana was interested in sex at all. Not as a source of physical satisfaction. As a source of power, yes—as a means of establishing control over other people, certainly. But not interested in sex in the way that a normal person is. As you said a few moments ago, Superintendent, so much in life, and especially in show-business, is illusion.'

'Did Thana say anything to you about the owners of the club?'

'Not really. She made one or two disparaging remarks about queers, that's all. But relatively good-humoured.'

'Do you think she would have made such remarks to Read or Cordwright direct? Teased them, or abused them?'

'Possibly, but if so it wasn't in my hearing.'

'Did you get the impression that she was afraid of anyone?'

'No—far from it. I got the impression that Thana had very few worries at all. For the time being, at any rate.'

'What about you girls,' said Spence turning towards Sue and Sandie. 'You haven't said very much at all. Did Thana mention that she was expecting a boy-friend on Wednesday night, or anything like that? Or mention that she was frightened of anyone?'

'No, not at all,' said Sue. 'Quite the opposite, as Ray says. There was just one thing she said to me on the Monday night after she came off, which was a bit unusual. She seemed very pleased with herself, and I said something about it being a good crowd. And she said no, it wasn't that—she was happy because she'd just found herself a new meal-ticket.'

'Ah,' said Spence. 'Did she now.'

After a few more questions Spence decided to bring the interview to an end. Deceivo rose to his feet to let his visitors out, his face once again wearing that expression of quiet amusement.

'Tell me, Superintendent,' he said, 'has there been a post-mortem on Thana's body?'

'Not yet,' said Spence. 'I'm going there next . . . Why do you ask?'

'Oh, no reason really. I was just thinking, though,

about what you said . . . about how your job involves peeling off the layers of illusion until you get to the reality. I think you'll find that where Thana is concerned you've still got a layer or two to go.'

23

They had travelled some distance on the road from Tallmead to Wellbridge before Laurel suddenly broke the long silence and asked a question.

'That Deceivo chap,' he said.

'What about him?'

'What do you think he meant when he said he thought we'd still got a few more layers of Thana to peel off before we got to the reality?'

'Damned if I know,' said Spence pensively. 'But the bastard's got me worried, too.'

Twenty minutes later, at 4.15, Spence and Laurel were uncomfortably seated on stools in the mortuary of Wellbridge General Hospital. The naked body of the dead striptease dancer who called herself Thana was stretched out on a table some ten feet in front of them, the breasts lolling apart, the head supported on a wooden block. Also present in the mortuary were Dr Oscar Dunbar, the Mortuary Superintendent, the Coroner's Officer, Dr Dunbar's assistant (female) and a police photographer who would record the proceedings on videotape.

Laurel was not at his best in such circumstances. The post-mortem on Thana was not the first such examination he had witnessed by any means, but he had yet to become hardened to the procedure: it still made him feel slightly ill. Spence, on the other hand, seemed immune to any form of squeamishness, and as for Dr Dunbar, the pathologist who was doing the actual work, he seemed to be positively enjoying himself.

'Come in, come in, gentlemen,' he had called cheerfully as the two detectives had entered. 'This promises to be one of our more interesting cases. It's not every day we get to see the inside of an international cabaret star, no sirree. Especially one as beautiful as this.'

It was Laurel's private opinion that Dr Dunbar's comments were in extremely poor taste, but he kept his thoughts to himself. And on further reflection he decided that perhaps Dunbar's oppressive good humour was a reaction to the revolting nature of his work; from time to time he had noticed the same heartiness among medical students.

Dunbar was wearing a red rubber apron over a green smock, with a tight-fitting green cap on his bald head. He began to work quickly and efficiently, dictating notes to his assistant as he proceeded, and occasionally pointing out to Spence the significance of certain wounds and marks on the body.

'She was certainly taking some sort of drugs, you know,' he announced as he made the first incision.

'Oh?' said Spence.

'Oh, yes. After you'd gone downstairs this morning we found a couple of bottles of pills in that dressing-table. I couldn't identify them straight off, no labels on them at all, but Forensic are getting them analysed. They should be able to tell you what they are fairly soon.'

Spence asked the Coroner's Officer if he knew whether fingerprints had been taken from the body and was assured that they had.

'Good,' he said. 'Her agent tells me that Thana told him her real name was Melody McFee, but I can't believe that's genuine for a minute. The name her parents gave her will probably emerge when we go through the papers at her flat, but at a pinch, if we can't find anything written, we might be reduced to checking her prints against Records.'

After a few minutes Dr Dunbar stood back a pace, his hands on his hips. He scratched his head and looked puzzled.

'What's the matter?' said Spence.

'Well, I dunno, really. It's just that—well . . .'

Dunbar's voice trailed off into silence and he resumed work, only to pause again a few minutes later and point something out to his assistant, who peered closely at what Dunbar was indicating.

'You see that? What do you make of it?'

'Hmm,' said the assistant. 'How very peculiar.'

'That's what I think, too.'

Dunbar spent the next few minutes disentangling intestines, a performance which Laurel preferred not to watch. Then he bent closely over the abdomen, frowning with concentration, and eventually gave an exclamation of triumph.

'Ha!' he said loudly. 'Well I'm damned.'

Spence moved restlessly on his stool; Dunbar's amateur dramatics sometimes annoyed him.

'Well, Ben,' said Dunbar with a gleeful expression, 'do you want to hear something really interesting?'

Spence was not amused. 'Go on, then,' he said irritably. 'Surprise me. I suppose you're going to say she was a virgin.'

'No,' said Dunbar, 'I'm not. I'm going to tell you that she wasn't a she at all . . . She was a man.'

Spence rose to his feet. The expression on his face was such that the Coroner's Officer hastily moved out of his way. Spence approached the autopsy table and looked the pathologist straight in the eye across the empty shell of a body which had once been Thana. Or Melody McFee. Or someone.

'Oscar,' said Spence dangerously. 'What the bloody hell are you talking about?'

'Why don't you listen to what I say?' asked Dunbar in pained tones. Spence wasn't the first angry policeman he had dealt with, and he remained totally unruffled. 'I mean just exactly what I said a few moments ago. This is not the body of a woman—it's the body of a man.'

Spence gritted his teeth. 'Then why, Dr Dunbar, has it got a handsome pair of tits, and no, repeat no, cock and balls?'

Everyone present listened with close attention.

'Because, my dear chap, this fellow, whoever he was, has undergone a so-called sex-change operation.'

Spence turned away from the body and went and sat down again. Laurel had never before seen his chief at a loss for words. If it came to that, Laurel couldn't think of anything to say himself, either.

'Oh, yes,' Dunbar continued cheerfully. 'It's quite common nowadays, you know. Well, relatively common. You can even get it done on the National Health if you can convince my psychiatric colleagues that it's necessary to preserve your sanity . . . It doesn't really change a man's sex, of course, it just gives him the outward and visible appearance of being a woman. I expect we'll find that those tablets in the dressing-table are hormones—reduce the beard growth, encourage the mammary development, and all that sort of thing . . . Oh, yes, this is a bloke all right, no doubt about it. Beautiful piece of work, too. Smashing piece of surgery. I mean from the outside you'd never guess, would you? It's only when you get inside and begin to poke around that you realize what's what.'

Spence turned to Laurel beside him. 'Well,' he said grimly, 'now we know what Deceivo was talking about. The cunning bastard—he guessed all the time, but he let me show off by taking the wig off his twins and making a little speech, and then he gave me a hint, just so I'd know later on that I'd made a fool of myself.' He gave a snort of exasperation. 'Ah well, I suppose I shall know better next time.'

He got up and approached the body again; he seemed to have recovered his equilibrium quite rapidly.

'All right, Oscar,' he said evenly. 'I'm not seriously questioning your judgement, but you are quite certain about all this?'

'Oh, yes,' said the pathologist with a grin. 'It's really quite a simple operation, you know. Just a snip here and a snip there, and Bob's your auntie.'

'Yes,' said Spence, 'so I recall hearing. And if I may summarize for a moment, what we have here is essentially the body of a man, with genitals removed, and with hormone treatment to reduce the masculine characteristics and produce the breasts?'

'Exactly,' Dunbar agreed. 'Plus long hair dyed blonde, plus make-up, plus nail varnish, and so on. Nothing to it, really. The feet and the elbows look a bit unfeminine though, once you start to look carefully.'

'Hmm,' said Spence. 'Well, you'd better finish off now and we'll talk about it in detail later.'

Dunbar nodded and followed Spence's suggestion. There was no further discussion until the post-mortem was complete; then, unusually for Dunbar, he offered Spence a complete summary of his findings on the cause of death.

'Right,' he said. 'This is the order of events as I see it. We'll talk about Thana as if she really was a her, for the sake of simplicity, otherwise, it gets a bit confusing. OK?'

'I suppose so.'

'Right. Well first of all she was knocked unconscious. Then she was tied up and gagged, probably while still unconscious, but in any case while still alive. Thirdly, burns were inflicted while she was still alive. And fourth, there was vomiting—doubtless caused by the combination of a head injury and the pain of the burns. Now, it was the vomiting which was the cause of death, interestingly enough. She choked on it and inhaled it into the lungs—hardly surprisingly, seeing she had a gag on. Finally, the frenzied stab wounds, which we not unreasonably thought this morning were the main cause of death, were in fact inflicted after the heart had stopped beating.' He paused. 'Does that help?'

'Yes,' said Spence thoughtfully, 'I think it helps a great deal. You see, our thinking so far is that this—well, this person—was tortured in order to make her say where she had hidden some blackmail evidence. Or at any rate to get her to admit that she was the person blackmailing the killer, something like that. So, the fact that she choked and died and was *then* stabbed is highly significant, I feel. I've been assuming up to the present that her killer found out what he wanted to know and *then* killed her. But the way you tell it, it looks as if she may have died before revealing anything, and that the killer stabbed her repeatedly in frustration. So that's encouraging—it means that if Thana did have some documentary evidence which she was holding over the killer's head, we may come across it somewhere in her possessions. She may have died before she revealed where it was.'

Spence turned to Laurel.

'Incidentally, make sure a check is run on Thana's fingerprints, will you, please. What Dr Dunbar has told us makes it essential. We've got to know who Thana really is, and as quickly as possible.'

24

Nothing he had heard at the autopsy had caused Spence to change his plan, which was to go next to Thana's flat in Roehampton. However, as it was now approaching 6 o'clock he decided to call in at his home for a bite to eat before setting out; he invited Laurel to join him. He also wanted to collect an overnight case as he had arranged to spend the night at his cousin's farm near Tinley.

Spence and his wife lived in a three-bedroomed detached house in a quiet avenue on the north side of Wellbridge. As they had no children, the house was more than large enough for the two of them; the garden, in fact, was too big. Julia Spence's work as a full-time lecturer, plus her outside interests and her husband's more than full-time job, ensured that the house was empty more often than not. Perhaps as a consequence, it had been burgled twice.

This particular evening Julia Spence was at home. She settled her husband and his companion at the kitchen table with drinks while she made them a quick snack. Laurel found himself thinking how nice it would be to find someone young and attractive to replace his own wife, who had been dead long enough now for him to be able to think of remarrying quite seriously. The thought prompted him to go and ring up his two teenaged children to warn them that he would be home late, they were fairly self-sufficient now, but he liked to let them know where he was.

While Julia was cooking, Spence gave his wife a rapid summary of the day's events, partly to clarify the major points in his own mind but also because he genuinely wanted to hear her comments. Julia's academic interest in psychology, together with some voluntary marriage-guidance work, gave her a useful combination of theory and practical experience. Spence himself was widely read in psychology and criminology, but he often found his wife's insights extremely valuable; most of his cases were discussed with her at some stage.

Julia listened attentively, with an occasional question, as Spence related the outline of the investigation to date. Then, as the two men ploughed their way through large plates of eggs, bacon, sausages, and assorted trimmings, Julia began to tread her way carefully through the facts.

'So,' she said, 'you have on your hands a murder case which at first sight looked to be the work of a sadistic psychopath . . .'

'Correct.'

'But which in fact you believe was committed by the person who also killed Patrick Meadows and his young son seventeen years ago . . . And the motive for this present killing is, you believe, to put an end to blackmail over the first murder, almost before the blackmail got started.'

'Again correct.'

'All right. So we'll set aside for the moment the idea of a pure sex murder. Now, you say that the victim, far from being the beautiful girl we imagined her to be, was in fact a plastic fantastic.'

'A what?' said Spence in surprise.

'A plastic fantastic—a man who has undergone a sex-change operation.'

'Well, if that's the right word for it, yes.'

'It may not be scientific,' said Julia, 'but it's graphic.'

Spence shrugged. 'OK. Carry on.'

'Now, one interesting question is this—did the killer, and/or anyone else, know that Thana was a man?'

'Well,' said Spence slowly, 'I think Deceivo guessed, yes, but he's an exceptionally astute feller.'

'And, of course, he works in show-business/cabaret circles where a lot of these creatures end up,' said Julia.

'Do they?'

'Oh, yes. They're narcissists, you see. They long to become beautiful women instead of men, and having become women, sort of, they long to be applauded and admired . . . I gather that several of the really top-class international striptease stars are in fact boys.'

'Well, well, well. Amazing what these lecturers can tell you,' said Spence to Laurel.

Julia ignored him and continued. 'Well, anyway, whether the murderer knew that Thana was a man or not is a question I'll leave with you to resolve. I'm not sure that it's relevant, anyway—blackmail is blackmail, whatever the sex of the person applying it. So let's make a further assumption, possibly unjustified, and assume for the moment that the man who did the killing seventeen years ago was the man seen then in the early hours of the morning, and was also the man seen by the chef walking away from the Blue Bazaar earlier today. And following on from that, are you sure that this person, whom Thana was blackmailing, is a village resident?'

'Well,' said Spence, 'that's what Thana said—or rather implied. That's if it was Thana who phoned Booth on Monday night, and I'm pretty convinced that it was.'

'All right,' said Julia. 'And I further gather that there are only a handful of people living in Tinley now who were there at the time of the original murders.'

'Absolutely spot on.'

'Well then, forgive me, Ben, but isn't your task a fairly simple one? I mean, what you're looking for is a person who is totally selfish and completely ruthless. He committed two murders seventeen years ago, for reasons unknown, and he's now committed another one last night. So he's able to maintain an outwardly normal appearance, able to live with the most hideous memories and the knowledge of appalling crimes, and yet not let all that affect him. He can apparently disguise his feelings to that extent. But what he can't disguise, I'm quite convinced, is his fundamental self-ishness—his lack of concern for the feelings of others. And so all you have to do is consider your suspects—people who were living in Tinley seventeen years ago and are still there now—and ask yourself which of these people has the necessary drive, the necessary nerve, the unflinching determination, to have his own way at all costs?'

Spence gestured to Laurel in mock despair. 'I can't think why we hadn't solved this by 12 o'clock this morning.'

'And I'll give you another thought to take with you on the way to Roehampton,' said Julia. 'You said that no one was ever able to identify the motive for the murder of Patrick Meadows.'

'That's so, yes.'

'But did anybody ever consider that perhaps it wasn't a case of a murderer wanting to kill Meadows, and then killing the boy because he was in the house at the same time. Did anyone ever consider the possibility that the murderer's main purpose might have been to kill the boy? And that it was Meadows who was killed only because he was sleeping under the same roof?'

Spence scratched his nose. 'No,' he said. 'I don't think anyone did.'

25

Before driving to Roehampton, Spence and Laurel called in at the mobile police office parked beside the Blue Bazaar. There Spence collected the keys to Thana's flat from Detective Sergeant Wilberforce; they had been found among her possessions in her room. He also arranged with Wilberforce for a particularly careful check to be made on Thana's other belongings at the club. He was convinced that she must have stumbled across some incriminating evidence connected with the Meadows murders, perhaps something which would not immediately be recognized for what it was; and despite the fact that the room had been ransacked by the murderer, he was hopeful that the evidence might yet turn up.

After leaving Tinley it took Laurel a further hour to drive them to Roehampton. Once there they announced their presence in the district at the local police station; then they made their way to Warmingly Mansions, a tall and expensive-looking block of flats in a quiet backwater.

Spence was impressed by the quality of the carpet in the entrance-hall to the flats, and by the general decor. 'Well,' he said, 'whatever else Thana was short of, she evidently wasn't short of money.'

They went up to the second floor in an immaculately clean lift, and Spence used Thana's key to open the front door of Flat 21. Inside the flat they found a long hall leading to a large, square living-room. Off the hall to the left were a bathroom and a kitchen, while to the right were a study and a bedroom.

The carpets, curtains, and furniture had all apparently been chosen with a total disregard for expense; everything was of the highest quality, if not always in the best of taste. The bedroom, for example, featured a blood-red carpet and two white walls; a third wall was formed by a built-in cupboard, also white, and the fourth wall was solid mirror. The curtains, bedspread, and drapes over the four-poster bed, were all pink.

'Not quite what I would have chosen myself,' said Spence drily, 'but entirely in character, don't you think?'

'I find it oppressive,' said Laurel with a slightly nauseated look on his face. 'Too rich and too opulent for me—let's search the place quick and get out.'

Together the two detectives went through the flat with all the professional skill they could muster. Short of tearing up the carpets and taking the side off the bath, they looked everywhere: behind the original oil paintings in the hall, underneath the Meissen porcelain in the living-room, and in the pockets of the white mink coat in the bedroom. They left the study till last, on the grounds that it was the room most likely to provide interesting results; and in that they were quite correct.

The pictures on the walls of the study were illuminating in themselves. A heavy antique desk stood opposite the door, in front of the window, and on the wall to the right were a dozen framed photographs of slightly *passée* film stars such as Arlene Dahl. On the left-hand wall were an interesting print of the village of Tinley in the mid-eighteenth century, and a Speed map of Southshire, which Spence declared was genuine. The wall opposite the window was virtually covered with framed still photographs from great movies of the 'thirties and 'forties.

It was in a bookcase to the right of the desk that the first important discoveries were made. One shelf was filled with a comprehensive collection of contact magazines published during the previous five or six years. In each of them several advertisements had been circled in red, and it rapidly became clear that Thana had placed some of the advertisements herself; others she had simply replied to. In either case a code number had been written against the advertisement; the number was cross-referenced with a folder in a filing cabinet standing to the left of the desk. Ten minutes' perusal of the files made the pattern absolutely clear.

'Sticks out a mile, doesn't it?' said Spence. 'I suppose we've got to believe Dunbar when he says that Thana was once a man, but he's clearly been living as a woman for a good many years. And it's also quite clear what he—no, damn it, let's go on thinking of her as Thana—it's also quite clear what she was up to.'

'Putting tempting adverts in sexy magazines,' said Laurel. 'Plus a reply to any ads put in by other people which look promising—'

'And then—blackmail on as big a scale as she could manage.'

'Right. So now we know how she could pay for this treasure-house of a flat.'

'Yes . . .' Spence shook his head in reluctant admiration. 'She was a clever bitch, there's no doubt about it. Judging by the few files I've looked at so far, it seems she never let anyone know her real address of her real name. And when I say real name, I mean the Melody McFee name, which wasn't real at all. And as for an address, she seems to have got her mail sent care of an address in Putney, which is probably a little shop offering accommodation addresses as a sideline. In every case where contact was made, she either met the victim at his place, or at a hotel, and as soon as the poor bastard had committed himself to something indiscreet in writing, or sent her a photograph of himself in the nude or whatever, she put the pressure on.'

'Yes. And payment was also made to the accommodation address,' said Laurel, looking up from the files in his own lap. 'This place in Putney seems to crop up fairly frequently—27 Norcrest Street.'

'Yes, same in mine.' Spence paused and looked up at the ceiling. 'Right then, let's just take stock of the situation. We could spend all night going through these files, but I don't think it's worth it. I think someone else should do it, apart from looking for one thing which I'll come to in a minute. But so far we haven't really found anything new. All we've done is confirmed that Thana was a blackmailer, which we were 90 per cent sure of already, though we didn't realize it was on this scale.'

'And that lends strong support to the idea that it was Thana who phoned Mr Booth—'

'Yes, it makes it a certainty in my view.'

'Which in turn confirms your theory that Thana was killed by the person she had just started to blackmail—'

'Namely, the person who was responsible for the two murders seventeen years ago . . . Yes. I think we can also safely assume that it was only when Thana actually got to Tinley—presumably after an absence of some years—that she realized who the murderer was, otherwise she would have contacted Booth with her query before. After all, she could afford a long-distance phone call easily enough . . . Now—we haven't found anything here to tell us who Thana really was, but I don't think that matters a great deal. I don't think her murderer knew who she really was, either—he just knew that she was a danger to him.'

'Her real name might be somewhere in these files or in the desk,' said Laurel. 'Is it worth a quick shuffle through the whole lot?'

Spence thought about it. 'Well, yes, I think it is. But not in the hope of finding Thana's identity—I think her prints will give us that because I'm fairly sure she'll have a record. But what I would like to know is whether this filing cabinet contains any information about any long-term residents of Tinley.'

Laurel scratched his ear. 'I thought you felt that she'd only just realized who the murderer was?'

'So I do. But I have in mind one particular resident of Tinley whom she was seen talking to, and who gave every appearance of having a guilty conscience about three miles long.'

'Oh, yes, you mean the Colonel.'

'I do indeed. Colonel Brian Host-Wall himself . . . Let's just flick through these folders and see if we can spot his name.'

It took a further seven minutes to find the file on the Colonel. Laurel, who picked it out, passed it to Spence, who sat back in the only easy chair in the room and studied its contents. After a while he looked up.

'Right then, this is the way it shapes up. Three

years ago the Colonel placed an advert in a magazine called Whiplash. "Middle-aged gentleman seeks severe chastisement by beautiful governess. Will travel. All replies acknowledged. Box number 447." And, naturally, Thana replied. "Dear Sir, etcetera, etcetera. Please write at length with full details of your more intimate wishes." Care of the usual accommodation address in Putney. And, sure enough, the bloody fool did. Several more letters were exchanged . . . Then they seem to have—yes, they met at a hotel in Knightsbridge, at which she appears to have given him what he wanted. After that he wrote again. Positively infatuated . . . cheap at the price, etcetera, etcetera. And after that she had him just where she wanted him. Here, take a look at this.'

Spence handed over a carbon copy of a neatly typed letter to the Colonel: it demanded, politely but very firmly, that the Colonel should send £50 every month, cash, to the Putney accommodation address—otherwise, Miss Jennifer Smart, as she called herself in this instance, would feel obliged to send copies of his *very* indiscreet letters to his wife, the local Vicar, the local post-mistress, the local newspaper, and so on.

'I bet it was that mention of the local post-mistress which really turned the scales,' said Spence with a grim smile. 'Can you imagine the result if Mrs Amble got a letter like that? My God, it doesn't bear thinking about. No wonder the Colonel paid up. The notes here indicate that he's been paying £50 a month for the past three years . . .'

'Kept careful records, didn't she?'

'Yes, she did indeed . . . Anyway, we've found what I suspected, namely that the Colonel had something to hide. I'm also inclined to think that it was the fact that the Colonel lived in Tinley which prompted Thana to ask her agent to get her a booking at the nightclub there. And having got there, something else, and God only knows what, revealed to her the identity of yet another victim—or rather a potential victim—someone she could *really* put the screws on.'

'You mean the evidence on the Meadows murders?'

'Yes.'

'What on earth could that something have been?' said Laurel.

'I don't know,' said Spence, 'and I'm beginning to feel that it's not as important as I once thought it was.'

'But that would be the key to everything,' Laurel insisted. 'After all, if we can find the evidence which Thana was going to use to blackmail the murderer with, then we'll know who the murderer is.'

'Well, that's true enough,' said Spence. 'And if you can find anything in this study, or in a safe-deposit box or whatever, which leads us to the killer, then I shall be delighted, of course. But I seriously doubt if it's here—and in any case we can reach the same conclusion by a more promising route. Look—Thana phoned Charlie Booth in the early hours of Tuesday morning, right?'

'Right.'

'OK. And what did she do on Tuesday afternoon?'

'Um—went to London, didn't she?'

'So Mrs Cordwright says, yes. And, if we assume that Thana stuck to her usual m.o., what did she do in London?'

'Well . . . presumably, if she followed the usual pattern, she sent a letter to the murderer, demanding payment, or else.'

'That's right. Now, I've no reason to suppose that

she came to this flat on Tuesday, but if she had any tangible evidence, such as a letter or something, then quite possibly she stuck it in a safe-deposit box or posted it to herself or something like that. But in any case, the main point is this—in her letter, if she stuck to the usual pattern, she would have asked for payment to be sent to the usual accommodation address in Putney, not so very far from here. And no doubt she called herself Miss Jennifer Smart, again as usual. So, what happened on Wednesday?'

'Well, on Wednesday morning, someone in the village got a horrible shock. He woke up and found that what he had thought was a secret for seventeen years, was suddenly not a secret any longer. It must have been the worst moment of his life.'

'No doubt,' said Spence. 'But our murderer is not a man who knuckles under without a fight. He's as hard as they come. Remember what my wife said? Completely self-centred and totally ruthless. So, what do you suppose he did?'

Laurel thought for a moment. 'Well, I imagine he came to Putney and tried to find out who Miss Smart really was, and where she lived.'

'Precisely. So why don't we go round to this accommodation address, and ask whoever runs the business whether anyone called on him yesterday afternoon? And if so, get him to describe that person to us.'

Laurel raised his eyebrows. 'Do you think it's going to be as easy as that?'

Spence grinned. 'Why not? It sometimes is.'

26

Spence used the phone in Thana's flat to ring the local police station and obtain directions to the address in Putney to which so many of Thana's victims had sent so much money. It turned out to be a narrow, ill-lit street lined with two-storey mid-Victorian terraced houses. Number 27 was a small newsagent's shop, much as Spence had expected.

It was dark now, and Laurel parked his Ford Escort under a street-lamp; then the two men walked back a few yards to the shop door. Two panes of glass in the door were cracked, and it was many years since the woodwork had seen a coat of new paint. Ancient metal adverts for Oxo and Brooke Bond tea were quietly rusting in the panels below the shop window.

There were no signs of life in the building, but there was a bell-push to the left of the door, and Spence kept his finger on it until a light came on somewhere within. The sound of someone clumping about and cursing was heard. After further thumps and bangs from the interior, a portly, slow-moving shape appeared silhouetted against a light at the back of the shop; the shape lurched towards the door and eventually wrenched it open.

Spence took his finger off the bell and with his left hand pushed the outraged and protesting newsagent firmly backwards. Then he stepped inside; Laurel followed him.

The opening of the door had let out a smell of bad drains and boiled cabbage, and at the best of times Spence was often out of sympathy with unkempt shop-keepers and their nasty, unsanitary premises. 'Put some lights on,' he said curtly. 'And then we'll talk.'

The newsagent was evidently well able to recognize plainclothes policemen when he saw them, and after a few token splutters he did as he was told. He led his visitors into a cluttered kitchen with bare brick walls; empty gin bottles littered the floor. There were two rickety chairs with round, perforated-plywood seats, and Spence and Laurel both sat down; the news-agent remained standing, moving nervously from foot to foot, his hands in his trouser pockets.

Spence let him stew for a moment or two and took a careful look at him in the meantime. He was in his mid-fifties, of medium height, and going bald; he had a large belly and he needed a shave. He peered near-sightedly at Spence and Laurel through thick-lensed glasses; he wore a shirt without a collar and trousers with braces; everything about him was scruffy and his teeth were appalling. Spence's instant dislike of the man intensified.

'A. I. Palmer, it says over the window outside,' Spence began. 'Is that you?'

"Um—er—yer.' Mr Palmer cast shifty glances from side to side. 'There's nothing here, you know,' he said anxiously. 'I got done five years ago and I had nothing stronger than *Penthouse* even then. But there's noth-ing like that here now.'

'Bloody liar,' said Spence. 'But in any case that's not why we're here . . . You've got a card in the window. "Accommodation address services" it says—

only you can't spell accommodation. "Inquire within" it says—and I am inquiring.'

'Oh—um—yes. That.'

'Yes,' said Spence. 'That. And kindly don't waste my time.'

Mr Palmer swallowed hard and jangled some coins in his trouser pocket. 'Well . . . What do you want to know?'

'I want to know who uses your services, and how.'

Palmer's eyes flickered desperately all round the room, finding no comfort anywhere. 'Well—it's—um—quite a few people use it now and then. Travelling salesmen, you know, that sort of thing.'

'Don't lie to me,' said Spence disgustedly. 'It's used by people who want to buy dirty books and write love-letters without their wives knowing, and we both know it. How much do you charge?'

'Um—25p a go.'

'And how does it work—do people collect from you or do you send the letters on?'

'Well, a bit of both. Most collect. Some I send on . . . I've never 'ad no complaints, mind. I don't know what's been said, but it's all lies, and I never knew what was in 'em, neither.'

Spence sighed. 'Just listen to the questions,' he said. 'And answer them. Tell me about Miss Jennifer Smart.'

Mr Palmer couldn't help it, despite the circumstances; he leered. 'Oh! Her.'

'Yes, her. How long has Miss Smart been using your services?'

'Oh, a long time. Good few years now.'

'And did she collect or did you send on?'

'Oh, collect, always. I never knew where she lived, no, never.'

'How often did she come here?'

'Oh, once every week or two.'

'And how did she get here?'

'Get here?'

'Yes.'

Palmer's eyes became fearful. 'How would I know?'

Spence stood up, all six feet and thirteen stone of him. Palmer looked startled and stepped back.

'You would know, you nasty little man, because you make it your business to know things like that. An old peeper like you would spot a bird like J. Smart 400 yards away, even without your glasses. You know all right and you're going to tell me.'

Palmer hastily decided that co-operation was the best policy. 'Yes, well, come to think of it she did come by taxi once or twice. But mostly on foot.'

Spence approached the newsagent and looked down at him hard.

'On foot?'

'Yes.' Palmer's voice squeaked.

'She never came by car?'

'Car?'

'Yes. By car.'

'No . . . Well . . . I mean. Possibly. Once or twice.'

Spence let the silence drag out. In the end Palmer had to ask. 'Why do you want to know?'

'I'll tell you why, Mr Palmer. I'll tell you exactly why. Miss Smart came to see you a few years ago, about using your accommodation address service, and you came to an arrangement together. You agreed to receive letters addressed to her here, and when she came to collect them from you, she paid you for them. Correct so far?'

Palmer nodded miserably. He took out his handkerchief and mopped his forehead.

'She didn't tell you her real address, and she didn't want you to post things on to her, and that interested you. What was even more interesting was the fact that she began to receive packages. Some packages addressed to J. Smart and some addressed to Miss J. Smart, or Miss Jennifer Smart. Interesting little packages, about the size of a paperback book. And after a while you steamed one open.'

'No, no, I never!'

'Well, whether you did or whether you didn't, you got the idea that someone, somewhere, was sending her money. Possibly a lot of people, if there were lots of different postmarks on the packages.'

'Oh, yes, there were, there were. Lots of different places they came from.'

'I see. Now, if you'd had any guts, of course, you'd have opened a package or two, but perhaps that's asking a bit too much of a man like you. Instead I suppose you just suggested, ever so politely, that perhaps your charge ought to go up to 50p a time. Or maybe even a pound.'

Palmer was sweating copiously. 'No, no, nothing like that. As a matter of fact—'

'Yes?'

'Well, she, Miss Smart, that is—she accused me of the same thing as you have—accused me of steaming one open, that is. Got quite nasty, and told me to keep my thieving hands off or she'd get her mates to duff me up.'

'So naturally you did as you were told.'

'Well—yer—I did.'

'Well, anyway,' said Spence, 'I'm not interested in whether you opened her letters or not. What really interests me is her car.'

'Car?'

'Yes. What kind was it?'

'Oh. I dunno.'

'You dunno?'

'No—I'm not very good on cars.'

'Perhaps not—but you saw the number, didn't you?'

Palmer was past caring now, only too delighted to tell the truth. 'Well, yer, I did.'

'And having seen the number you wrote to the council which issued the road-fund licence, didn't you, Mr Palmer? You told them you had reason to believe that this vehicle had been in collision with your own, and you asked who it was registered to, didn't you, Mr Palmer?'

'Well, yes, yes, I did, yes.' Palmer wiped the sweat out of his eyes and kneaded his handkerchief in his hands.

'And surprise, surprise, you found out it was registered to a Miss Melody McFee.'

'Um—yes, yes, I did.'

'And where does Miss McFee live?'

'Um—Warmingly Mansions, Roehampton.'

'That's right. And what does she do for a living, Mr Palmer?'

'She's a—um—er—stripper.'

'Yes. So she is. You found that out too.' Spence stepped back and relaxed the pressure a little. 'Why did you want to find out who she was?' he asked amiably.

'Well—I dunno really. I was just . . . interested, like.'

'Interested?'

'Yes. I mean—not every day you see a bird like that. And then there were these little packages. Like you say, I thought they had money in 'em. I never looked, mind you, never looked.' Palmer shook his head violently and then straightened his glasses. 'But I was concerned, see—wondering if she was breaking the law. I didn't want to get into trouble, did I?'

'No,' said Spence, 'you didn't. And you don't want to now, do you, Mr Palmer?'

Palmer agreed vehemently. 'No, no, I don't.'

'So—tell me about the other man. The one who came yesterday.'

'Other man?'

Spence clenched his fist and Palmer panicked. 'All right, all right! I'll tell you.'

'What time was it?'

'Oh—um—4 o'clock. Before the rush, anyway.'

'Go on.'

'Well . . . He stood on the other side of the road for a bit, watching. Smoking his pipe, and watching. Some of 'em do, you know. They like to wait till the shop's empty before they come in. Get bit shy, like.'

'I see. So he waited till the shop was empty.'

'Yer . . . Yer.'

'Then what?'

'Well, he come in, and asked about the accommodation address service. And then a lady come in, and we broke off. And then he asked a few more questions . . . Anyway, after a bit he come to the point.'

'He wanted to know J. Smart's address.'

'Yes.'

'Did he know J. Smart was a woman?'

'No, come to think of it, he didn't, no.'

'Not till you let it slip.'

Mr Palmer looked at his boots, somewhat abashed. 'Yer, that's right.'

'Stupid, that—you could have earned an extra fiver from that. Anyway, we haven't got all night . . . The long and short of it is, this man wanted J. Smart's address, and he was willing to pay you for it, right?'

'Yes.'

'And so after some argy-bargy, you made a deal.'

'Yer. That's right.'

'And how much did he pay you?'

Palmer mumbled.

'What?'

'Fifty . . . Fifty quid. I tried to get more but he turned nasty. Got me worried.'

'All right. So for fifty quid you told him who J. Smart was, and what she did for a living. Correct?'

'Yes.'

'Right. Now describe this man to me. Exactly. And don't make any mistakes.'

Palmer gulped. 'Well. He had a mac on. An old one. Fawn sort of colour, with a greasy collar . . . Bit big for him, I thought.'

'Hat?'

'Yer. Oh yer. A trilby.'

'Colour?'

'Um. Grey.'

'With a band on?'

'A what?'

'Was there a band round the hat?'

'Um—can't remember.'

'What about his face?'

'Well—ordinary.'

'Come on, dammit, think.'

'Well—pale. Pale face. And glasses. Black glasses.'

'You mean they were sun glasses?'

'No, no, they had black frames. Like you get on the National Health.'

'Was he clean-shaven?'

'Um—no. No, I think he had a moustache. Yes, he had. And a stringy neck, I remember that. Fairly old, he was, older than me, anyway.'

'What colour hair?'

'Grey.'

'You're sure?'

'Yer—certain. Quite long for a bloke his age. Grey, like his 'tache.'

'Was he tall, fat, or what?'

'Well—quite slim really. Smallish sort of bloke. Smoked a pipe all the time.'

'Yes, so you said. Didn't tell you his name, I suppose?'

'No, no, he didn't.'

Mr Palmer didn't seem to realize that Spence had been joking.

Soon afterwards Spence and Laurel left the newsagent's shop and returned to Laurel's car. Palmer seemed pleased to see them go.

Spence rubbed his hands together. 'Good, good, good,' he said briskly. 'We're making progress.'

Laurel wasn't so sure. 'Are we?' he said doubtfully. 'The bloke old Palmer just described to us doesn't remind me of anyone back in Tinley at all.'

'No? What about the Colonel?'

'Well, the Colonel's an elderly bloke, agreed. But his hair's not grey for a start. It's dark brown.'

'So it is, and it's probably dyed by the look of it. And the Colonel doesn't wear glasses, either. But dammit, man, use your imagination. Obviously our killer disguised himself. For instance, the Colonel could have sprinkled some talc on his hair to make it grey, and put on a pair of glasses, just to put us off the scent.'

Laurel was not convinced. 'Well, perhaps so. But the Colonel doesn't seem to have the guts for the job, somehow.'

'Yes, I agree with you, and I don't think it was the Colonel either, as a matter of fact. But what about the Vicar—the description fits him, more or less.'

'Well, sort of,' Laurel agreed unenthusiastically. 'But I was hoping that Palmer would describe Lester Read or David Cordwright. We already know that they both came up to London yesterday afternoon—and went their separate ways—so I was expecting it to be one of them. But neither of them could have disguised himself to look like the bloke Palmer described.'

'Don't be so sure,' said Spence. 'Read's an amateur actor, remember, and Cordwright's quite capable of putting on a pair of glasses and a hat and mac, and sticking a pipe in his mouth.'

'Oh, well, if you're going to argue like that . . .' said Laurel.

'Yes, I am going to argue like that,' said Spence forcibly. 'One of those long-term Tinley residents has committed three murders, and by God I'm going to find out who it was before I'm very much older . . .'

He clenched his fist and punched the dashboard to emphasize his points. 'Look, it all fits. Monday, Thana found out somehow who it was that committed the old murders and she rang Charlie Booth. Tuesday, she came to London and posted a blackmail demand in the name of J. Smart—not giving away her sex, you see —no clues to the killer. Wednesday, however, the killer gets the letter, reacts immediately by coming to London and finds out who J. Smart really is. And Wednesday night, last night, he tortures and kills Thana . . . All we have to do is sort out who came to Putney on Wednesday afternoon. As you say, we already know that Cordwright and Read were in London yesterday —but the Vicar and the Colonel could have been too, quite easily.'

'Well, maybe,' said Laurel. 'But I'm disappointed that the description isn't a closer fit. I wonder if old Palmer realizes how important he is?'

'Probably not,' said Spence, 'and I deliberately didn't tell him. It would only make him nervous. We'll do a job card to get someone to help him do an Identikit picture of his visitor—then maybe we shall have an even better idea of who it was.'

'What about an identity parade?' suggested Laurel.

'Not yet, no. Much too dangerous—counsel would rip us apart.'

'Hey,' said Laurel, 'I've just had a thought.'

'What's that?'

'Well, perhaps Read or Cordwright just hired themselves an old pensioner to come round and ask Palmer the right questions. They could have picked out a bright old boy in the Library reading-room and it would be a doddle. Perhaps that's who Palmer saw.'

'Well, perhaps,' said Spence. 'I'm not jumping to any conclusions one way or the other just yet. There's only one thing I am sure of—whoever our murderer is, he's very resourceful and bloody dangerous.'

27

Spence said very little during the drive back to the Blue Bazaar. There was still a great deal he didn't know, but an idea was beginning to form in the back of his mind. He used the time taken up by the journey to check and re-check the facts against various theories.

As soon as they arrived back at the Blue Bazaar Spence sent Laurel home. He himself, however, headed for the mobile office parked at the side of the night-club, where a light was still shining. Inside the mobile office Spence found that Detective Sergeant Wilberforce had also gone home for the night, and that only his former boss, Charlie Booth, remained.

'It's all right,' said Booth with a grin. 'I haven't come back and taken over. I've just been mooching around the village, that's all—talking to people—and I thought I'd wait here till you got back . . . Have a drink.'

He indicated the bottle of whisky in front of him and poured Spence a glass to stand beside his own. Both the bottle and the glasses were on Spence's list of standard equipment for the office.

'Thanks,' said Spence. He sat down wearily and glanced across the desk at the older man, who looked surprisingly fit and relaxed, considering his medical record. 'Well,' said Spence, 'anything interesting happen while I've been gone?'

Booth chuckled. 'No one's confessed, if that's what

you mean. But you can rule out the chef, Colin Marples.'

'I already had,' said Spence. 'More or less. I suppose the forensic tests were negative, were they?'

'Oh, yes. It's all here—' Booth indicated a sheaf of paper—'but what it boils down to is that they couldn't find any physical evidence that he'd knocked out and stabbed our friend Thana. No blood in the bathroom, no blood on his clothes, nothing at all anywhere. No prints on the knife, either.'

'Wiped clean?'

Booth nodded.

'Hmm. Well, not surprising, really. I always did think the murderer put that knife in the chef's room to try to deceive us. I'll ring Tallmead station in a minute and get them to take the poor devil home.'

Booth rested his chin on his palm. 'How've you spent your time since I last saw you?' he asked.

'Well, I had chats with the three owners after lunch. The two men first, then Mrs Cordwright. And after that I saw the other half of this week's cabaret, Deceivo and company.'

'Oh, yes? Anything startling emerge?'

'No, not really. It was a useful exercise, though— it gave me a chance to assess them all individually, as people. And that Deceivo's a sharp one—he knows a lot more than he lets on.'

'Yes, I bet he does. I gather you were at the post-mortem, too.'

'Yes. Did you hear about it?'

Booth took a sip of whisky and nodded. 'Yes. I must say I was a bit surprised to hear that Thana was really a man. Or had been a man.'

'I still don't know who she or he really was,' said

Spence. 'I've been to her flat but there was nothing there to help me. But I'm hoping that Records will come up with the answer before long.'

'They already have,' said Booth. 'They rang through about 9 o'clock. Thana, back in the days when she was still a young man, got a suspended sentence for stealing from an employer, about eleven years ago.'

'Oh? And what was her real name?'

'James Barndean,' said Booth.

'Barndean,' Spence repeated. 'That's the Vicar's name . . . Any relation?'

'Yes,' said Booth. 'It's his son.'

'Well,' said Spence after a pause, 'that explains a good deal. This is the lad you told me about—the one who left home when he was eighteen.'

'Yes.'

'I see . . . Does the Vicar know?'

'Not yet, no. I've been sitting here thinking, wondering how to go about telling him. He knows subconsciously, of course. He saw Thana on Monday afternoon, and it gave him a nasty turn, but I doubt whether he really understood why—he hasn't put two and two together yet. As far as he's concerned he just saw a very erotic-looking young woman who might easily have been his own daughter. Not a nice thing for a Vicar to see at the best of times.'

'No . . . Anyway, we now know how Thana came by her local knowledge. She, or he, would have been about thirteen at the time of the Meadows murder—is that right?'

'Yes, roughly. I found out afterwards that James was beginning to be a bit of a naughty boy even at that age. What the choir-boys got up to in the organ loft in those days was apparently nobody's business. And when his mother died a year later he really went off the rails.'

'Why did he leave home—just wanted to see the bright lights, do you think?'

'Well, yes. But things were beginning to get a bit hot for him round here. When clergymen's sons go bad they really go rotten, you know. The fact is, James was a thief, and people knew it. And he was also a notorious queer. He went to Tallmead as a day-boy, but he used to go back there at nights and run through whole dormitories at a time.'

'Did he indeed . . . And if I've got my facts right, David Cordwright would have been about three years older than James.'

'Yes, that's right.'

'And Patrick Meadows's son, Peter, he would have been about three years younger—correct?'

'Yes. But what are you think about—the fact that both James Barndean and David Cordwright turned out to be queer?'

'I don't know, really,' said Spence. 'I'm just trying to get the picture clear in my mind, that's all . . . Any idea what happened to young Barndean after he left home? When did he transform himself into Thana?'

Booth shook his head. 'No idea. Not really. I did hear once, very vaguely, that someone had seen him hanging round Piccadilly, which isn't surprising. He probably served his time on the meat-rack. And after that, who knows? He might have found a rich patron, or gone into show-business, and he probably went abroad for the operation. He was always a good dancer, was James—he had some ballet training as a youngster, and his mother was very keen, so that's where he learnt to perform. And after the sex-change I suppose he got himself a new name, a new hairdo, and that was it. It's no wonder that nobody round here recognized him.'

Spence refilled his own glass and Booth placed a hand over the top of his.

'Laurel and I spent about an hour in Thana's flat,' Spence continued. 'She's lived in Roehampton for the last few years apparently. She made a lot of money one way or another, much of it from blackmail, and she's got a filing cabinet there which will yield a list of victims as long as your arm. Including, I may say, Colonel Brian Host-Wall.'

Booth grunted. 'Huh. The Colonel is a fool. He gave honourable service in the war, I believe, but after that he just came back here and sat on his money, and nothing decays a man faster. He should have found himself a proper job to do. The world has changed and he's tried to stand still, and I gather that now even his money doesn't go as far as it did . . . But tell me more about how this blackmail was conducted—what was the m.o.?'

'Pretty simple. Contact magazines to provide victims, plus an accommodation address and a series of false names.'

'Ah,' said Booth. 'Now we're getting somewhere. Perhaps that's how she put the bite on in this case.'

'It undoubtedly is,' said Spence. He proceeded to tell Booth about his visit to the grimy newsagent's shop, and how Mr Palmer had already been visited on the previous afternoon by a man wearing a trilby hat and smoking a pipe.

Booth's eyes began to gleam with interest. 'This is a

bit more like it. At least we've got someone who's seen the man we want at close quarters, in broad daylight.'

'Well, yes,' said Spence. 'But don't get too carried away. The description Mr Palmer gave us doesn't sound exactly like any of our suspects, and it's my belief that the murderer is deliberately misleading us again. Look at the features that the witnesses have told us about, both seventeen years ago and again today. What do people tell us they saw? Answer, a hat and a pipe. And now the newsagent adds further details: glasses, a moustache, grey hair, and a mackintosh. None of those things are really permanent physical features, they can all be put on or taken off at a moment's notice, and all would result in a radical change in a man's appearance.'

'All right,' said Booth. 'So let's try to narrow it down a bit. I gather you're convinced that Thana's murderer was also the murderer of Patrick Meadows, and that he's a long-term resident of Tinley.'

'I am, yes.'

'Well, there aren't more than a handful of them, and it all boils down to where they were yesterday afternoon at 4 o'clock. Let's go through the list. You've got Walter Underwood, who hardly counts—he's not rich enough to blackmail, and in any case he was almost certainly here in Tinley. But you can always check. Then you've got the Colonel, who has a very hot motive—he was already being blackmailed by Thana.'

'And he's got a stringy neck, too,' said Spence. 'That's one physical feature the newsagent did mention.'

'All right. Next, another long shot, the Reverend

Barndean. I'd stake my pension that it's not him, but we must be objective. If he realized that Thana was his own son, considerably tarted up, he could easily have killed him out of sheer revulsion. And, finally, you've got Cordwright and Read, and you already know that they were in London at the relevant time.'

Spence was very quiet. 'Yes,' he said. 'I'll give it some thought . . . But in the meantime, we've got another problem with the Vicar. He has to be told about his son tonight, before the papers get hold of it. Who's going to break the news to him?'

'I am,' said Booth firmly.

'All right. I won't argue with that. But just do one thing for me—ask him where he was at 4 o'clock yesterday afternoon.'

'Yes,' said Booth. 'I will.'

For an hour after Booth had left, Spence read through reports, jotted down instructions on job cards, studied a map of the village, and thought.

At midnight he decided to call it a day. He picked up his own car from the car park and drove to his cousin's farm, where he had arranged to spend the night. On his way he made a short detour to look in at the vicarage. Booth's car was still parked outside, and there were lights on in the downstairs rooms. After a moment Spence drove on.

When he arrived at the farm he had a brief chat with his cousin George, who was waiting up for him, and then he retired to bed.

He slept for three hours and then woke up. He found that the facts of the case were all clear in his mind, and he could summon a picture of each suspect into his brain just like projecting a slide on to a screen. He thought of them all in terms of the newsagent's description.

After perhaps half an hour Spence had decided who had killed Thana, how and why. Proving it, of course, was something else—but that, he felt, could wait until after breakfast.

He turned over and went back to sleep again.

28

At 8.30 the following morning Booth telephoned Spence at the farm to report on his conversation with the Reverend Albert Barndean.

'Before you start,' said Spence, 'I think I ought to apologize to you. I saw your car still parked outside the vicarage late last night, and I suppose I ought to have come in and had a word with the Vicar myself. But I'm afraid I funked it.'

'No, no, you did the right thing,' said Booth. 'It was best that I should tell him on my own.'

'How did he take it?'

'Oh, pretty well, considering . . . He's going to retire shortly. In the meantime he's going to go away for a few days—stay with friends. If you want him for anything I know where he'll be.'

'OK. Did you ask about Wednesday afternoon?'

'I did, yes. He spent it helping his housekeeper to put up a new cupboard in the kitchen. So, I think you can safely cross him off your list.'

'Thanks,' said Spence. 'I don't think I'll need to bother him again.'

By 9 o'clock Laurel had joined Spence at the mobile office, and after Spence had given him the details of Thana's identity they set off together to see the Colonel. Spence had no great hopes of learning anything dramatic, but he wanted to get the interview out of the way.

The Colonel's large, rambling manor house was situated once and a half miles to the north of Tinley, at the end of a long, straight road. The front door was opened by the Colonel's wife, Emily Host-Wall, whose face bore the scars of long and deep depressions. She seemed heavily sedated, and Spence was doubtful whether she quite understood who she was admitting to the house.

In due course the Colonel was interviewed alone, and faced with the evidence of his embarrassing letters to Thana he could hardly do otherwise than admit that she had been blackmailing him. He wept, and complained pitifully that he had not been able to sleep recently. Spence believed him. More to the point, the Colonel claimed that on the Wednesday afternoon of that week he had been playing golf with three other retired gentlemen, one of them a JP and al' of them eminently respectable. Spence arranged to have the story checked but he didn't doubt that it was true.

'Pity about that,' said Laurel as they came away from the manor house. 'He had a jolly good motive.'

'Yes,' said Spence. 'But he didn't have the strength for it, that's the point. The psychological strength, I mean. That's the key to this whole matter, and don't you forget it.'

By 10 o'clock they were back in the mobile office. Spence ordered coffee and then brought in Detective Sergeant Wilberforce for a conference.

'Right,' he said. 'Now with any luck we're going to crack this case by lunchtime, so listen carefully. For better or for worse I've been assuming for some time Thana was murdered by the same hand that killed Patrick Meadows and his son seventeen years ago—in other words, that the man with a hat and a pipe, who's been seen on three occasions now, is a long-term resident of Tinley. OK . . . Now, so far this morning we've eliminated both the Vicar and the Colonel, and I'm also going to eliminate Walter Underwood, on the following grounds: one, he hasn't got the guts for it, two, he isn't wealthy enough to be worth blackmailing, and three, Mrs Amble told me at a quarter to 9 this morning that he was in her shop at half-past 4 on Wednesday afternoon. So, who does that leave?'

'David Cordwright and Lester Read,' said Laurel promptly.

'So it does,' said Spence with a smile. 'All right, let's just think for a minute . . . Thana—alias James Barndean—came back here last Sunday for the first time in twelve years. But the James Barndean who came back here last Sunday was a very different person from the one who left, all those years ago. James had become Thana, and she was much wiser in the ways of the world than James had been—a much more astute psychologist. And what I'm going to do this morning is make a little wager. I'm going to bet that my wife and I, put together, know at least as much about human nature as Thana did.'

Laurel raised an eyebrow but said nothing.

'Basically,' said Spence, 'what I think happened is this. On Sunday and Monday Thana was introduced to the owners of the Blue Bazaar, all of whom she'd known before, in her childhood, or boyhood. But this time Thana looked at the relationship between them with fresh eyes. And suddenly the motive for the original murders of Patrick Meadows and his son was as clear as day . . . It was my wife who pointed me in the right direction: she said that perhaps we ought not to be looking for a motive for the murder of Patrick Meadows—that it was more a case of looking for a motive for the murder of the little boy. Now, we all know what sort of men are interested in little boys. And Thana herself gave us a clue—in fact two clues. One in the telephone call she made to Booth, and another in the act of dying. You see, the post-mortem itself tells you how her murder was committed—and I'm not talking about the stab wounds.'

Laurel and Wilberforce exchanged glances which indicated that neither of them had the faintest idea what Spence was talking about.

'Right, gentlemen,' said Spence briskly. 'I will now explain to you precisely who killed Patrick Meadows and his son, and who killed Thana, and why.'

During the next quarter of an hour Spence proceeded to explain his theory to a fascinated audience of two. At the end of his explanation he asked for comments.

'Well,' said Laurel slowly, 'even if you're right, it's going to be hellish difficult to prove.'

'Almost impossible,' Spence agreed. 'But we'll do our best. And this is how we'll tackle it . . . In a minute or two we'll ring up the owners of the night-club and get them all over here. Laurel and I will take them up to Thana's bedroom, where the murder was committed, and we'll put some psychological pressure on. In the meantime, you, Wilberforce, will take a couple of men, collect a search warrant from the local JP whom I lined up at breakfast-time this morning, and see what you can find. What you're looking for is quite simple: the clothes worn on the night of the murder, and/or the blackmail letter from J. Smart, alias Thana, alias James Barndean, etcetera. I imagine that the letter's been destroyed by now, and possibly the clothes have as well, but we can but look. If your search produces anything positive we may be able to make an arrest. If not—well, we shall just have to go back to first principles.'

A few minutes later Wilberforce departed, with clear instructions on what to do and when. Spence then put through a phone call to Cordwright and Read's house and asked them if they would be kind enough to join him at the Blue Bazaar as soon as possible.

'Well, if you insist,' said a doubtful David Cordwright. 'But we've just sat down to have coffee—and my mother's here, we're having a little conference about business.'

'Oh, well, bring your mother along too,' said Spence cheerfully. 'I was going to invite her anyway. What I have in mind won't last very long. But finish your coffee first—there's no great rush.'

29

Mrs Cordwright, her son David, and Lester Read all arrived at the Blue Bazaar in Read's Jaguar XJ6, about half an hour later.

In order to give Wilberforce and his men adequate time to complete their tasks, Spence then took the three owners of the nightclub on a tour of the premises, asking a lot of pointless questions and quietly observing their reactions. Eventually, when he sensed that irritation, impatience and anxiety, in varying degrees, had all been firmly e ´ablished in their minds, he led the three of them upstairs to the bedroom which had been occupied by Thana.

The window in the bedroom was open, but the atmosphere was still close and unpleasant. Mrs Cordwright wrinkled her nose with disgust.

'Is it really necessary to bring us in here?' she asked.

'Yes, it is,' said Spence, without elaboration.

Laurel had arranged five chairs in the room, in such a manner that the two Cordwrights and Lester Read would be sitting facing himself and Spence. He closed the door after everyone had entered and then took out his notebook.

'Really, Superintendent,' said Mrs Cordwright forthrightly, 'I do hope we're not going to be expected to sit here long. It's a room which will always have the most unpleasant connotations for us. And in fact I can't imagine why you've brought us up here at all.'

'Patience, patience, Mrs Cordwright,' said Spence. 'All will become clear in the end.'

'Well, I hope so . . . Poor David is already looking unwell, and I can't say I blame him. I feel quite upset myself.'

'Oh, please, mother,' groaned Cordwright in protest, but he certainly was looking very pale, and his forehead was sprinkled with sweat. Spence examined him with some satisfaction; he was delighted to see that he was already heavily undermining the morale of at least one of the three owners.

'Well now,' he began, 'I've brought the three of you up here because I feel that we're very close to bringing this particular murder investigation to a successful conclusion. And it's my belief that each of you, in your different ways, can provide me with vital information. In this connection, perhaps I ought to point out to you that you are not obliged to say anything unless you wish to do so, but what you do say may be put in writing and given in evidence. Do you understand?'

'Well, yes, Superintendent—we understand,' said Read doubtfully. 'But I can't say I like the implications very much.'

'You don't have to like them,' said Spence. 'You just have to understand them . . . Now, very briefly, let's review the events of the past week. Last Sunday a stripper who called herself Thana arrived at the Blue Bazaar. She mentioned to Mr Cordwright that she had met him before, but the truth is she had met all of you before. In fact she grew up in this village as a child. And she wasn't a she at all—she was a man. A man by the name of James Barndean. The Vicar's son.'

The reactions were not perhaps as dramatic as Spence might have expected. Lester Read gave a snort of surprise and amusement, Mrs Cordwright gasped and forgot to close her mouth after it, and David Cordwright was already so utterly miserable and ill-at-ease that the information had no apparent effect whatever: he simply glanced up at Spence and then returned his gaze to the floor, his hands clasped between his knees.

'So,' said Spence. 'Now you know who Thana really was.'

Lester Read took out his pipe and a tobacco pouch. 'Well,' he said, 'it is a bit of a surprise, I must say. But it explains a few odd remarks that Thana made. And she wasn't the first transsexual stripper we've had here by any means—and I doubt if she'll be the last.'

Spence looked at David Cordwright. 'I suppose you and James Barndean were quite good friends,' he suggested. 'Years ago.'

Cordwright shuddered. He looked as if he might be sick at any moment. He shook his head. 'No. No . . . He was younger than me—three years younger. Nobody would have recognized him after all those years, and a sex-change operation. Nobody at all.'

'Well, it doesn't matter much anyway,' said Spence. 'But it's important that you should realize that Thana wasn't quite the stranger here that you all thought she was. She knew the village very well. That's why she came here, you see. I think originally she came back here for a bit of quiet amusement—to have a little snigger at the ways of the country bumpkins, ways she had long since abandoned. But once she got down here, something unexpected happened . . . You see, among other things Thana was a highly proficient and well-organized blackmailer. And after she'd been here a day or so, she came across something which gave her the key to a mystery from the past. She discovered who had committed the murders of Patrick Meadows and his ten-year-old son, seventeen years ago.'

David Cordwright cast an anguished glance at Lester Read, who pretended not to notice and went on filling his pipe.

'Thana remembered that crime very well, of course. In her earlier existence as James Barndean, she'd been thirteen years old at the time, and Detective Chief Superintendent Booth often came to see her father to get information from him.'

Mrs Cordwright folded her arms and sighed impatiently; her gaze was directed out of the window.

'So,' said Spence, 'perhaps we ought to consider just what is was that Thana saw, after an absence of twelve years, which made the identity of the murderer as plain as day to her. Now it's my belief that it was a simple matter of psychology, and of homosexual psychology in particular. All you have to bear in mind is that Thana herself was a sort of reformed homosexual, if I may use that expression, and that she was looking at the owners of the Blue Bazaar in the light of her accumulated experience, after a long period of time.'

At the mention of homosexuality Mrs Cordwright turned to look sharply at Spence; the angle of her jaw rose a little and her whole demeanour became more aggressive.

'The important thing to remember,' said Spence, 'is that it wasn't just Patrick Meadows who was murdered —it was also his son. And the original investigators very naturally spent all their time looking for motives for the murder of the father, thinking that the boy was killed as an afterthought. But they should, of course, have been thinking about motives for the murder of a little boy.'

Lester Read began to light his pipe, but his attention was wholly focused on Spence.

'Now I'm well aware that not all homosexuals are interested in little boys, just as not all heterosexual men are interested in little girls. Far from it. And some of my best friends, and so on and so forth. Nevertheless, it is a fact that some homosexual men like to have contact with young boys. And living in the village of Tinley at the time of the first murders were two men whom we now know to have been homosexual: James Barndean, alias Thana, and David Cordwright.'

'Superintendent,' said Mrs Cordwright in a voice that would have put fear into the heart of many a sergeant-major. 'I do hope you are intimately familiar with the law of slander.'

Spence ignored her totally and continued to address David Cordwright. 'It's my belief that Patrick Meadows's son was murdered because the boy was involved in some sort of homosexual activity. And it's also my belief that the other half of that relationship was you, Cordwright.'

David Cordwright weakly opened his mouth as if to begin speaking but his mother stopped him.

'Say nothing, David,' she commanded firmly. 'Say nothing at all. Just don't lose control of yourself.' Mrs Cordwright leaned forward and placed a hand on her son's knee. Cordwright flinched and gasped, and after a moment his mother took her hand away again.

Spence continued.

'What happened on Sunday and Monday of this week was that Thana looked at David Cordwright as a grown man, and realized what must have been happening seventeen years ago. She was probably vaguely aware of some hanky-panky at the time, of course—but seventeen years later the connection between the sexual relationship and the murders was suddenly crystal clear. She knew instinctively who had committed the murders, and why. And, of course, being a greedy girl, she decided to blackmail the murderer . . . On Monday night she checked with Mr Booth that the murderer could still be convicted of the crime and on Tuesday she went to London and sent a letter demanding the first payment. She sent it under the asexual name of J. Smart, and asked for payment to be sent to her at an accommodation address in Putney.'

Spence assessed the reactions of his assembled audience. Read was relaxed and completely absorbed by the narrative, Cordwright was on the point of collapse, and Mrs Cordwright seemed to be controlling her fury with difficulty.

'On Wednesday morning the blackmail letter arrived. What an appalling shock it must have been for the recipient. For seventeen years all had gone well. Most people had long since forgotten the murder and in fact most people now living in the village didn't even know about it. And then, suddenly, out of the blue, this devastating demand from a mysterious Smart person . . . Dreadful. But our murderer is not one to give up easily. People don't change much, you know, and the murderer's instinct for self-preservation was just as strong as ever. The accommodation address which Thana had used was a shop run by a man called Palmer, and on Wednesday afternoon Mr Palmer had a visit from a man who wore a hat and smoked a pipe. By a curious coincidence the owners of the Blue Bazaar were all in London on Wednesday afternoon, too . . . Anyway, this man with a pipe paid a good price for details of J. Smart's real identity. And when he heard that she earned her living as a stripper, he knew immediately who he was dealing with. And, being a ruthless, selfish, totally amoral individual, he went back to Tinley determined to put an end to this blackmail nonsense once and for all.'

'You say this Palmer person actually saw the murderer?' asked Mrs Cordwright scornfully.

'He did, yes.'

'Then he can presumably identify him?'

'I doubt it,' said Spence. 'You see, the description Mr Palmer has given us is of an elderly man with grey hair and a moustache, wearing a hat, glasses, and a mac.'

'Precisely my point,' said Mrs Cordwright triumphantly. 'That description bears absolutely no resemblance whatever to my son. Or, for that matter, to Mr Read.'

'That is precisely my point too," said Spence evenly. 'You see, it's my belief that Mr Palmer's visitor had deliberately put on a hat and glasses and smoked a pipe, so that those features alone would be remembered.'

Mrs Cordwright's contempt was unlimited. 'Oh, well, really,' she said, 'I've never heard such ridiculous nonsense in all my life.'

'Perhaps it is nonsense and perhaps it isn't,' said Spence. 'We shall soon know when my men get back.'

David Cordwright stopped gazing at the carpet and

raised his panic-stricken eyes to Spence's face. 'Get back from where?'

'David!' His mother almost shouted, and anything that David Cordwright might have been about to say was instantly suppressed; he slumped in his chair again.

'The rest of the story is pretty straightforward,' said Spence after a pause. 'Thana thought she was safe behind a false name and an accommodation address, devices which had proved very satisfactory on numerous other occasions. So she didn't even lock her bedroom door. The murderer had no difficulty in getting in here in the early hours of the morning. He knew that the only other person sleeping in the building was the chef, and that he, poor fellow, was deaf. And so the murderer got into this very room with no trouble at all. He knocked Thana unconscious with an iron bar, tied her up, heated a knife from the kitchen on the gas fire, and tried to persuade her to tell him what proof she had of his guilt. Unfortunately, however, Thana choked and died. Died right there, almost exactly where you're sitting, Mr Cordwright. So the murderer, still thinking clearly in spite of all the stresses and strains on him, searched this room for any incriminating evidence of the old murders. And then he went away, leaving the knife in the chef's bedroom in an attempt to implicate him. Funnily enough, the chef woke up at that stage, and saw a man in a hat, smoking a pipe, walking away. A nice touch, that pipe—sort of a trademark, you might say. And so, for the last couple of days, despite having committed that hideous crime, the murderer has been going about his business as usual, living a reasonably normal life.'

Cordwright began to sob; he put his head in his hands and his whole body shook. Lester Read moved his chair closer to Cordwright's and put his arm round his friend's shoulders, quietly soothing away the pain. Read seemed quite self-possessed and un-shocked, as if he had been expecting something like this to happen for some time.

It was while Cordwright was regaining control of himself that there was a knock on the door. At Spence's call the door was opened by Detective Sergeant Wilberforce.

'Ah,' said Spence, 'excuse me a moment.'

He got up and went out of the room, leaving Laurel to brave Mrs Cordwright's incensed stare. After perhaps three minutes Spence returned and sat down again. Cordwright had stopped crying now and was wiping his eyes.

'Superintendent,' said Mrs Cordwright in a voice full of menace, 'I think that I can safely say that so far the three of us here have been co-operating with you to the utmost of our ability. We have exercised the greatest possible self-restraint under the greatest possible provocation. I hope you will understand if I say that I now intend to take my son home.'

'You're not leaving just yet,' said Spence firmly. 'Not until I've finished. So stay where you are.'

Mrs Cordwright could hardly believe her ears and seemed about to argue. But after a moment she lowered her shoulders and gave in.

'Oh, very well,' she said disgustedly. 'But say what you have to say quickly.'

'Very well, I will. Earlier this morning, I instructed one of my officers to obtain a search warrant. He has just returned from completing the search made under that authority, and he has shown me what the officers found.'

All three owners of the Blue Bazaar suddenly became very alert and interested.

'They found exactly what they were looking for—eventually. It was hidden in a loft, in a dark and obscure corner by a chimney. Presumably it was left there to be burnt at a later date—a much later date, when all the fuss had long been forgotten. What my men found was a sack, and it contained the following items: one suit, with bloodstains; one trilby hat; one mackintosh. Also a pair of shoes, a pair of socks, a shirt, and a tie. A pair of glasses. A stick-on moustache, of the type used in amateur dramatics. And a pipe. In other words, what we found were the clothes worn by the murderer, both during the visit to Mr Palmer's shop on Wednesday afternoon, and when the crime was committed, in the early hours of Wednesday morning.' Spence looked hard at David Cordwright. 'Do you remember owning a dark-blue pinstripe suit, Mr Cordwright?'

Cordwright shook his head, his eyes filled with tears.

'You should do—it has your name in it.'

Lester Read spoke up. 'Look here, Superintendent, I think I ought to make one thing clear. You seem to have got the impression that David and I went shopping separately on Wednesday afternoon. But that's not the case at all—we were together all the time. He couldn't possibly have gone to Putney. I'm willing to swear to that.'

Spence shook his head. 'Nice try, Mr Read,' he said

kindly. 'But don't go getting yourself into trouble when it's not necessary. You see, you're jumping to the wrong conclusion.'

'Am I?'

'Yes. You're assuming that we found these clothes in the loft of the house you share with Mr Cordwright. But we didn't. We found them in Mrs Cordwright's house.'

Spence turned to look Mrs Cordwright full in the face. As he had expected there was no dramatic change in her expression.

'How did they come to be there, Mrs Cordwright?' he asked.

Mrs Cordwright's mouth closed into a hard, thin line; she folded her hands in her lap and looked down at them.

She said: 'I've got absolutely nothing to say.'

30

It was 7 o'clock in the evening before Spence was finally able to get away from Tinley. On his way home he looked in at Charlie Booth's house to bring his former boss up to date on the case.

'It was the post-mortem that gave me the hint,' said Spence, when he was well into his first glass of Booth's whisky. 'It occurred to me then that if a man could successfully masquerade as a naked stripper, then it would be relatively easy for a woman to masquerade as a fully-clothed man. All she did was take a suitcase of clothes with her to London—she told her son and Lester Read that it was a fur coat she was going to get altered. Once she got to London she went into a ladies' loo and put on the suit and the mac, and of course she came out looking like a woman in a trouser suit, more or less. In the street she put on the hat and the glasses and stuck a pipe in her mouth, and after that she went into a gents' toilet and stuck on the moustache. Dead easy.'

'Yes, it could be done easily enough,' said Booth. 'Tell me—when Laurel gave me a ring to let me know that Mrs Cordwright had been charged, he said that you'd told him that Thana had supplied a clue to who did it in her phone call to me.'

'Yes, and I think it was a deliberate clue at that,' said Spence. 'I think Thana was laughing at us when she referred to the investigation *dragging* on for so long.'

'Ah, yes, I see what you mean.'

'It was the kind of thing that would have amused her, I think. And Mrs Cordwright herself was dangerously frank with us—she told Laurel and me quite openly that she'd felt ill on Wednesday morning.'

'Yes. I bet she felt ill, too. I bet she felt as sick as a dog.'

'Once I'd decided that it must be one of the owners of the Blue Bazaar it was pretty clear it must be her. She was by far the strongest and most determined personality—she'd demonstrated it over and over again.'

'Yes,' said Booth. 'I agree. All right—now you've arrested Mrs Cordwright and charged her. But how are you going to prove your case?'

Spence sipped his whisky before continuing. 'Well, in the pocket of the suit which we found in her loft we also found the blackmail letter which Thana sent her, still in its original envelope. Mrs Cordwright no doubt intended to burn it later, like the suit. She must have taken it to London with her, in case she needed to convince the accommodation address people that she had to contact J. Smart urgently or something like that. Anyway, there it was. The letter demanded £500 in return for keeping quiet about the fact that Mrs Cordwright had killed Patrick Meadows. And the really interesting thing was this—I'd suspected from the beginning that Thana had some sort of tangible evidence to blackmail the murderer with. And the letter to Mrs Cordwright contained a Xerox copy of part of Patrick Meadows's diary.'

'Meadows's diary?' Booth was astonished. 'We never found a diary.'

'I know you didn't. But Thana did.'

'Where in God's name did she come across that?'

'That's what I asked myself. So we started looking . . . Thana's bedroom at the Blue Bazaar had obviously been ransacked by the murderer, and our people had also searched it thoroughly, but Laurel and I decided to start there and go over it again anyway, just to make sure. And the interesting thing was this—there was a huge Victorian dressing-table in the bedroom, the sort of thing nobody wants these days. And when I crawled underneath it, I found what the Victorian manufacturers no doubt referred to as a secret drawer. Not really very secret but not the sort of thing you would find unless you had reason to suspect it was there. I've been told this afternoon that concealed drawers like that were a big selling-point in Victorian times—the lady of the house could keep her pearls in them.'

'And Meadows's diary was in this drawer, was it?'

'It was. So the question I asked myself then was this—is that where Thana found it, or was it simply where she hid it? Hid it, that is, after she'd been to London and Xeroxed the important bits. Anyway, we soon found the answer to that. We looked up the photos of Meadows's bedroom in the old murder file, and there was the same dressing-table, as large as life.'

'You mean the dressing-table in Thana's bedroom at the Blue Bazaar is the same one that once belonged to Patrick Meadows?'

'That's right.'

'Well I'm damned . . . I wonder how many pairs of hands it passed through before it got there?'

'Only one, I think,' said Spence. 'There's a big second-hand furniture dealer in Tallmead—man called Reggie Fawkes.'

'Oh, yes, I know him.'

'This particular dressing-table has Reggie's mark on the back, so we called him in. He remembers it perfectly, mainly because it came out of a murdered man's bedroom. But he's had the piece in his shop three times all told, and what really helped is that he remembers who owned it before Meadows—a certain Mrs Barndean.'

'Ah—the Vicar's mother.'

'Yes. So that's how Thana came to know about the concealed drawer—her grandmother no doubt showed it to her when she was a child. After Mrs Barndean died Reggie Fawkes bought the dressing-table with all the rest of her stuff and sold it to Meadows. And then when Meadows was murdered it was sold to an elderly man in Tallmead—again through Reggie Fawkes—and finally it came back through Fawkes's shop to the Blue Bazaar, when they were starting up. I suppose that it must be about a hundred years old, give or take a decade, and it's probably had a dozen or more owners, all told.'

'Do you think Mrs Cordwright knew it had once belonged to Meadows?'

'I doubt it. Fawkes kept his knowledge very much to himself—he was afraid it would discourage buyers. And I doubt whether Mrs Cordwright was ever in Meadows's bedroom apart from that one occasion— when it was dark and she had other things on her mind than the furniture.'

The former head of the Southshire CID puffed on his pipe for a moment. 'Well now,' he said, 'we've decided that Meadows kept his diary in the concealed drawer of his dressing-table, and that after his death it just lay there for seventeen years because no one else knew about it.'

'That's right.'

'But why did he bother to hide it there at all?'

'Oh, because of the nature of the thing. It was a very private journal, with accounts of all his fantasies and sexual frustrations and so on. Not at all the sort of thing for a young boy to see.'

'I don't know who searched Thana's bedroom yesterday,' said Booth, 'but I know who searched Meadows's room all those years ago. It was Alf Simmonds. And it's a good job he's already dead, or he'd have died of shame when he heard that he'd missed a thing like that.'

'There would be no reason for him to be ashamed,' said Spence. 'That drawer was designed not to be found. It's well hidden, with a catch on it to prevent it opening by accident when the dressing-table is moved.'

Booth nodded. 'If you say so. So our assumption then is that on Sunday or Monday Thana recognized the dressing-table as the one her granny had owned, had a look in the drawer for old times' sake, and found the diary. But what exactly did the diary say? It could hardly say, "I was murdered by Jennifer Cordwright", could it?'

'No. it couldn't. And I suppose most people reading that diary—or journal is perhaps a better word— wouldn't have realized its significance. It was only because Thana had grown up in the village, and knew both the Cordwrights and Meadows, then and now, that she understood what it meant.'

'Yes, I see. And what did it say precisely?'

'Well, it showed that I'm not quite as good a judge of psychology as I thought I was. You see, I had this theory that Mrs Cordwright was mainly interested in killing the boy, not his father.'

'And wasn't she?'

'No, not really. My guess was that she killed the boy because he was a source of homosexual temptation to her son David—and possibly a willing participant with him. But that wasn't really the case . . . The last entry in Meadows's diary was written late on the Sunday evening, Sunday the seventh of August. It had been a beautiful warm evening, and young Peter Meadows had been down by the river. Now a lot of odd things happen on river banks on summer evenings, and what happened that particular Sunday I don't know exactly. And the boy's father didn't know, either. But David Cordwright made some sort of pass at young Peter, or exposed himself or something. Anyhow, it was some sort of homosexual assault, and the boy was badly frightened, although not physically hurt—the autopsy showed no signs of any physical interference. And the long and the short of it was, Patrick Meadows told David Cordwright in no uncertain terms that he would report him to the police on Monday morning.'

'Which gave Cordwright a powerful motive.'

'Indeed it did. But Thana knew the Cordwrights well, remember, and she knew which of them was capable of murder and which wasn't. Anyway, exactly what happened next we can only conjecture at this stage—Cordwright is not willing to talk about it yet, and his mother certainly isn't. But my guess is that Cordwright went home badly shaken. His mother no doubt realized immediately that something was wrong, and he probably told her he'd been falsely accused—that Meadows had mistaken him for someone else, and so on and so forth. The usual panic-stricken lies. I expect Mrs Cordwright understood the truth well enough, but what we do know, from Meadows's diary, is that she immediately went to see Meadows to have it out with him. She started by being aggressive and ended up by begging and pleading, but neither method cut any ice with Meadows. He didn't like her to start with, and she rubbed him up the wrong way entirely.'

'Well, that's not surprising,' said Booth. 'She was a snobbish, hard-line Tory with a big sixteen-year-old son at a public school—and he was a Socialist widower with a badly-shaken ten-year-old kid. Oil and water aren't in it.'

'No. Anyway, the way matters ended up that night, Mrs Cordwright was left believing two things. One, Meadows and his son had so far told no one else of the incident, because their house was a bit isolated from the rest of the village. And two, Meadows intended to go to the police in the morning. He had no phone and no car, and the nearest police station was in Tallmead.'

'Yes, I see,' said Booth wearily. 'So the motive for the murders was to protect her beloved son from this foul slur on his character—to protect him from an accusation which would have been made the following day. She fought for him again later on, when he was accused of soliciting—and she won that time, too. And to commit the crime, she disguised herself as a man, in case anyone saw her.'

'Yes—the old amateur dramatics touch. And seventeen years later she did it again when she had to.'

There was silence for a few moments while Booth poked the bowl of his pipe; he seemed unhappy about something.

'What's her son's attitude to all this?' he said at last. 'You say he's not talking.'

'Well, he's told me a bit, and he'll tell me more in due course. He broke down and had a good weep when it was all over. After that I prised a few facts out of him. He'd always known in his heart of hearts this his mother had killed Meadows and the boy, though she had never admitted it outright. When she came back from her interview with Meadows on the Sunday night, she told David that Meadows had agreed to drop the whole business—that it had all been a misunderstanding and that the matter was was closed, never to be mentioned again. But the next day, when he heard of the murders, David was shocked speechless. Literally speechless, he says—claims he couldn't speak for nearly twenty-four hours. And then, over the years, his mother dropped some pretty big hints. She reminded him from time to time of all the things she had done for him. And when she really wanted to pressurize him she would remind him of how she had settled the Meadows business, as she called it. David says he was physically sick twice when she brought that up, but both times the reminder had the desired effect—he did what his mother wanted . . . The worst thing was, he felt he couldn't confide in anyone, not even Read.'

'I'll tell you what surprises me a bit,' said Booth thoughtfully. 'I wouldn't have thought that Meadows would have been so adamant about going to the police if his son wasn't physically hurt. If it had got to

court, Mrs Cordwright would have fought that case
to the bitter end. It wouldn't have been a happy experience for a ten-year-old boy, and a lot of mud
would have been left on both sides.'

'That's just the point,' said Spence. 'Meadows's
diary makes it clear that he didn't really intend to
go to the police at all. He was well aware of all the
difficulties and snags, and he just wanted Mrs Cordwright and her son to sweat for a few hours. He'd
actually made up his mind to take no further action
whatever . . . It's all quite plain in the diary. I've
brought it with me as a matter of fact. I thought you
might like to read it.'

There was a long pause while the former Detective
Chief Superintendent fiddled with his tobacco pouch.

'No,' he said eventually. 'No, I don't think I will.'

Dell Bestsellers